The body of a murdered prostitute, a black nylon stocking round her neck, is found in a fashionable West End hotel. A few hours later, across London, a lorry is hijacked, the driver abducted and left trussed up in a field, while another man is shot dead, his corpse dumped in the boot of a stolen car.

To Detective Chief Superintendent Tommy Fox of the Flying Squad the lorry heist bears all the hallmarks of one Thomas Walter Harris – known as Tango Harris on account of his nifty footwork at the New Cross Palais during his somewhat murky youth – and the dead man worked for Harris's rival gangleader, Billie Crombie. Together, the two gangs – involved in every imaginable form of nefarious activity – make up the nastiest gathering of villainy that Fox has encountered for some time.

As usual, Fox wants to put his unique stamp on an investigation he sees as his chance to bring about the taming of Tango Harris. But first, he must prove a link between two seemingly unconnected murders. And Tango Harris has always kept one step ahead of the law . . . until now.

The Taming of Tango Harris

Graham Ison

MACMILLAN
LONDON

First published 1993 by Macmillan London Limited

a division of Pan Macmillan Publishers Limited
Cavaye Place London SW10 9PG
and Basingstoke

Associated companies throughout the world

ISBN 0–333–59202–6

9 8 7 6 5 4 3 2 1

A CIP catalogue record for this book is available from
the British Library

Phototypeset by Intype, London
Printed by Mackays of Chatham PLC, Chatham Kent

Chapter One

It was pouring with rain.

It had slowed the traffic.

Windscreen wipers worked overtime as drivers peered out, doing their best to see the vehicle in front. Moving slowly, bumper to bumper. A forest of red, white, and winking amber lights.

On the pavements, pedestrians were bent beneath inadequate umbrellas, shoes soaked, trousers wet and devoid of creases, stockings wet and muddy.

Rain ran along the gutters in fierce little rivers, coursing towards drains that were blocked with leaves.

And it was windy . . . and bloody cold.

Detective Superintendent Gavin Brace stood gazing out of the window, shoulders hunched, hands in pockets, and asked himself what in hell he was doing there. The simple answer was that he was there to investigate a suspicious death. The more complex answer was that he was the only remaining detective superintendent in the area major investigation pool not investigating a murder . . . until now. But that seemed often to be the case on Eight Area. The fact that he had been obliged to cancel his leave – due to start the following day – did not enter into it. But then it never did in the Metropolitan Police. The Commander Operations had apologized, half-heartedly, and told Brace that he would just have to get on with it.

Outside, two white vans pulled into the kerb, and a number of men got out. The scientific team. ''Bout bloody time,' said Brace, turning from the window. 'Now all we want is a pathologist and a few detectives. Where the hell is everybody, Geoff?'

Detective Sergeant Jagger walked across the room and picked up a clipboard. 'This is the list, sir, but they've been told to report to the nick.'

Brace scanned the list of support staff detectives supposedly available from the pool, but each had to be located and telephoned. 'I suppose you've told someone that I need at least another three here?' he said, handing the board back to Jagger.

'Yes, sir. They should be arriving very shortly.'

'Story of my life,' said Brace, and glanced back to the bed, and to the body that lay on it, a black nylon stocking tight around the neck. There were scratch marks where the girl had tried to free herself from the ligature and her nose had bled heavily. Brace reckoned she was about twenty-eight . . . maybe thirty. Good-looking girl with blonde hair. Wet blonde hair. But not natural blonde hair. He knew that because she was naked. He looked around the room and fretted inwardly, anxious to get on with the enquiry. The maxim, the sooner you start the sooner you finish, was probably truer of crime investigation than of anything else. The only difference with crime was the later you started, the less chance you had of finishing at all. Satisfactorily, anyway. Of getting a result, as policemen are wont to say.

The door opened and a uniformed PC poked his head in. 'Fingerprints and photographic are here, sir.'

'Send 'em in.'

The technicians of murder entered the room, carrying their cases and tripods and all the other paraphernalia of their trade.

'Evenin', guv.' The older one looked at the body on the bed. 'What a bloody waste,' he said. 'Tom, was she?'

'Probably,' said Brace. He wasn't certain that the girl was a prostitute, but all the signs were there. Expensive dress and scanty colourful underwear, all abandoned in the bathroom. Water all over the floor; the signs perhaps of jollifications under the shower. Brace had seen all that

2

from the bathroom door, and stopped anyone else from entering until the fingerprint officers had examined the floor. A footprint could be as valuable as a fingerprint.

The duty assistant manager at the hotel – panicking – said that she wasn't registered.

'Oh?' Brace frowned. 'How come I don't know who she is yet, but you do?'

The assistant manager backtracked. 'I mean that this room was not booked to a woman. Any woman.'

'A visitor then?' Brace raised an eyebrow. He knew what the assistant manager had meant.

'This hotel has a reputation—' The assistant manager immediately regretted saying that.

But Brace latched on to it, just for the hell of it. 'Yes,' he said, 'I'm beginning to think you're right.'

'No, Inspector, I mean—'

'It's superintendent. *Detective* superintendent, and yes, I know exactly what you mean.'

'Well, if it's at all possible to be discreet—'

Brace looked at the assistant manager with a sour expression. 'You've got the naked body of a woman who's probably a prostitute in one of your nice expensive rooms,' he said, 'and you ask me to be discreet. You've got to be joking, mister. Anyway, who was the room booked to?' He paused. 'And for Christ's sake don't say Mr Smith.'

The assistant manager glanced down at a computer printout in his hand. 'John Phillips,' he said.

'Well, at least that shows a bit of initiative,' said Brace. He held out his hand. 'Let's have it.' He scanned the brief details of John Phillips. Address in Richmond. Nationality British. And that was it. He handed it to DS Jagger. 'Log that in the property register, Geoff.'

'But—' The assistant manager looked distressed.

'Yes?' Brace rounded on him.

'Well, my records, Superintendent—'

'It's evidence . . . probably. If you want a photostat copy, my sergeant will give you one. When he's got time.'

'Evening, Gavin.'

3

Brace swung round. In the doorway was a woman in a dark dress. Long grey pigtail. Fortyish.

'Ah, good. How are you, Pamela?'

'Fine.' Pamela Hatcher, a Home Office pathologist, put her bag down on the floor and cast a professional eye at the body. 'What are you doing back on your old patch?' Brace had been the detective chief inspector at West End Central police station at Savile Row before his promotion.

'I'm the last available superintendent in the pool tonight. Should have been going on leave tomorrow, too.'

'Bad luck. What've you got? Any idea?'

'Not a clue,' said Brace. 'Could be a tom. Everything points to strangulation with a ligature.' He grinned. 'But no doubt you'll destroy that theory for me in a minute.'

Pamela Hatcher smiled. 'I'll try not to,' she said. 'Just give me the go ahead when I can start.'

'Right.' Brace watched the fingerprint men at work. The photographers were taking a breather. They'd done all the basic shots and were now waiting to see if they were needed for anything else that might turn up when the detailed search of the room started.

'Got something here, guv.'

Brace crossed to the dressing table and took the magnifying glass from the senior fingerprint man. He trained it on a mark on the white laminate inlay and peered closely.

'We'll get twelve points off that, guv, but whether it'll mean anything is another thing.'

Brace shrugged and handed the glass back. It was always the way. You got a good print, but there was nothing in the records. So it went into the scenes-of-crime prints and waited for the day that another crime at another scene matched it. Then you waited for someone to come into custody. Then you got a phone call – in the middle of the night, usually – and you went to some distant police station and you started asking questions. Like, 'Where were you on the night of October the twelfth?' or, 'What were you doing in that place at that time?' Then a solicitor turned up and advised his client

– the prisoner – to say nothing. It was all very frustrating.

'Lift it,' said Brace.

The fingerprint officer got out his roll of Sellotape. 'We've got a footprint in the bathroom,' he said, 'but there's nothing we can use. No discernible characteristics.'

'There wouldn't be,' said Brace with a shrug. 'It's all yours,' he added, turning to the pathologist.

Pamela Hatcher nodded briefly and opened her case. 'Who was the first officer on the scene?' She looked round at the group of policemen.

'I was, I suppose,' said DS Jagger. 'The first CID officer, anyway.'

'That wasn't the question,' said Brace acidly.

'Well, the area car was here first, guv.'

'And where are they now?'

'Back on patrol. Why? Was there—?'

Brace ignored him and turned back to the pathologist. 'What did you want to know?' he asked.

'If there were any windows open when police arrived,' said Hatcher. 'It'll make a difference to my temperature readings.'

Brace turned to Jagger. 'Well, were there?'

'No, sir. They were closed, as they are now.'

'I hope you're not making that up.'

'No, sir, of course not.' Jagger looked hurt as though his professional expertise had been impugned.

'All right to move the body?' Hatcher asked.

'Do your worst,' said Brace.

Skilfully, despite her slight build, the pathologist turned the body on to its face and, producing a thermometer, started to take temperatures.

'Anyone found a handbag?' Brace addressed the scientific team and his sergeant.

'Not yet, guv,' said Jagger. 'Still looking.'

Brace looked across at the senior lab man. 'You finished now?' he asked.

'Yes, sir.'

'Good. Let's take the place apart.'

5

It was a standard hotel room. A bath towel had been used and abandoned on the bathroom floor, and the bed had been used – at least, the body was on it – but whatever had taken place before the murder had not entailed pulling back the covers. The plastic folder containing stationery, and another advising guests about the services of the hotel, yielded nothing of value. Countless guests had left fingermarks on them, but they were overlaid, one upon the other. There was nothing that experts could 'read'.

'Found a handbag, guv,' said Jagger. 'Under the bed.'

Brace took the small suede bag and emptied its contents on to a table. It contained a solid powder compact, a lipstick, some loose change, and fifty pounds in ten-pound notes. But there was nothing to indicate the identity of the owner.

By now three other detectives had arrived, the first from the major investigation pool. 'Oh good,' said Brace, 'the cavalry's arrived.'

The detectives looked apprehensive. 'I was tied up with—' one of them began.

Brace held up a hand. 'I don't want to know,' he said, 'but now you're here, there's work to be done. Get down among the staff. See if anyone remembers a woman fitting the description of the deceased coming into the hotel . . . or the man Phillips. The name's bound to be duff, knowing my luck. Start with the linkman outside, and work your way up to the floor waiter.' The detectives hesitated. 'Well, don't stand there,' said Brace. 'Get on with it.'

'I've done all I can here, Gavin.' As she spoke, Pamela Hatcher examined the rectal thermometer she had been using and then looked at the other instrument with which she had been measuring the temperature of the room. Then she did a few calculations in her notebook. 'Been dead about three hours. That's the nearest I can get for the moment. Might have to amend it after I've done the PM.'

Brace nodded. 'Thanks, Pam.' The time of death

6

wasn't really material. He knew that Phillips had booked in just before six o'clock that evening and the chambermaid had knocked at around seven to turn down the bed. A Portuguese girl who spoke hardly any English, she was not at all surprised to see a naked woman on the bed. But then she had moved closer and seen the staring eyes and the protruding tongue . . . and the stocking round the neck. She hadn't screamed; she had closed the door and fetched the duty assistant manager. This was, after all, a respectable hotel where screaming chambermaids could lose their jobs.

'There's a briefcase in the wardrobe, guv,' said Jagger. He swung the door open wide and paused. 'OK to move it?' he asked the fingerprint officer.

The FPO stepped across the room and glanced down at the black executive case. 'I'll give it the once over, just in case,' he said and then laughed. 'Just in case! I like that.'

'Well?' Brace looked over the FPO's shoulder.

'Yeah, there's a few here, guv. Best thing's to take it down to the lab and examine it there. I can open it for you if you want.'

'You can bet they'll only be her prints anyway,' said Brace gloomily.

'I'll let you know as soon as I can,' said the FPO.

'OK,' said Brace. 'In the mean time, open it up, will you.'

The FPO placed the case on the bed and carefully, with plastic-gloved hands, opened it. Inside was a small machine, the type that prints out credit-card vouchers. There was also a copy of such a voucher, dated that day. The only other items in the case were a pair of scanty red briefs, trimmed in black, and a spare pair of black nylons.

'This,' said Brace, picking up the voucher, 'is too good to be true. If this is the killer, why in hell did he leave it here? He must have known.' He laughed, a short grating laugh. 'It's signed by John Phillips for five hundred pounds in favour of . . .' He handed the slip of paper to

7

Jagger. 'Mountjoy Services. I must say this girl had a sense of humour,' he added.

It was raining in Romford, too.

At about one o'clock in the morning, just as the unknown prostitute's body was being removed from the hotel in the West End of London, four men were sitting in a car. They were slumped down in their seats so that any inquisitive passing police car would assume that it was empty. But they were pretty safe anyway – or thought they were – because it was dark and the windows were steamed up. No one could see in, and the occupants couldn't see out, except when the driver rubbed the windscreen with his gloved hand and risked switching on the ignition to clear the outside with a couple of sweeps of the wipers.

And they were tooled up. On the floor lay two sawn-off shot-guns, a hand-gun, and two or three pick-helves.

They were waiting for an articulated lorry that they knew would pass them very soon, on its way to Harwich. Their concentration on the road ahead made them a little careless of what might be behind, and the first they knew of danger was when the doors of their car were wrenched open and they were dragged out by a number of men wearing ski masks.

All four were beaten unconscious and dumped out of sight behind trees which lined that part of the road. The job was neatly finished just as an articulated lorry passed them. One of the attackers slipped behind the wheel of the car they had just seized and drove off, followed by the remaining three in their own car . . . or at least, in the car which they had feloniously acquired some two or three days previously. They followed the artic until it pulled into a lay-by. Stopping immediately behind it, the four villains spilled out.

One of them pulled open the door of the cab. 'Out!' he said.

The man who was holding the lorry driver at gunpoint jumped down. 'You took yer bloody time,' he said and then was thrown against the side of the lorry as one of the others put a single round through his temple.

They put his body into the boot of the car they had taken ten minutes previously and one of them drove it to a cul-de-sac just off Colchester Road and left it there.

On the first floor of New Scotland Yard, Detective Chief Superintendent Tommy Fox, operational head of the Flying Squad, nodded an acknowledgement to the DC who had just told him that the last of the Squad's teams was back safely, and then went home to bed.

Chapter Two

It was still raining five hours later, which did not do a great deal for the comfort and welfare of Wayne Parish. Wayne Parish was a long-distance lorry driver, except that right now he wasn't driving. He was trussed up like a chicken and lying in a fold in the ground on a golf course alongside the A12 . . . or Eastern Avenue, as the *habitués* of Romford prefer to call it.

The woman who found Parish – she was about twenty-five and dressed in a multi-coloured tracksuit – was pounding round the golf course as though her life depended upon it . . . which she had convinced herself it did. She stopped and stared. 'What's up with you?' she asked.

Parish's answer was restricted by the large strip of sticking plaster across his mouth and he merely managed a loud groan.

After a careful appraisal of his predicament, the woman pulled the sticking plaster off, causing Parish to utter several words not normally uttered in the presence of women. 'Well, untie me, for Christ's sake,' he added.

Gingerly, the woman started to release him. 'Are you one of those sado-masochist people?' she asked.

'No, I'm bloody not,' said Parish, vigorously rubbing his arms and legs in an attempt to restore the circulation. 'Where's the nick?'

'In Main Road.'

'Where the hell's that, then?'

The woman pointed. 'Other side of the golf course and turn right,' she said. 'Just past Oaklands Avenue.'

'How far's that then?'

'About a mile and a half, I suppose.'

'Well, sod that,' said Parish.

'What d'you want the nick for, anyway?'

'Because I've been robbed, you silly cow.' And Parish stumbled on to Eastern Avenue without so much as a word of thanks.

He had almost reached the flyover at the Southend Arterial Road before he saw a police car. He stepped out into the road and waved.

The police car stopped and the driver wound down his window. 'You trying to get run over?' he asked.

'I've been robbed,' said Parish.

'There's been another one, guv'nor,' said Detective Inspector Jack Gilroy.

Fox looked blandly at his DI. 'I suppose, Jack, that you are going to elaborate on that rather bald statement.' Carefully, he teased the cuffs of his shirt out of the sleeves of his Gieves and Hawkes suit and flicked aimlessly at imaginary specks of dust on his lapels. Fox was well known at Scotland Yard for the fastidiousness of his dress, but the Queen's Gallantry Medal, awarded for tackling an armed criminal, and which now lay buried at the back of one of the drawers of his desk, belied any suggestion that he might be a fop. Many criminals – and quite a few policemen – could testify to Fox being a very hard-nosed and unremitting detective.

'Another lorry heist, guv.' Gilroy sat down in a chair opposite Fox's desk and smoothed out one of the message flimsies in his hand. 'Bloke called Parish set off from his depot in East London with a lorry-load of Scotch *en route* for Harwich and the Hook of Holland ferry when he found that he was not alone.'

'Oh dear,' said Fox mildly.

'A bloke surfaced from the sleeping quarters of the cab and shoved a shooter in his ear. Then he suggested to Parish that he should stop in a lay-by.'

'And he did, presumably?'

'Yes, sir.'

'Very wise. And what happened next in this exciting saga, Jack?'

'He was met by a group of heavies who tied him up, left him on Romford golf course, and drove off into the night with his booze.'

Fox shook his head slowly. 'There is no doubt, Jack,' he said, 'that there are some wicked people in this world. Romford, you say?'

'Yes, sir.'

'If only they'd gone a few miles further, Jack,' continued Fox wearily, 'they'd have sailed over the border of the Metropolitan Police District and that' – he waved a limp hand towards the message flimsy – 'would have been resting on the desk of the head of Essex CID.' He stood up. 'How many's that now?'

'Seven, sir.'

'Then it's time to do some sorting, Jack. Any descriptions?'

'Four blokes in ski masks. All of 'em Mr Average.'

'Well,' said Fox, 'there's a surprise.'

'But not the only surprise, guv. At about the same time that Master Parish was being rescued from his bonds by a jogging bird in a tracksuit, the CID at Romford were wondering what the body of a known villain was doing in the boot of a stolen car just off Colchester Road.'

'Colchester Road?'

'Yes, sir. Even nearer the Essex boundary.'

'There's no justice in this world, Jack,' said Fox.

'No, sir. Probably the same view that the said deceased hood took when they topped him.'

'Oh, I don't know, Jack. Sounds like justice to me. No, I was thinking more of the unreasonable attitude of the toe-rags who left the body there. What's wrong with Southend?' Fox shook his head wearily. 'Who was the victim, incidentally?'

Gilroy glanced down. 'Carter. Frank Carter. Aged thirty-seven. Eight previous, but only three that are worth anything . . . all for armed robbery. Last one earned him a five-stretch. Been out nine months.'

'Method?'

'Shot, sir. Preliminary examination seems to indicate that a nine-millimetre pistol was used.'

'Who did he run with?' asked Fox.

'Billie Crombie, guv.' Gilroy leaned back in his chair with an expression of wry amusement on his face.

Fox stood up and turned to face the window. Carefully, he separated the slats and peered down into Victoria Street. Then he turned to face Gilroy again. 'Did he now. Well, isn't that interesting, Jack?' He sniffed loudly. 'I think it's time to do some sorting,' he said again. 'We shall consult with the commander. Forthwith.'

Commander Alec Myers, Fox's immediate boss, glanced up warily when Fox, accompanied by Gilroy, entered his office. 'Morning, Tommy.' He indicated chairs with a sweep of the hand.

'Morning, guv.' Fox carefully eased the cloth of his trousers over his knees as he sat down.

'What's on your mind, Tommy?'

'Lorry hijackings . . . and related villainy.'

'You talking about the Romford job, Tommy?'

'Jobs, sir,' corrected Fox. 'Yes.'

'Go on then.' Myers sat back and waited. He knew instinctively that Fox was going to ask for money or men . . . or both. But today, he had a surprise for Fox.

'Off the top of my head,' began Fox airily, 'it would seem that certain persons are conspiring to take the piss out of the Old Bill in general and the Heavy Mob in particular . . .' Fox had spurned the use of the slang term 'Sweeney' ever since a television programme about the Flying Squad had used it for a title. He preferred the term Heavy Mob, a far more common nickname among the criminal fraternity.

'So you want to take over this Romford job, is that it?' Myers took a cigarette out of the open packet on his desk and then pushed the packet towards Fox.

'More than that, guv'nor,' said Fox. 'If what I hear is true, last night a lorry-load of Scotch was nicked on Eastern Avenue on its way to Harwich and the Continent.

13

The heist appears to have all the hallmarks of one Thomas Walter Harris, known to friends and enemies alike as Tango Harris on account of his nifty footwork at the New Cross Palais during his somewhat murky youth.' He leaned forward to flick ash into the commander's ashtray. 'And Frank Carter, one of Billie Crombie's brethren, was found – shot to death – in a side turning in Romford . . . the morning after the night before.'

'So what have you in mind?'

'I should like to concentrate on these two little teams, sir . . . the Tango Harris and Billie Crombie mobs. They're at it, the pair of them . . . together with the nastiest collection of villainry that has been gathered together for many a long year.'

'And you want the men to do it, I suppose?'

Fox looked hurt. 'Can't improve on what I've got, sir . . . with one or two exceptions.' He grinned and cast a sidelong glance at Gilroy.

'Yeah, but how many, Tommy? You can't use the whole of the Flying Squad. There are other things going on, you know.'

Fox looked thoughtful. 'About a dozen, guv?'

'All right,' said Myers.

'All right?' Fox was disconcerted by the readiness with which the commander had agreed to his request.

'As a matter of fact, Tommy, the DAC Specialist Operations has just telephoned me, suggesting that you over-see an investigation into these hijackings . . . and anything else that happens to turn up. He said that you could have two dozen men if you needed them, but as you say you can get by with twelve . . .'

'Oh, that's only for a start, sir,' said Fox hurriedly, and then tried to recover his lost ground. 'But I propose to leave the present investigating officers *in situ* and just co-ordinate.'

'Of course, Tommy.' Myers nodded affably. 'But I want to be kept fully informed,' he said as Fox reached the door. 'And so does the DAC.'

'Do I ever leave you in the dark, guv?' asked Fox, pausing with his hand on the doorknob.

14

'Yeah . . . most of the time.'

'Reckon you can manage with a dozen blokes, guv?' asked Gilroy when they were back in Fox's office.

'A dozen's more than I need, Jack.'

'But—' Gilroy stopped.

Fox laid a finger alongside his nose. 'I shall filch more when I need them. In the mean time, I like to let the commander think he's got his own way. Makes him think he's in charge.'

'Well, isn't he, sir?'

Fox gave Gilroy a severe glance. 'Of course he is, Jack. Of course he is.'

Fox gazed round the small conference room. Apart from Gilroy, there were, among others, DI Denzil Evans, DSs Percy Fletcher, Ron Crozier, and Ernie Crabtree, and DCs Bellenger and Rosie Webster, the tall, striking blonde who overawed villains and policemen alike.

'We are going to sort out the Harris and Crombie gangs,' announced Fox. 'And if anyone mentions a word of what we're doing to anyone outside this squad, I shall break off my criminal enquiries personally to put the said officer back into a tall hat.' He glared at the assembled detectives. 'And that's the *best* they can hope for.' He lit a cigarette and watched the smoke drift upwards. 'We are starting off with the twelve of you, but if we need more, we shall acquire them. However, for the time being we shall see how we go. Now, Denzil, what do you have to tell us?'

DI Evans struggled to his feet only to be waved down again by Fox. 'This is going to be a protracted enquiry, Denzil. Save your strength.'

'I've been on the blower to Romford, guv,' began Evans. 'A lorry driver—'

'That would be Wayne Parish, I take it?'

Evans signed inwardly. 'Yes, sir, Wayne Parish. Well, he was dispossessed of his valuable cargo at about one o'clock this morning by a team of four heavies. About three hours later, a patrolling PC—'

15

'They have such things in Romford?' enquired Fox mildly.

'Apparently, guv.' Evans struggled on; it was always the same with Fox. 'Anyway, this PC found a car in a cul-de-sac, did a quick check on the PNC and found it had been nicked three days ago in Wandsworth. And in the boot, he found the recently expired body of Frank Carter.'

'What an extraordinary business.' Fox acknowledged the dutiful laughter. 'I think, Denzil, that I shall pay a visit to this Romford. Get a taste of the action first hand, so to speak. In the mean time, Perce,' he continued, nodding towards DS Fletcher, 'put yourself about, my son. Beat on the ground and see what comes up.'

'What are you after in particular, sir?' Fletcher looked slightly nonplussed.

'Anything in particular will do, Perce,' said Fox.

Tommy Fox swept into the incident room at Romford police station with an enthusiasm that frightened the life out of the assembled detectives. Nick Dorman, the detective superintendent assigned from the area major investigation pool, had never met Fox before . . . but he had heard of him. And that was enough.

'Good afternoon, sir.'

'You've got a body you don't know what to do with, they tell me.' Fox strode across the incident room and examined the action book. Humming an unidentifiable tune – which further discomfited Dorman – he rapidly absorbed what had been done so far.

'We've got a positive ID from fingerprints, sir.'

'Yes . . .' Fox drew the word out slowly. 'Well, you would have,' he said. 'With the sort of form that Frankie Carter's got, you could hardly avoid identifying him, could you? Now, what about this lorry heist?' He changed tack with a disconcerting suddenness. 'How far have you got with that?'

'The local DCI's handling that, sir,' said Dorman.

'Oh, really?' Fox looked surprised. 'Separate from this topping, is it?'

Dorman looked uncomfortable. 'Well, there's nothing to connect the two, sir,' he said, not wholly convinced that he was right.

'One of Billie Crombie's foot-soldiers, wasn't he, this Frankie Carter?'

'Yes, sir.'

'How far has the DCI got with the lorry hijacking?'

'I understand that the vehicle's been found abandoned, sir, but as I say, that's not my enquiry.'

'Where?'

'Eltham, I believe, sir.'

'Any fingerprints?' Fox's questions came one after the other, like a rapid burst of machine-gun fire.

'Are you talking about the murder or the hijacking, sir?'

'Yes,' said Fox.

'Still waiting for the results from the car the body was found in, sir,' said the unhappy Dorman. 'But I can't really say anything about the heist.'

'The heist is down to Tango Harris.' Fox leaned back in the detective superintendent's chair, a triumphant grin on his face.

'Can we be sure, sir?'

'You might not be,' said Fox, 'but I'm bloody certain. The MO's identical. Harris lets Crombie set it all up and then steps in and snatches the gear. And you've got the body of one of Crombie's runners. And Tango Harris and Billie Crombie are sworn enemies. Beginning to get my drift, Mr Dorman?'

'You think they're connected, then.' Dorman suddenly realized that life on the area investigation pool was nowhere near as bad as it might be if he were on the Flying Squad.

'Well,' said Fox, standing up. 'It might be a good idea if you got alongside the local DCI and compared notes. Get hold of the papers on the other six lorry hijackings that have occurred in recent months and have a look at them. But I can tell you this. On each occasion, a nasty man with a gun suddenly appeared from the back of the cab when the driver was bowling along in the night, doubtless listening to Capital Radio or some such entertainment, and before he could say Chris Tarrant, he was tied up in a field somewhere. It's only a suggestion, mind. But you might just find that Tango Harris took out one of Billie Crombie's men, just to give him a bit of a warning that lorry blaggings weren't his exclusive preserve. Got the idea?'

'Yes indeed, sir.'

'Good. Now, Frankie Carter, deceased. What can you tell me?'

'One nine-millimetre round through the head, sir. Death was instantaneous.'

'Would be, I should think,' said Fox. 'But that much I know. No witnesses, of course.'

'No, sir.'

'Can't understand people not wanting to help the police,' said Fox shaking his head. 'Any joy with the rope?'

'The rope, sir?' Dorman was having a job keeping up with Fox.

'The rope that Parish was wearing. He was the driver of the lorry, wasn't he?'

'I'm sorry, sir, you'll have to speak to the DCI about that. He's down the corridor . . . in the other incident room.'

'Perhaps you'd give him a ring, get him up here. I think you need to put this all together.'

The Romford DCI, John Godwin, appeared minutes later. 'Enquiring about our hijacking, sir?'

'Yes. What can you tell me? That I don't already know.'

'Bloke called Wayne Parish, guv'nor.'

'I know,' said Fox. 'Had any joy with the rope that he was tied up with? And from which I understand he was disentangled by a butch jogger thundering round the golf course. Up at the lab, is it?'

'Er, yes, sir. Well, on its way.'

'Splendid.' Fox beamed round at the other detectives in the incident room who were all doing their best to look

18

busy. Despite Fox's warning to the members of his select squad, the bush telegraph of the CID had been at work and the news that he was co-ordinating the enquiries had preceded his arrival at Romford. 'Well, I can see you're on top of it, Mr Dorman. Anything I can do to help, don't hesitate to give me a bell . . . or you, Mr Godwin.'

'No, right, sir. Thank you very much,' said Dorman.

Fox leaned confidentially towards the detective super-intendent. 'I have a consuming interest in Tango Harris and Billie Crombie,' he said. 'And I am going to have the pair of them.'

'Time somebody did,' said Dorman, half to himself. And for one passing moment he actually felt sorry for Tango Harris and Billie Crombie.

Chapter Three

The chief security officer of the credit-card company was an ex-CID officer called Sharp. 'I remember you,' he said, as he shook hands. 'You were a DC on Eight Area about three years ago.'

'That's right, guv'nor,' said Detective Sergeant Jagger. 'And I remember you, too.'

Sharp waved a deprecating hand. 'I'm not in the job any more,' he said. 'Call me Ron. What can I do for you?'

Jagger laid the voucher which had been found in the hotel room on Sharp's desk and gave him brief details of Brace's investigation into the murder of the so-far unidentified woman.

Sharp laughed as he stood up. 'Gavin Brace has caught a good one there,' he said. 'Won't keep you long.' When he returned, minutes later, he was clutching a slim folder. 'The principal and sole proprietor of Mountjoy Services is called Gina West,' he said, 'and she seems to be in a very good way of business.' He raised a sceptical eyebrow at Jagger. 'Average take is about eight thousand quid a month.'

'Sounds like a busy up-market tom all right,' said Jagger. 'Got an address for her?'

Sharp pushed the file across the desk. 'Help yourself.'

'Is that where she lives?'

Sharp shrugged. 'Haven't a clue, mate. Frankly we don't care. We pay *her* the money, not the other way round. Probably an accommodation address, but you might get lucky.'

20

'Bloody rich, isn't it? Toms using credit cards.'

'Rich is the word,' said Sharp. 'But why not? Prostitution's not illegal. Only soliciting for it . . . as you well know.'

'Yeah!' Jagger sighed and made a few notes from the file. 'Been at it for about three years, according to this.'

'That's how long she's had a supplier's account with us. Could have been on the game a lot longer than that. Before she got into the plastic.'

'That sounds kinky,' said Jagger.

Although never quite sure whether he needed one in such circumstances, Brace had taken the precaution of obtaining a search warrant. Then he and Jagger made their way to the block of elegant service flats in St John's Wood where Sharp's records showed that Gina West lived.

There was no answer when they rang the bell, but they eventually contacted the caretaker, who described himself as the 'con-serge'. He looked suspiciously at the search warrant and shook his head. 'Well, I don't know,' he said. 'I mean these is good-quality flats. We don't have no *hoi polloi* in here. No rough. I reckon I'll have to speak to my boss.'

'Let me put it to you in simple language,' said Brace. 'This is a search warrant, issued by a magistrate. Now you can telephone the managing agents, the managing director . . . or your MP if you like. But while you're doing that, we shall be putting in Miss West's door with a sledgehammer. On the other hand, you could get the duplicate key which you undoubtedly have and open the door for us. There, that plain enough for you?' Brace always got irritable with petty functionaries.

The caretaker mumbled and disappeared into his flat, returning moments later with a key. Then the three of them took the lift to the third floor in silence.

A twenty-minute search merely confirmed that Gina West was a prostitute, albeit high class. The wardrobe was stocked with expensive clothes . . . of two varieties. There was a collection of good-quality dresses, suits, shoes, and underwear, bearing the labels of some of the best-known fashion houses in both London and Paris. Then there was the other collection, also expensive, consisting of the colourful apparel – bras, briefs, suspender belts, and sheer black stockings – favoured by whores the world over, and which she probably called her business clothes.

'Found any corres, Geoff?' asked Brace.

'Just,' said Jagger, emerging from the bedroom. He sat down on the leather sofa, placed a bundle of papers on the coffee-table and started to sift through it.

'Anything interesting?'

'Her passport for a start.' Jagger handed the document to Brace.

'Well, that's her all right.' Brace glanced briefly at the photograph and dropped the passport on to the table. 'Anything else?'

'Yes, sir. Bank statements showing substantial weekly payments by cheque. No name, of course. Just the cheque number.' Jagger looked up. 'I'll bet they were to her ponce.'

'Could be. Means talking to the bank.' Brace looked round the room. 'I've got a hunch,' he said suddenly. 'Let's do the kitchen.'

'The kitchen, guv?' Jagger wondered what his governor knew that he didn't.

'Yeah!' Brace stood up. 'Found some interesting things in kitchens in my day.'

But Brace was wrong. Half an hour later, having emptied just about every container and packet in the kitchen cupboards, he turned his attention to the rest of the flat.

It was Jagger who found it, in an envelope taped to the back of a picture in the spare bedroom.

'What've you got?'

'Insurance, guv.'

'Insurance? What sort of insurance?'

'The best, I think. Hang on.' Jagger walked through to the sitting room and picked up the bank statements. 'Great!' he said, after a moment or two's reading. 'Got the bastard.'

'What is it?'

'It's a list headed "Payments made to Billie Crombie in the name of F. Richardson", and each one of them matches an entry on the bank statement.'

'So Crombie's her ponce,' said Brace thoughtfully. 'It looks as though she made that record in case she got topped.'

'Smart girl,' said Jagger. 'Gina West was obviously a copper-bottomed professional.'

'I didn't notice that, Geoff.'

'What, guv?'

'That she had a copper bottom.'

Gavin Brace had a blind spot when it came to accountancy. He could work out his pay-slip and that was about all, but DC Tanner had worked in a bank for two years before becoming a policeman, and he knew his way round figures. Which was why Brace had given him the job of analysing Gina West's accounts.

'Well? Anything interesting?'

'Not really, sir,' said Tanner. 'All looks pretty kosher. There are the usual payments out: gas, electricity, TV, rent. That sort of thing. Oh, and couturiers. She spent a lot on clothes.'

'I noticed,' said Brace drily.

'The only interesting thing is that the payments to Richardson' – Tanner glanced up – 'alias Billie Crombie, ceased about eight weeks ago.'

'According to the bank statement, you mean.'

'Sorry, sir, I don't quite follow—'

'She might have paid in cash or through another account that we haven't traced.'

'That's possible, sir,' said Tanner. 'Or she might have started paying a different ponce.'

'That's a thought,' said Brace. 'On the other hand, she

23

might have decided that she could go it alone. And that might just be why she got topped.'

'You're not going to like this, sir . . . I think,' said DS Jagger, clutching a printout from the Police National Computer.

'What?'

'I ran Billie Crombie through the PNC, just to get an up-to-date on him.'

'And?'

'Apart from being an SO11 target criminal—'

'Which we knew.'

'Yes, sir, which we knew, but apart from that, there's a marker on the computer.'

Brace's eyes narrowed. 'What sort of marker?'

'No enquiries without reference to Detective Chief Superintendent Fox of the Flying Squad, sir.'

'And that,' said Brace, standing up, 'is all I need.'

The car stopped, engine still running. The three men inside looked quickly up and down the narrow street and donned stocking masks. Then the older one, sitting next to the driver, spoke. 'Don't hang about, then. Get on with it.'

The man in the back opened the door nearest the pavement and got out. Leaning back into the car, he grabbed the two four-pint plastic containers – they had originally held milk – and strode across the pavement. Stopping in the doorway of the restaurant, he placed them on the ground and calmly lit the rag fuses in the top of each.

Once the flames had caught, the man kicked the door open violently and hurled the two containers inside.

The petrol in the containers ignited with a sudden dull explosion, and within seconds the whole of the bar area of the restaurant was engulfed in flames. The barman, who had just skirted his counter with a trayful of drinks, caught the full effects of the blast and staggered away screaming, his whole body a mass of flames.

The man who had thrown the petrol bombs walked swiftly back to the car, which sped away, leaving a throng of curious pedestrians on the pavement.

The whole operation had taken less than a minute.

Tommy Fox was seated at his desk drinking a cup of coffee and reading *The Times*. 'Gavin, dear boy, to what do I owe this unexpected pleasure?'

'Billie Crombie, sir.'

'What about Billie Crombie?'

'There's a marker on the PNC which says no enquiries without reference to you, et cetera—'

'Yes, I know. I put it there. Have you got an interest in the odious Mr Crombie, Gavin?' Fox swung in his chair and stretched out his legs.

'Sort of, sir. He features quite strongly in the Gina West murder.'

'How strongly?'

'Looks as though he was her ponce.'

'Oh, is that all?' Fox looked disappointed. 'Well, that comes as no surprise, Gavin.'

'But it seems she stopped paying him about eight weeks ago.'

'So?'

'Motive for murder, would you say?'

'D'you know, Gavin, I might just say that, yes.' Fox grinned. 'Or she'd got herself another ponce. Is there any evidence that Crombie really was her ponce, though?'

Brace told Fox about finding Gina West's notes secreted behind the picture in her spare bedroom. 'But there's no corroboration, sir,' he added. 'Apart from the bank statements. We've checked with the bank and they confirm that the payments she listed were made to F. Richardson. So we tried Richardson's bank.'

'And?'

'They say that they don't have an address for him, whoever he is. Seems he told them he worked abroad. They don't mind apparently, so long as there's money in his account. And there is. More than a hundred grand.

25

He goes in to cash a cheque very occasionally, but no one can remember what he looks like. Usually payments from the account are against cheques that he's issued to someone else. Straightforward traders for the most part. Marvellous, isn't it?'

'What else have you got?'

Brace explained about the credit-card voucher that had been found in Gina West's briefcase at the hotel. 'We've had a go at the hall porter to see if he put Gina West in touch with Phillips, but if he did he's not having it. And we're checking all her previous clients. At least those who put their payments through Mountjoy Services by credit card. It's a mammoth task and it'll be a waste of time, but it's got to be done, I suppose.'

'There's something odd about that credit-card voucher,' said Fox when Brace had finished. 'I don't see a killer leaving what amounts to a calling card. Either it's a set-up, or Phillips isn't your man. All you've really got is a piece of paper on which Gina West claims to have paid Crombie large sums of money. Sums of money that her bank account shows were paid to F. Richardson. And you've only got Gina West's post-mortem word for it that Richardson is Crombie. You haven't confirmed that yet, I suppose.'

'No, sir. I was considering interviewing Crombie and putting it to him.'

'Don't bother, Gavin. At least, not yet. You'll achieve nothing . . . except to alert him. In no time at all, there'll be more solicitors than you can shake a stick at, all claiming that their client's being harassed. No, let's wait until we've something to screw the little bastard with.'

'D'you mean that you're taking the enquiry over, sir?' Brace looked hopeful.

'Good Heavens, no, Gavin. Whatever gave you that idea? Apart from anything else, I'm much too busy. Some thoughtless bastard has just torched one of Tango Harris's restaurants.' Fox tapped a message flimsy and gave Brace a malevolent smirk. 'On your old patch, too.'

*

26

The barman was dead, burned to death by the violent conflagration caused by the two petrol bombs, which had in turn ignited the liquor and wrecked the whole of the bar area. By the time police had arrived, the clientele, most of whom had been dining at the rear of the building, had fled. To the chagrin of the owner, now surveying the smoking ruins from the street, none of them had paid.

'I thought you said this was one of Tango Harris's dives,' said Brace. 'That bloke over there is Morrie Isaacs. Been the owner for about five years.'

'That's right,' said Fox. 'But when I said it was one of Tango's joints, I meant it was under his protection.' He shot a sideways look at Brace. 'If you get my meaning, Gavin.'

'Then why the hell hasn't someone done something, guv'nor. If I'd known, I'd've had a go at him when I was stationed here.'

'It's not that easy, Gavin. Put simply, no one will talk. Go and ask Morrie if you don't believe me. Ask him how much he's into Tango Harris for every week, and he'll tell you he's never heard of Harris.' Fox lit a cigarette. 'That's the trouble with being tucked away on the area pool, Gavin. You fail to get the broad overview.'

Brace stuck his hands into his overcoat pockets. 'I haven't even got enough CID officers to do my own work, let alone anyone else's,' he said. 'But I'll tell you this, guv, someone needs to sort these bastards out.'

'And I'm just the man to do it,' said Fox. 'Let's have a word with Morrie.'

'Mr Fox, Mr Brace . . .' Isaacs held out his hands, palms uppermost. 'Who would do such a thing?'

'Dry your eyes, Morrie,' said Fox. 'They're only crocodile tears anyway. And if you don't know who this little lot's down to, then it's time you gave up. You still paying Tango Harris his weekly stipend?'

'Who?'

'Thomas Walter Harris, also known as Tango. Often in here with his smelly little friends.'

27

'Oh, *that* Mr Harris. He's only a customer, Mr Fox. A valued customer, I may say.'

'Do leave off, Morrie. By this time tomorrow you'll have convinced yourself that the chip-fryer caught fire, I suppose.' Fox fixed Isaacs with a cynical stare. 'Well, just in case you get too complacent, let me remind you that a man is lying dead in there . . . murdered. And you may care to advise your friends that I intend to take you and them apart. Got it?' And steering Brace out of Isaacs's earshot, added, 'Anything I can do to help with your murder, Gavin, just say the word, but don't talk to Crombie or Harris without my say-so. Apart from anything else, I'd love to come along for the ride.' He moved towards his car and paused. 'Oh . . . and the best of luck.'

'Well, Mr Dorman, and how are your enquiries going?' Fox looked expectantly around the incident room at Romford.

In fact, Nick Dorman was not having a great deal of luck and the arrival of Tommy Fox did nothing to improve his despondent feeling that he was hammering his head against a wall. A wall of silence. 'DCI Godwin and I have put our enquiries together, sir, but there are no witnesses to the hijacking and no witnesses to the murder of Frank Carter. And certainly no one saw the car being dumped where police found it.'

'Doesn't surprise me. Must be something in the air in Romford that stops people from seeing things. Pollution, I suppose. How far have you got?'

'The rope that Parish was tied up with has yielded nothing, sir,' said Godwin. 'And he can't – or won't – tell us anything. The car that Carter's body was found in was stolen—'

'You told me that. Nicked from Wandsworth. What about the lorry . . . abandoned at Eltham, I think you said?'

Both Dorman and Godwin were unnerved by Fox's ability to grasp all that was going on at Romford and had to think very quickly to keep up with him. 'We've examined the lorry, and the car, and come up with nothing,' said Dorman. 'The lab's been over them both. There's nothing.'

'Tyres? Did they do the tyres?'

'The tyres, sir?' Godwin looked puzzled.

'They must have run the load into a slaughter somewhere. It's just possible that there might be something on the tyres that'll steer you in the right direction.'

Godwin sighed. 'I'll get on to it, sir,' he said, wondering why the hell the head of the Flying Squad kept pestering them.

'Splendid,' said Fox. 'But if Tango Harris is behind it, you haven't got a hope in hell.' And with that encouraging comment, he left and made his way back to New Scotland Yard.

Penny Sinclair was a tall, willowy blonde. She would be twenty-nine next July and had been a prostitute for ten years. At the age of twenty-five, she had become Tango Harris's live-in lover until, six months ago, she had been supplanted by a girl called Melody. With angry resignation, she had returned to her flat in the West End and resumed a life of high-class prostitution. But she still saw him and, foolishly hoping for reinstatement, would go running to Buckhurst Hill whenever Harris flicked his fingers. But she had to admit, if only to herself, that her willing response to Harris's demands was fuelled as much by fear as a desire to regain the protection and doubtful prestige of being the boss's woman.

Billie Crombie, himself the ponce of a not inconsiderable number of call-girls in London, knew about Penny Sinclair and her relationship with Tango Harris. And Crombie was still seething about the death of Gina West. He, like Fox, was certain that Harris was responsible. With his two sons, he had torched Morrie Isaacs's restaurant – just as a little lesson – but knew that it was no great inconvenience. After all, the insurance company would pay out, so the arson attack had done Harris little real harm . . . except to his ego.

So he held a council of war with his two sons.

'It's a dog's dinner, guv'nor,' said Fox as he settled into one of Commander Myers's chairs.

Myers gazed at Fox over his half-glasses and smiled. 'These area detectives not coming up to snuff, Tommy?'

'Oh, they're all right, guv'nor. Gavin Brace particularly. Trouble is they're all nibbling round the edge.'

'Round the edge?' Myers knew what Fox meant, but he enjoyed playing him along.

'We've got gang warfare here. Tango Harris and Billie Crombie. Within the space of about forty-eight hours, a lorry was hijacked in Romford by Tango Harris, and one of Billie Crombie's foot-soldiers has been topped. Added to that, one of Crombie's toms was murdered in the West End – that's got to be down to Tango Harris – and one of the restaurants under Harris's protection was torched.'

'How d'you know all this, Tommy?'

'It's in the crime books at Romford and West End Central, sir.'

'No, I meant how d'you know that Harris did the Romford heist, topped Carter, and murdered a tom. Or that Crombie set fire to a restaurant run by one of Harris's stooges?'

Fox stood up. 'I don't, sir,' he said. 'But I bloody well intend to prove it.' He paused, hand on the doorknob. 'I'm going to get in among this little lot. Hard!'

Myers sighed. 'Do it your way, Tommy. You always do, anyway.'

Chapter Four

Penny Sinclair was accustomed to getting telephone calls asking her to go to elegant hotels, there to indulge the sexual whims of those men prepared to pay for her expensive services. Consequently, when she received a call at six o'clock that evening, she dressed carefully in erotic underwear and, shunning tights, put on the more provocative suspender belt and sheer black nylons. Slipping on high heels, she dismissed the need for a dress, and donned a shiny black belted raincoat. Then she picked up her handbag and emerged from her flat to hail a cab.

When she arrived at the hotel she casually dropped an envelope on the hall porter's desk, as was the practice in her trade, before making her way to the third floor.

And that's when it all started to go wrong.

Gary Crombie opened the door, smiled, and invited her in. It was not until she was well into the room and the door was closed firmly behind her that she saw Gary's brother Kenny sitting on the bed. In his right hand was a fearsome-looking knife and he was tapping the palm of his other hand gently with its six-inch serrated blade.

Penny turned quickly, the colour draining from her face, but Gary was leaning against the door with a malevolent smile on his face.

'We're going for a little ride, darlin',' he said. 'And if you do as you're told, you won't get hurt.'

'What's this about?' asked Penny, her voice breaking with the near hysteria which threatened to engulf her.

'Shut up,' said Kenny, rising from the bed and pointing his knife towards the girl. 'We're going downstairs and you're going with us. Like there was nothing wrong. But don't forget that I've got a knife and I shan't hesitate to use it. Got the idea?'

Penny nodded dumbly. She too knew of the death of Gina West and was scared out of her wits.

Kenny placed the knife in a special holster under his jacket and gestured towards the door. They walked casually down the corridor, at one point Gary nodding to a chambermaid, until they reached the fire exit. With a quick look up and down, Gary pushed his way through it, followed by the girl with Kenny bringing up the rear. Quickly, they descended to the ground floor and out through the escape door. In the alleyway at the side of the hotel, the two Crombie brothers bundled the girl into their Rover. Gary took the wheel and Kenny sat in the back next to Penny, once more taking his knife out and laying it menacingly on his lap.

They drove for an hour, being careful to observe speed limits and traffic lights, out through the City and on to Leyton, Wanstead, and Woodford until they reached Tango Harris's secluded house, in an equally secluded lane, at Buckhurst Hill.

Coasting the last few yards, Gary stopped the car just short of the house, doused the lights and turned in his seat. Grinning at Penny Sinclair, he said, 'Take your clothes off. All of them.'

'And if I don't?' Convinced that she was about to be murdered, Penny Sinclair developed a little late bravado.

'If you don't, you'll get hurt . . . nastily. Do it and you'll be all right.' And to emphasize what his brother had said, Kenny lifted the knife and touched the girl's throat with its point.

As quickly as she could in the confined space of the car, Penny stripped off her minimal clothing.

Leaving his brother to guard the girl, Gary walked forward a few yards and peered through the ornamental iron gates of Harris's house towards the hut that was just inside. There was a light on and the security guard could be seen, with his back to them, watching television.

Stealthily, Gary returned to the car and opened the

32

rear door. 'Out!' he said in a menacing whisper and grabbed the girl's wrist.

Penny was shivering uncontrollably now, both from fear and the cold. 'What are you going to do?' she asked, unable to keep the panic from her voice. She could not believe that these two men had brought her all the way to Buckhurst Hill just to rape her. They could have done that in the comfortable surroundings of the hotel from which they had abducted her. That, more or less, is what she had gone there for. And if she hadn't got paid . . . well, it wouldn't have been the first time.

Pushing the girl the few yards to the gates, Gary and Kenny Crombie forced her up against the cold metal bars and handcuffed her so that she was fully stretched with her hands high above her head.

'Reckon that'll teach him,' said Kenny with a smirk. He gazed wistfully at the naked, helpless girl and then placed a strip of sticking plaster across her mouth.

'Not quite,' said Gary and taking a felt-tip pen from his pocket scrawled a message across the girl's stomach. 'With love from Billie,' he said slowly, speaking as he wrote.

They drove for two or three miles before stopping at a phone box. Gary leaped out, dialled 999, and asked for the police. 'I've just seen a funny thing,' he said when he was connected. 'There's a naked girl chained to the gates of Tango Harris's house in Buckhurst Hill.' He declined his name and address, got back into the car, and together he and his brother roared away into the night, laughing and throwing items of Penny Sinclair's apparel out of the car windows at intervals along the way.

The crew of the police car knew where Tango Harris lived and arrived five minutes after receiving the call. They tried the key of their official handcuffs, but it didn't fit those securing the hapless, shivering girl.

By the time the fire brigade arrived, noisily, and the lane was full of flashing blue lights, the security guard had woken up to the fact that something was going on. He called Tango Harris.

Harris arrived at the gates just as the fire brigade freed

33

Penny Sinclair and a gallant fire-fighter put a coat round her, but he wasn't quick enough to prevent Harris from seeing the message that Gary Crombie had written on the girl's stomach.

After both Penny and Harris had denied knowing why anyone should do such a thing – or who 'Billie' was – the police left to record the incident as a domestic disturbance. Harris took Penny up to the house, gave her a large brandy, and told Melody to find her some clothes. Then he telephoned Alfie Penrose who was by way of being his chief of staff.

'I'm not having it,' said the furious Harris. 'I'm not having that bastard taking the piss. Straight-forward villainy I can deal with, but this man Crombie has got to be teached. Got it?'

Penrose undoubtedly got it, received a terse briefing from Harris, heavily larded with obscenities, and set out to find a man called Randy Steel.

All in all, Tango Harris was not a happy man.

Fox was unhappy about Wayne Parish's statement. He had brought a copy of it back from Romford and had read it several times.

Then he had telephoned Detective Chief Inspector Godwin and told him to fetch Parish in again.

Finally, he had sent for Denzil Evans and the pair of them had returned to Romford.

Wayne Parish was lounging in a chair in the interview room, dressed in jeans and a blue T-shirt, the sleeves of which were stretched over the bulging muscles of his upper arms. He had no previous convictions, but, from Fox's point of view, he looked as though he ought to have had.

'I am Detective Chief Superintendent Thomas Fox . . . of the Flying Squad. And this is Detective Inspector Evans.' Fox sat down opposite Parish and lit a cigarette.

'That's very bad for your health, you know,' said Parish.

'So's getting mixed up with Harris and Crombie,' said Fox.

'Never heard of them,' said Parish. 'Sound like a couple of overcoats.' He remained lounging, an expression of veiled contempt on his face.

'The only overcoats they're interested in are wooden ones. And as you've got in between them, you're in some danger of acquiring one.' Fox blew smoke in the air and was pleased to see that Parish sat up, the half-sneer vanishing from his face. 'So you have heard of them.'

'Well, yeah. I mean I've heard 'em mentioned . . . down the gym where I work out, like.'

'Work with weights, do you?' asked Fox mildly.

'Yeah.'

'Interesting,' said Fox. 'So do Harris and Crombie.'

'Oh yeah?'

'Yes,' said Fox. 'They usually attach them to people before they drop them in the river.'

Parish fidgeted in his chair. 'What you telling me all this stuff for?'

'Just so you know who you've got mixed up with,' said Fox. 'Which is nearly as bad as getting mixed up with me.'

'What d'you mean . . . mixed up?'

'What was your cut?'

'Eh?' Parish pretended to look astonished at Fox's question. 'I dunno what you mean.'

'My dear Mr Parish, are you telling me that this gang of blaggers happened on your lorry with its expensive load quite by accident?'

'Well, I dunno, do I? I was only the driver.'

'Only the driver.' Fox carefully rolled ash from his cigarette and glanced at Evans. 'He was only the driver, Denzil.' Fox thumbed through the copy of Parish's statement and then prodded at a paragraph with his forefinger. 'Now then, you say that you were driving along, without a care in the world presumably, when out of the sleeping quarters at the back of your cab there appeared a man with a gun. Right so far?'

'Yeah, well, I told the other copper that.'

'I know,' said Fox. 'He was the one who painstakingly

wrote it all down. Then you pulled into a lay-by under the directions of the gentleman with the gun . . .'

'Yeah!' Parish was beginning to feel uncomfortable.

'Then, you say, a further four men appeared out of the gloom, tied you up and dumped you on a nearby golf course.'

'Yeah, that's right. Why are you going over all this again?'

'Well, it's like this,' said Fox, stubbing out his cigarette end. 'It often happens that witnesses leave out vital pieces of information. Either they forget them, or the trauma of the occasion has blocked them out.'

'What the hell are you going on about? I told the other copper that's what happened.'

'But you didn't mention the shot, Mr Parish.'

Behind Fox, Evans glanced briefly at the ceiling. His governor was at it again. Taking a wild guess just to see what happened. Whenever Evans tried it, he usually fell flat on his face, metaphorically, of course. But time after time, he had seen Fox get away with it.

'The shot? What shot?' Parish shifted his feet and looked down at the table.

'When the man who was in your cab jumped down, there was a shot. Yes?'

'Well, there might have been.'

'Might have been. Well, either there was or there wasn't.'

'Well, there was a noise . . . sort of like a shot, I s'pose.'

'That's my problem, you see.' Fox brushed his hand across the statement. 'Just what I was saying. People forget things.' He leaned forward. 'Now, Mr Parish, the question I ask myself is, why should you leave out something as vitally important as the sound of a shot? You see, there was no other traffic about. Quiet as a grave. You said all that in your statement. No traffic, no noise, no nothing. Just you, a silent lorry, and five hoods who looked as though they'd recently flown in from Klosters.'

'I never said nothing about that.'

36

'Yes you did, but not in as many words, I'll give you that, but you did say they were wearing ski masks.'

'Yeah, well, they were,' said Parish, by now thoroughly mystified by Fox's line of questioning.

'And because you got down from your cab on the same side as the man who had held you up in the first place, you couldn't possibly have avoided seeing a body on the ground.' Fox took another wild guess.

'I can't say as how I noticed,' said Parish.

'Amazing,' said Fox and glanced at Evans once more. 'Isn't that amazing, Denzil?'

'Indeed, sir,' said Evans, unsure what sort of response Fox wanted from him.

'Good.' Fox stood up and took a stroll round the room. 'Now we're motoring, as they say.' He turned and leaned over Parish. 'My problem is this, Mr Parish. It seems likely that you were witness to a murder. And yet you say nothing about it. Not a word. Which leads me to believe that you were a party to this audacious theft, and that you hope to collect a portion of the take, so to speak. So I ask you again, what was your cut?' Then Fox sat down again and waited.

Parish had started to sweat. 'Here,' he said, 'I want my solicitor.'

'You've got one, have you? A solicitor, I mean.'

'Er, no, not exactly.'

'Oh well. Not that I can see what you want one for anyway . . . unless you're about to confess to a crime, Mr Parish?'

'This is harassment.'

'Yes,' said Fox mildly. 'Quite possibly, but as you are not a suspect, it doesn't matter, you see.'

'But you just said that I—'

Fox held up a hand. 'Don't take any notice of me, Mr Parish,' he said. 'Just thinking aloud.' And he smiled at Parish. It was unnerving.

'Look,' said Parish eventually, 'I'll be honest about this.'

'Oh, splendid. It's about time.'

37

'I did hear a shot, and I did see a body lying on the ground.'

'And what was said by these hoods?'

'Nothing.'

'Nothing?'

'Well, when the first geezer, the bloke in my cab, pulled a shooter on me, he just said as how to keep driving. Then a bit later on he told me to pull into a lay-by. Then we waited. No more than two or three minutes, I s'pose. Then this other lot turned up in two cars. One of 'em said, "Out!" That's all anyone said. The bloke what pulled me jumped down first and got shot—'

'Just like that?'

'Yeah. Then the other four blokes bunged his body in the boot of one of the cars and one of 'em drove off. The others tied me up and gagged me. Then, like I said, they bunged me in the other car and dumped me in this field.'

'The golf course?'

'Yeah. Leastways, that's what the law said when they picked me up.'

'And why didn't you tell the other officer all this, Mr Parish?'

'I never wanted to get mixed up in it, did I. See, in my game—'

'What? Lorry driving?'

'Yeah. Well, the word was out among the drivers that Harris had been pulling a few artics, see. And he's got a bit of a nasty reputation. Well, I could see that if I didn't keep my trap shut, I'd likely get topped an' all.'

'What d'you mean, word was out?'

'Well, it's about nine or ten hours across to the Hook. Sometimes I do Dover to Ostend – that's four and a half hours – and the drivers all have grub together. And we get talking, see.'

'Fascinating,' said Fox. 'And presumably mention was made of the fact that on the last few occasions such robberies occurred, a man had crept out of the sleeping quarters of the cab and produced a gun with which to persuade the driver to take a certain course of action?'

38

'Well, yeah.'

'But you got into your cab and didn't check to see if you'd got a stowaway.'

'Never thought about it.' Parish avoided Fox's gaze.

'Careless,' said Fox. 'Either that, or you fully expected a man to pop out somewhere between your depot and Harwich. See my predicament, Mr Parish?'

'Well, you don't expect it, like. Do you?'

'Oh, I do, Mr Parish. I go about confidently expecting villains to pop up from beneath every bush.'

Parish glowered at Fox but said nothing.

'But I suggest that you didn't expect to be tied up and dumped on a golf course,' Fox continued. 'That was when things started to get slightly iffy. Is that a good guess?'

'I dunno what you're on about.'

'What I'm on about, Mr Parish, is that you thought that you'd be left in the cab after the load had been taken. That you would be tied up – a sort of token tying up, you might say – and that later, at an agreed time, you would free yourself and drive all the way to the nearest nick . . . and lay a complaint.' Fox leaned back and studied Parish. 'But you didn't expect anyone to get shot, and you didn't expect to get dumped on a golf course. That about it?'

'Look, I've told you all I know,' said Parish. He desperately wanted to wipe the sweat from his face, but didn't dare to.

'All right,' said Fox, standing up and giving the impression of having suddenly tired of the whole thing. 'Another officer will be in shortly to take a full statement from you, Mr Parish. Then you can go.'

'Here, hold on. Is that it?' Parish jumped to his feet in alarm.

'Unless you can think of anything else,' said Fox.

'What about protection?'

'What about it?'

'Well, you said I was in danger, and now I've told you all this, they might come after me.'

'Who might?'

'Well, Harris, I s'pose . . . or Crombie.'

'Yes,' said Fox thoughtfully. 'I suppose they might. I'll see what I can do.'

As Fox strode through to the incident room, Evans caught up with him. 'Aren't you going to nick him, guv?'

'Is that what you'd do, Denzil?'

'Well, you seem to think he's implicated.'

'Undoubtedly, Denzil, undoubtedly. But there's no evidence. The minute we get him into court, his mouthpiece is going to claim duress and suggest to his client that he stays shtum. And we'll have blown it. The plan, Denzil, is to use young Mr Parish to trap Messrs Harris and Crombie.'

'How, sir?'

'It's fairly evident to me, Denzil, that Billie Crombie was all set to hijack Parish's lorry, probably with the assistance of the said Parish, but his little team was jumped by Harris's mob just before the heist. Frankie Carter got blown away and Tango's lot took over where Crombie's lot had been obliged to leave off. Simple.'

'Well, that's it, then, guv.'

'Alas, Denzil, that is not it. There are some vital elements missing.'

'Like what, sir?'

'Like witnesses, Denzil,' said Fox over his shoulder as he threw open the door of the incident room. 'Your murder, Mr Dorman' – Fox strode across the room – 'is definitely tied up with Mr Godwin's hijacking.'

'Really, sir?'

'Oh yes. Mr Parish in there is falling over himself to make another statement.'

'That's good news, sir.'

'Thought you'd be pleased. Oh, and by the way, he'll need round the clock protection, just in case Tango Harris decides to have a pop at him. Or Billie Crombie for that matter. But discreet protection. The sort that Parish won't notice, because I am anxious to know who he talks to.'

'But where am I going to get the men for that, sir?'

40

Dorman looked appalled at the prospect of having to assign at least twelve policemen to an apparently endless task.

'My dear Nick,' said Fox, using Dorman's Christian name for the first time, 'there are twenty-eight thousand police officers in the Metropolitan Police. I'm sure you'll be able to find one or two that aren't doing anything in particular. Try Community Relations Branch.'

Chapter Five

The race had started and the shouts of encouragement were deafening. The group of seven or eight men in the stand nearest the restaurant leaped to their feet as the dog they had backed forged ahead, yards clear of his nearest rival. The men had arrived together, intent on enjoying a good night out. Getting a few down them, was how they had put it. One of them, the owner of the winning greyhound, was obviously the host and the others in the group deferred to him.

Because of the noise, no one heard the shot.

But suddenly the dog's owner clutched at his chest and let out an involuntary gasp, little more than a sigh. At once, the force of the bullet threw him backwards, over the seat, so that he fell awkwardly, spread-eagled with his head hanging down.

At first none of his companions realized what had happened and, thinking that he had fainted, turned to help him. One of them started to pull him up. Then he saw the blood. 'Christ!' he yelled. 'He's been bloody shot.' Relinquishing his hold, he looked round, desperately, as if seeking the attacker.

A woman pushed officiously through the crowd. 'I'm a nurse,' she said and placed her fingertips on the injured man's throat, searching for a pulse. She shook her head and stood up. 'He's dead,' she said. 'Someone had better call the police.'

Police area car call-sign Papa Three was not far away from Catford Greyhound Stadium when it got the call to a shooting. But the crew didn't rush there, not until

42

they were assured that armed back-up was on its way.

When eventually the two PCs, supported by the crew of the gun car and the whole of the territorial support group, fought their way through the crowd, they found that the stand had been cleared, and was being kept clear, by uniformed security guards under the direction of the stadium's chief security officer, a retired policeman. Lying now on his back between the seats was the overcoated figure of the dead man. There was a dark pool of blood near the body.

'What have we got, guv?' asked one of the PCs. 'Apart from the obvious,' he added with a nod towards the body.

'There was a race going on,' said the security officer, 'when suddenly there were shouts and screams from here. One of my blokes sprinted up to have a look . . .' He gestured at the body. 'And that's what he found. Now you know as much as I do.'

DS Jagger and DC Tanner had done a lot of leg work as part of their particular enquiry into the murder of Gina West.

John Phillips, the man who had apparently paid five hundred pounds for Gina West's services, had a credit-card account which was managed by a bank. Because of that the police had deemed it necessary to obtain a warrant signed by a crown court judge before attempting to get details of it. That problem overcome, Jagger had learned that Phillips had held the card for only three weeks and, so far, no charge had been made against it. Phillips, said the bank, had an address in Richmond and that is where the credit card had been sent. The bank asked if there was a problem. Jagger said that there was . . . but it wasn't the bank's problem.

The property was a Victorian house converted into flats. Disinclined to make a cold call on someone who might be a murderer, Jagger and Tanner first undertook some discreet enquiries. The girl who lived in the flat beneath the one apparently rented by Phillips told them it was occupied by a young man who had moved in only two weeks previously. His name, she said, was Jason Morley and she had never heard of anyone called Phillips.

Jagger and Tanner decided to telephone Brace to see what should be done next. They thought that it was a bit risky to tackle Morley alone – he might, after all, turn out to be Phillips – but on the other hand they didn't want to go in heavy handed. Brace was unsympathetic. 'D'you want me to come down there and hold your hand or something?' he asked. And then rather spitefully, added, 'You're not on television, you know. You're real policemen. I think.'

'Come in,' said Jason Morley. 'Will this take long? I've just put a pizza in the microwave.'

The mention of food reminded the two detectives that it was a long time since they had last eaten. 'I hope not,' said Jagger as he and Tanner entered the flat cautiously. 'We are attempting to trace a Mr John Phillips.'

Morley took the pizza out of the microwave and carried it through into his tiny living room. Then he turned off the television. 'Must have been the previous tenant,' he said. 'I've only been here about two weeks.'

Jagger nodded at the pizza. 'Don't let us stop you,' he said.

'If you don't mind,' said Morley. 'I usually eat in town, but I've got a date this evening . . . here in Richmond.'

'Did you meet the previous tenant at all?'

'No. This place was empty and I dealt with the solicitors. I answered an ad in the evening paper. Lucky to find it really. Moved in within twenty-four hours.' Morley laughed. 'Not that I had much to move.'

Jagger glanced round the room. Piles of books and files covered most of the available surfaces and there were several large cardboard boxes on the floor. There were suits laid over the back of the settee and two or three pictures standing against the wall.

'I know,' said Morley, following Jagger's gaze. 'Bit of a state really, but I just don't seem to have had the time to get straight.'

'Does the name Phillips mean anything to you at all, Mr Morley?'

Morley shook his head slowly. 'No, I'm afraid not.'

'Was there any correspondence here when you arrived, by any chance?'

'No, nothing. Oh, just a minute though. There was something.'

'Oh?'

'A letter did arrive. Must have been four or five days ago.'

'For Phillips?'

'I don't know. It was an unfamiliar name, that's all I can remember.'

'D'you still have it?'

Morley stood up and ran his hand round his chin. 'I don't know what happened to it,' he said. 'I meant to send it back to the post office . . . or drop it into the solicitor. It was knocking about for a few days and then I forgot all about it.' He looked vaguely round the untidy room. 'I suppose I must have thrown it away,' he added and looked apologetic. 'Will that get me into trouble?'

'Shouldn't think so,' said Jagger to whom the finer points of the several Post Office Acts were a complete mystery. 'It's just that it might have helped us.'

'What's this all about, incidentally?' Morley sat down again and poked at his pizza briefly before abandoning it altogether. 'Would you like some coffee?'

'No thanks,' said Jagger. 'We don't have the time.' He and Tanner stood up. 'If anything should come to mind, or you find the letter, I'd be obliged if you let us know.' He scribbled his telephone number on a slip of paper and laid it on the small table beside the pizza. 'It is quite important. It's a murder enquiry.'

The following day, Jagger and Tanner delved deeper. They tracked down the owner of Morley's flat, but he said that he had nothing to do with the running of the property. He told the detectives that his solicitors acted as managing agents and took care of lettings, rent collection, and all the other day-to-day problems . . . among which he seemed to include giving the police any assistance which might help them with an investigation into a murder.

Despite the fact that he was on the point of closing, the solicitor was much more helpful. He knew Mr Phillips – in fact, he had seen him a couple of times – and although he had held the lease of the flat for only a very short time, there were no complaints about him. Phillips had apologized for having to abort the arrangement before he had even moved his things in – a matter of business, he had explained – and happily paid a sum of money in compensation. And in cash.

After a quick phone call to West End Central police station, Brace had told DS Jagger to show the solicitor a photograph of Billie Crombie and, just for good measure, one of Tango Harris. The solicitor had studied both photographs carefully and had eventually decided that the man he had dealt with was more like Crombie . . . although he might have been Harris. But, in any event, he had worn spectacles. Neither Crombie nor Harris had ever been known to wear glasses.

But the solicitor did have a previous address for Mr Phillips.

And about the time that the chief superintendent in charge of Lewisham Division was telling his commander that he had a murder at Catford Stadium, DS Jagger and DC Tanner arrived back at Brace's office with that address . . . and the lease which Mr Phillips had completed in his own hand.

Fox was in the Old Star opposite St James's Park tube station when Denzil Evans appeared. 'I suppose you want a drink, Denzil?'

'Thanks, guv. A Scotch, if I may.' Evans decided to accept this rare offer from Fox before imparting his news. He knew that once he told Fox there would be no more drinking. That they'd both be off again, racing round the Metropolitan Police District.

'Good health,' said Fox.

'Cheers, guv,' said Evans and took a sip of his whisky. 'By the way, Mr Brace has just been on the phone.'

'That's nice.'

'His lads have tracked down Phillips, the bloke whose voucher was found in Gina West's briefcase . . . along with her credit-card machine.'

'Nicked him, has he?' Fox lit a cigarette and absent-mindedly offered one to Evans.

'I don't smoke, sir. And no, he hasn't nicked him. He thought he'd better ask you first.'

'Ask me first? What the hell for?'

'Seems his leg men traced Phillips to a flat in Richmond . . . but he'd gone. Only been there a few weeks, it seems.'

'Are you going to get to the nub of this, Denzil?'

'Yes, guv. The address that Phillips gave before he moved into Richmond is the same as Tango Harris's address in Buckhurst Hill.'

Fox burst out laughing. 'I don't believe it,' he said. 'Tango Harris isn't going to leave a trail that'd take us straight to him.'

'That's what I thought, sir,' said Evans. 'But that's not all. We've just had a message from Lewisham.'

'Anything important?'

'Well, you could say that our workload's just been cut in half.'

'Could I indeed?' said Fox. 'Are you going to stop talking in riddles, Denzil, and tell me this joyful news?'

'Yes, guv. Billie Crombie's just been shot dead at Catford Dog Stadium.'

'Good gracious me,' said Fox, and confounded all Evans's expectations by ordering another round of drinks.

'Very soon, Tommy, every superintendent on every area major investigation pool will be working on some aspect of the Harris versus Crombie war.' Dick Campbell held the post of Deputy Assistant Commissioner Specialist Operations, a cumbersome title invariably foreshortened to the acronym DACSO. As deputy to the Assistant

47

Commissioner, he was the virtual head of London's CID and, as a former commander of the Anti-Terrorist Branch was, unusually these days, a working detective who had come up the hard way.

'Except that Crombie lost, sir.'

'Only in name,' said Campbell. 'Someone will take his place.'

'Undoubtedly,' said Fox.

'It's time for you to co-ordinate the enquiries, Tommy. I don't want two toe-rags like Harris and the late Mr Crombie tying up all our resources. Take a hand, Tommy. Get in among them. D'you need more men?'

'Not for the moment, sir. I've got the whole of the Flying Squad.'

'I don't want the whole of the Squad tied up either. What's your next move?'

'I'm going to have Harris in and give him a talking to, sir.'

Campbell looked pensive. 'I doubt that you'll get any joy there. There's no evidence . . . is there?'

'None at all, sir.'

'Well, then . . .'

'It'll make him more cocky if he thinks we're clutching at straws.'

'Well, aren't we?'

What Tommy Fox had not told DACSO was that he already had Tango Harris under observation. Detective Inspector Henry Findlater, sometime head of the surveillance team in Criminal Intelligence Branch, had mounted a twenty-four-hour coverage of Harris's luxurious home in Buckhurst Hill. Fox knew Harris wouldn't do anything which would play into the hands of the police – he was too fly for that – but he didn't want to take a team out to Harris's house with the intention of arresting him only to find that he was somewhere else.

But first, Fox had a call to make.

*

48

The incident room at Catford police station appeared to be in a state of chaos, but Detective Superintendent David Blunt, not long promoted from the onerous task of being DCI at Wandsworth, knew what everyone was doing. Or was supposed to be doing. 'Come to see how we're getting on, sir?'

'Are you getting on?' Fox always went to the heart of the matter.

'We've got HOLMES in, sir,' said Blunt.

'Sherlock Holmes?' Fox knew what Blunt meant, but had an almost pathological dislike of the ever-increasing use of abbreviations that the Metropolitan Police tended to indulge in.

'The Home Office Large Major Enquiry System, sir,' said Blunt patiently, not sure if Fox was pretending not to know.

Fox gazed at the bank of computer screens. 'Has he caught anyone yet?' he asked and lit a cigarette. He perched on the corner of a desk. 'Never mind all that electronic gismo,' he said. 'What's the SP?'

'Billie Crombie and about six of his hoods were watching the seven-thirty at Catford. They were standing all round him, but suddenly he fell to the ground, dead. If he'd been in the owners' box, where he should have been, he'd have been behind glass and that would probably have made him more difficult to hit. But Billie Crombie liked the common touch.'

'Is that it?'

'Well, there's not a great deal more, guv'nor. Pathologist's report indicates that he was shot with a single round, probably from a high-powered rifle, from as much as six hundred yards away. No one at the stadium saw a thing . . . and there were thousands there.'

'No,' said Fox reflectively, 'they wouldn't have done. There's something about greyhound racing that takes the average punter's mind off trivial things like people getting shot.'

'Even more so when they found out who the victim was,' said Blunt cynically. 'One mention of the name

49

Crombie and everyone went shtum. We've started house-to-house all round the place, and we've checked the buildings from which the shot could have come—'

'Don't tell me,' said Fox. 'Witnesses queuing up.'

'We should be so lucky,' said Blunt.

'It's got to be down to Tango Harris, Dave.'

'I know, sir. The problem is proving it.'

It was a large, expensive house in Hertfordshire on the very fringe of the Metropolitan Police District. Leaving their car in the roadway, DS Jagger and DC Tanner crunched their way up the gravel drive.

A very superior-looking man answered the door. He was about forty-eight, tall, and casually dressed in cords and a yellow sweatshirt adorned with some meaningless logo on the pocket.

'Mr Martin?'

'Yes.'

'We're police officers, sir. We were wondering if you could assist us in some enquiries we're making.'

For a moment, Martin looked puzzled, but then he opened the door wider. 'Oh, er, well you'd better come in, I suppose,' he said and led the way into a large sitting room. 'This is my wife.' He waved a casual hand at a woman seated in front of a large log fire. She looked very 'county' in her red sweater and navy-blue skirt, stockings, and shoes. 'These are police officers, my dear,' said Martin.

Mrs Martin gave Jagger and Tanner a faintly disapproving glance. 'Oh really?' she said and carried on watching television.

'This is a rather delicate matter, sir,' Jagger began. He and Tanner had now done twenty of these enquiries but still enjoyed the reaction. But the pompous Martins looked like being the best so far.

'That's perfectly all right, Officer,' said Martin. 'I have no secrets from my wife.'

'If you're certain, sir.'

'Absolutely, Officer.'

Jagger shrugged, took out his pocket book and thumbed through it until he found the entry that referred to Jack Martin. 'It concerns certain transactions with a company called Mountjoy Services.' He looked up expectantly. 'We're enquiring into the death of a Miss Gina—'

'Oh, I see,' said Martin hurriedly. 'On second thoughts, perhaps you'd better come into my study. Don't want to interrupt my wife's viewing, eh?' He glanced quickly at his wife, apparently absorbed in some programme about wildlife, and almost pushed the two detectives from the room.

Ten minutes later, Jagger and Tanner were walking down the drive again. Another Mountjoy Services customer had been eliminated from their enquiries. Jack Martin had satisfied them that at the time of Gina West's murder he had been out of the country on business.

Out of the country he may have been, but he wasn't out of the wood.

'What was so delicate about Mountjoy Services, Jack,' asked Martin's wife coldly, 'that you couldn't discuss it in front of me?'

'Oh, just a trivial business matter, dear.'

Mrs Martin fixed her husband with a steely gaze. 'Have you been kerb-crawling again?' she asked.

'Whatever makes you think that?' asked Martin.

'Because I've been married to you for twenty-two years, Jack Martin,' said his wife.

Chapter Six

Harris's house was in a private road not far from Epping Forest. The large gardens were screened front and back by trees, and the entrance was guarded by a pair of tall iron gates . . . and a guard in a small cabin.

Findlater had explained all this to Fox and had expressed concern that getting in without alerting Harris might be a problem.

Fox, however, did not see it as a problem. Leaving his own car and the three others containing most of DI Jack Gilroy's team parked down the road a little, he strode up to the gate and peered through the bars. 'Oi!' he shouted.

A uniformed guard from one of the lesser-known security firms peered out of the small hut. 'What?'

Fox pointed at the map he had in one hand and gestured to the guard. 'Can you tell me . . . ?' he began, and then appeared to study the map more closely.

The guard strolled over to the locked gates. 'What's up, mate?' he asked.

'What is up, dear boy,' said Fox, 'is that I am Detective Chief Superintendent Thomas Fox . . . of the Flying Squad, and I have a warrant to search these premises. Now you have two options. You can either unlock these gates without alerting Mr Harris, thus earning the undying gratitude of the Metropolitan Police, or you can raise hell and qualify for several years in chokey for obstructing officers investigating a murder . . . or two. The choice is yours.'

The security guard managed to look both doubtful and worried until Fox produced his warrant card. Then he held up his hands. 'You'll get no trouble from me, guv'nor,' he said. 'I'm only the relief anyway. Don't even know the geezer who owns the drum.'

'Splendid,' said Fox. 'I knew you'd see it my way. Now then, just unlock the gates and we'll say no more about it.'

Nervously fumbling in his haste, the security guard eventually managed to open one of the gates just enough to admit Fox.

'There are a few more of us, I'm afraid,' said Fox with an amiable smile as he signalled his motorcade to move up. 'And I think it might be a good idea if you came with us.' He opened the door of one of the cars and propelled the luckless security guard into the back seat.

'But I—' began the guard.

'Just so that you won't be tempted to make any telephone calls, or press any mysterious buttons,' said Fox, and wandered back to his own car.

The four cars crunched to a standstill on the wide expanse of gravel at the front of the house and Fox and his team alighted. The security guard remained, hunched miserably in the back seat where Fox had put him, and contemplated getting another job.

'Tell me, friend,' said Fox. 'Where is Mr Harris – who you don't even know – most likely to be at this time of the morning?' Fox glanced at his watch. He had deliberately picked mid-morning for his raid, secure in the knowledge that villains always expected to be 'spun', as they called it, in the small hours.

'Dunno,' said the guard.

'I beg your pardon?' Fox stuck his head through the open window of the car so that his face was close enough to the security guard's to give him some cause for alarm.

'Er, he's usually in the pool. Round the back.'

'Splendid,' said Fox. 'Jack.' He turned to Gilroy. 'We'll go the back way. And you, Rosie. Less formal, if you see what I mean. And you . . .' He turned back to the guard. 'You will arrange to admit my officers through the front door.'

'But—'

Fox shook his head. 'No "buts", dear boy,' he said.

Fox, Gilroy, and Rosie Webster walked round the house until they reached what looked like a large summer-house. Fox shielded his eyes and peered through the glass.

On the far side of the swimming pool, a bare-footed Tango Harris was seated on a wheeled sun-lounger. Dressed in a terry bathrobe, he was sipping at an evil-looking concoction in a long glass. He was in his fifties and over the years his bushy grey hair had thinned quite dramatically on top, leaving him looking like a benevolent monk.

Poised on the edge of the swimming pool, about to dive in, was a naked and curvaceous blonde who could not have been more than twenty-five.

'I'll bet you a pony, Jack,' said Fox, 'that she is not his daughter.' He pushed aside the sliding door and stepped inside. 'Tango,' he bellowed. 'Long time, no see.' The blonde screamed and fell in.

Harris made to stand up, but knocked over the drink he had just put down on the small shelf built into the side of his sun-lounger. Pieces of broken glass scattered everywhere. 'Fox! What the bloody hell—?'

'Don't move,' said Fox sternly. Harris froze, expecting to see guns: he knew the Flying Squad of old. 'There's glass everywhere, Tango. You'll cut your dainty dancers to ribbons.'

Harris picked up his spectacles and put them on. 'What the bloody hell's this all about?'

'Well, you've just answered one question. You do wear glasses.'

'What are you going on about, Fox?'

By now the blonde had made her way to the edge of the pool and was crouching down in the vain hope that the water would cover her lack of costume. 'Tango,' she said plaintively. 'I've got nothing on.'

'I know,' said Harris.

54

'What shall I do?'

'Get out and piss off,' said Harris. 'I'm talking business. Oh,' he added, 'and get on the blower to Olly.'

'Stop!' said Fox and turned to Rosie Webster. 'Go with Mr Harris's secretary . . .' He paused to give the word sarcastic emphasis. 'And make sure she doesn't use the phone. I'll decide when Tango can call his mouthpiece.'

'It says in the Police and Criminal Evidence Act that I'm entitled to speak privately to my solicitor,' said Harris.

'Oh, very good,' said Fox. 'But not if I think it'll hinder my enquiries.'

Harris leaned back in his sun-lounger. 'That's only if you've arrested me,' he said.

'I have. You're nicked.'

Harris leaped out of his chair and stood on a piece of broken glass. He yelled and promptly sat down again, examining the sole of his foot. 'I've cut me bloody foot now,' he said.

'Pity you didn't do that before I nicked you,' said Fox mildly. 'Now one of my officers will have to write a report about it.'

'How the hell did you get in here anyway?' asked Harris, dabbing at his cut foot with a handkerchief.

'Through the front gate. How else? I did consider landing in the garden in a police helicopter, but the Commissioner wouldn't authorize the expense . . . not for a tuppeny-ha'penny villain like you, Tango. And talking of front gates, my spies tell me that you've got into the habit of draping naked blondes on them.'

Harris gave Fox a sour look. 'Are you going to tell me what this is all about?' he said.

'Sure.' Fox sat down on the sun-lounger opposite Harris. 'Jack, get the lads going, will you.'

'Here,' said Harris. 'What's the game?'

'We're searching the premises, Tango.'

'I hope you've got a warrant.'

Fox withdrew a sheet of paper from his pocket and handed it to Harris. 'There you are, Tango. Your very own copy. That's in the Police and Criminal Evidence Act, too.'

'Talking of which—' Harris began.

Fox held up a hand. 'I know, I know. You've got to be told what you're arrested for. In very simple terms, Tango, for the murder of Gina West, a prostitute.'

'Do what?' Harris stopped nursing his foot and looked at Fox in amazement. 'You must be bloody joking.'

Fox shook his head slowly. 'It's no joke, Tango.' He nodded towards the door. 'Who's the bird, incidentally?'

'Melody.'

'That's nice. Melody who?'

'Eager,' said Harris.

'And is she?'

'That's what she calls herself. Melody Eager. Don't suppose it's her real name. Don't suppose Melody's her real name, either.'

'No, I don't suppose it is. On the game is she?'

'She better hadn't be. She's employed as my companion.'

'Is that a fact?' said Fox. 'Pity you don't give her a clothes allowance then.'

'What's all this about a murder? Who did you say? Gina someone.'

'Last Friday evening, at a hotel in the West End of London, a prostitute by the name of Gina West was found murdered. The murderer paid by credit card, Tango. And we have traced the holder of that credit card all the way here. To you, in fact.'

Harris leaned forward and peered at his foot again. Then he looked up. 'What d'you take me for?' he asked. 'Firstly I never pay for it, and secondly, if I did I certainly wouldn't pay for it with a credit card that could be traced back to me.'

'That's what I thought,' said Fox. 'I put it down to your advancing years.'

'It's a bloody stitch-up, that's what it is. A pound to a pinch it's bloody Billie Crombie.'

'Quite possibly. She was certainly working for him. But

56

as someone topped him last night, he's out of the race.'

'Topped? Billie Crombie?' Harris contrived to sound surprised.

Fox laughed. 'Oh, do leave off, Tango.'

'At what time did you start asking the prisoner questions, sir?' The custody officer at West End Central police station was very conscious of the law.

'Haven't asked him anything yet,' said Fox without pausing as he walked through the charge room. 'Get Mr Brace down here, will you.'

'Yes, sir. And Mr Harris's solicitor's here.'

'I'll bet he is,' said Fox as he made his way into the interview room.

Tango Harris was lolling in a chair, a half smirk on his face. 'What have you been doing, Fox? Poking around for some evidence to fit me up with?'

Harris's solicitor placed a hand on his client's arm and shook his head. Then he faced Fox. 'Mr Harris knows absolutely nothing about Miss Gina West, or her murder,' he said. 'And I should like to register my protest at the way he is being demeaned and harassed when a simple question would have proved categorically that he had nothing to do with this alleged crime.'

'What simple question is that?' asked Fox, nodding to Gavin Brace as he slipped silently into the interview room.

'Did you think to ask him where he was on the night in question?'

'On the night in question.' Fox savoured the phrase. 'That's nice. Sounds like pure Agatha Christie. All right then. Where were you on the night in question, Tango?'

'Clubbing . . . up west,' said Harris.

The solicitor smiled benevolently. 'And there are several people who can testify to that fact.'

Fox looked severely at the solicitor. 'You may go,' he said.

The solicitor opened his book and started to make

copious notes. 'If you are going to exclude me from the interview,' he said as he wrote, 'you'll be required to give the reasons in writing.'

'You can stay if you wish,' said Fox, 'but your client can go. And may I thank him on behalf of the Commissioner for his ready assistance in this matter.'

The solicitor looked shocked. 'You really mean Mr Harris may go?' he asked, wanting to be absolutely clear on the point.

'Of course. Why ever not?'

'But you arrested him for murder.'

'I wouldn't go that far,' said Fox. 'He kindly offered to assist me in my enquiries. Mr Gilroy will show you out. Oh, and if you find that you've unfortunately collected a parking ticket, let me have it and I'll get it cancelled.'

At the door of the interview room, Harris paused. 'What's your bloody game, Fox?' he asked. It seemed to be one of his favourite expressions.

'Game? I'm not playing games, Tango. See you in court.'

'Is that a threat, Chief Superintendent?' asked the solicitor.

'No,' said Fox. 'A promise.'

The long line of black limousines stretched all the way down Verdant Lane, Lewisham.

'Looks like a Criminal Records Office outing,' said Fox.

'There'll be a few old friends here, guv'nor, that's for sure,' said Gilroy.

The hearse containing the mortal remains of Billie Crombie nosed its way into Hither Green cemetery. The coffin was almost completely hidden by colourful wreaths, the largest of which bore an elaborate floral design emblazoning the message: IN LOVING MEMORY OF MY DEAR BILLIE. NOT FORGOTTEN.

'How tasteless,' muttered Fox.

The car immediately behind the hearse contained a blowsy redhead dressed all in black, her heavy veil failing

58

to disguise the fact that not only had she had a hard life, but had undoubtedly kept a cosmetics firm in full-time employment. Her gloved hands clutched a single red rose to her ample bosom.

'Who's that, guv?' asked Gilroy.

'That,' said Fox, 'is Arlene Fogg, common-law wife of the dear departed Billie Crombie. And they don't come much more common than she does. What's more, I'll lay seven-to-four on she chucks that rose on Billie's box when he's planted.'

'How long's she been with him then?'

'Going on twenty-five years, I should think,' said Fox. 'Her father used to run a stall in Deptford market and moonlighted as a street bookie, but he moved on to better things. War surplus, secondhand cars, and the usual bit of blagging. I think he even got captured for having lead off a church roof in the fifties. Very enterprising in those days, the local villains.'

Fox and Gilroy strolled into the cemetery and watched the procession, now on foot, re-forming itself into a huge human arena around the grave. The six pallbearers, clearly unused to anything approaching hard work, struggled with the coffin.

'Gordon Bennett!' Fox stopped beneath a tree and lit a cigarette. 'Would you look at that collection of toe-rags.' The pallbearers, clearly taking the broad view of what amounted to suitable attire for a funeral, wore suits that ranged from black to light green, with jackets that appeared to be about three sizes too big. Their multi-coloured ties had been slackened off to reveal unfastened collar buttons on the vilest shirts Fox had ever seen. With obvious relief, they placed the coffin on the wooden stretchers over the grave and stood up, easing muscles that manifestly took exception to such physical exertion.

'Ah,' said Fox, 'now this ought to be interesting.'

'What's that, guv?' asked Gilroy.

'Arlene Fogg might have been Billie's common-law, but that scrubber over there with the Sylvester Stallone hair-do, who goes by the unlikely name of Sharon Scrope, was his bit on the side.' Fox pointed his cigarette at a girl of about twenty-seven with dyed blonde hair who was forcing her way through the assembled mourners. She wore a very tight, very short black skirt, and her ample breasts bulged out of a low-cut matching jacket that was nipped in severely at the waist.

Suddenly Arlene Fogg leaped into action. Stepping in front of Sharon Scrope, she placed her hands on her hips. 'And what's a slag like you doing here?' she demanded.

'Come to pay my respects,' said Sharon.

'Well, you can piss off and pay 'em some place else,' said Arlene, and pushed Sharon violently in the chest.

Sharon staggered back a yard or so, but recovered her balance and stepped forward again. 'I done more for him than what you ever did,' she shouted.

'Yeah, and most of it on yer back an' all. Well if you think there's anything in his will for you, you've got another think coming, you saucy cow.' And Arlene seized Sharon's jacket and ripped it open.

'This could get a bit tasty, guv,' said Gilroy.

'Quite likely, Jack, quite likely,' said Fox. 'However, as an experienced police officer, I do not, at this stage, perceive a breach of the peace . . . or even an apprehended breach of the peace. These things have a habit of sorting themselves out. Apart from which,' he continued, 'there used to be a piece in the good book which said that police should not interfere with the innocent amusements of the working classes.'

Sharon, her breasts now fully exposed to the obvious delight of at least the male mourners, leaped at Arlene and delivered a forearm smash that would have brought applause from those who regularly watched the wrestling at Lewisham Town Hall. Arlene, hat dislodged to a ludicrous angle, responded by belting Sharon across the side of the head with her heavy handbag.

Sharon lurched backwards and fell on to the coffin, moving it enough to dislodge the supports, and she – and the coffin – fell into the grave.

'Oh, the cow, the little cow,' screamed Arlene. 'Look what the disrespectful bitch has done.'

A young man jumped forward and held on to Arlene. 'Here, hold up, Ma,' he said. 'Leave it be.'

'You get rid of that cow,' Arlene shrieked.

'All right, Ma, but leave it.'

'Who's the hero, guv?' asked Gilroy.

'That's Gary Crombie, eldest son and heir apparent to the Crombie empire, Jack. And the other one – the tosser pulling Sharon out of the hole – is his younger brother Kenny.'

Several of the mourners ushered Sharon Scrope away from the graveside and she limped towards the gate, holding the remains of her torn jacket together with one hand while clutching a shoe with a broken stiletto heel in the other. Pausing at a sufficiently safe distance, she delivered her parting sally. 'I'll have you, you shrivelled-up old bag,' she screamed.

'Piss off,' bellowed Arlene, not to be outdone in the matter of last words. 'I'm sorry about that, Vicar, but I was provoked,' she said, turning back to the clergyman who, throughout Arlene's exchange with Sharon, had waited patiently to complete the committal.

At last, Billie Crombie's ornate coffin, having been hoisted out and replaced on the stretchers, was lowered once more into the mud of Hither Green cemetery. The crowd, deferring to Arlene, stood back while she examined the long, double-banked row of floral tributes. Suddenly she stopped, causing Gary Crombie to cannon into her. 'Oh my Gawd!' she cried in a keening voice. 'Look at that. Just look at that.'

'What's up, Ma?' asked the ever solicitous Gary.

'Look what that sod's been and done.' Arlene stooped and tore the label from the large wreath. 'You wouldn't credit it, would you?' she asked the congregation at large.

'What is it, Ma?' Gary Crombie craned his head to read the label that Arlene was flourishing.

'That bastard Harris. Tango Harris has sent a bloody wreath. To my Billie's funeral. Oh my Gawd, it's too much, too much for a widow to bear, I tell you.' And with that, Arlene started kicking violently at the wreath so that great chunks of it flew up in the air.

Gary Crombie took hold of one of his mother's arms and his brother Kenny took the other. 'Leave it, Ma,' said Gary. 'Just leave it.' The Crombie brothers steered their mother away towards a waiting limousine, nodding to Fox as they passed him. 'Hallo, Mr Fox,' said Gary. 'Nice of you to come and pay your respects.' Then he bent to his mother again. 'Don't you fret, Ma,' he said. 'We'll sort Tango Harris out. We'll do for the bastard.'

Fox sighed. 'Here we go again, Jack,' he said.

Chapter Seven

'Mr Fox! Nice to see you again.'

'You don't mean a word of that, Morrie.' Fox and Gilroy seated themselves at one of the tables in Morrie Isaacs's restaurant and surveyed the work that was going on in the bar area at the front of the building following the arson attack. 'I see you're open for business again.'

Isaacs shrugged. 'Got to earn a living, Mr Fox. Keep the wolf from the door.'

'Talking of wolves, Morrie, how did Tango Harris take this?'

Isaacs lowered his voice. 'Not pleased, Mr Fox. Not pleased at all. Said it was his favourite restaurant and he didn't like having to go some other place.'

Fox nodded understandingly. 'I suppose you'll get a refund for the time you were closed, eh?'

'A refund? I'm not sure I quite—'

'A refund of what you usually pay Tango Harris. After all, if you pay for protection and then don't get it, you're entitled to your money back.'

'I don't know what you're on about, Mr Fox.'

'I'd be inclined to sue him. Was there a written contract, at all?'

'Mr Fox . . . please. I'm in a very difficult position here. I mean, you just sitting here will drive away business.'

'Really? Well you do surprise me, Morrie. Here am I, investigating a dastardly murder on your premises – your own barman, no less – and you get nervous about it. What would Tango Harris expect? That we'd just forget about it?'

'We've all got a living to make, Mr Fox,' said Isaacs, wringing his hands.

'It's a hard life, Morrie, but tell me again what happened.'

Isaacs let out an audible sigh. 'I don't know, Mr Fox, honest. I never saw a thing. I was in the back when I heard shouting and that. I run out and see the whole of the bar in flames. And Harry – he was the barman, God rest his soul – was lurching about all over the place, screaming like a stuck pig. Looking like a human torch, he did. Someone picked up an ice-bucket and chucked it over him, but it never done no good.'

'And no one saw anyone throw anything?'

Isaacs shook his head. 'Nothing, Mr Fox.'

'That's an extraordinary thing, Jack, don't you think?' Fox glanced at Gilroy. 'Here we are in the heart of London's West End and someone sets fire to Morrie's nice restaurant. And no one sees a thing.'

'Stranger than fiction, guv,' said Gilroy, playing his usual part of feed-man to Fox.

'Ah, yes, Jack. Fiction. There's a lot of it about these days.' Fox switched his gaze back to Isaacs. 'Seen Gary Crombie in here recently, Morrie?'

'Who?'

Fox leaned menacingly close to Isaacs. 'Morrie,' he said, 'I don't think you realize how many arrows I've got in my quiver.'

'Quiver, Mr Fox?'

'Yes, Morrie. Not what you're doing now, but something toxophilites keep their ammunition in.'

'You've lost me a bit there, Mr Fox.'

'Well, for a start, there's the fire brigade to look at your fire exits and other precautions. They'll be practically living here after what happened, I shouldn't wonder. Then there are the environmental health officers,' Fox started ticking off the titles on his fingers. 'Love poking about in kitchens they do, in their unending quest for cockroaches. Not that they need go into the kitchens here to find cockroaches, of course.' He glanced round at the

64

few diners that Isaacs had managed to attract back. 'And last but not least, there are the VAT inspectors.' Fox leaned back in his chair and lit a cigarette. 'And all for the price of three telephone calls, Morrie. After all, the television adverts for BT keep telling me to make that call.'

'If you don't mind me saying, Mr Fox,' said Isaacs, looking at Fox's cigarette. 'this is a no-smoking part of the restaurant.'

'Like the bar you mean?' said Fox. 'But let me tell you about the Vatmen. They can be very nasty indeed. Once they move in and start examining the books, they could be here for weeks. D'you do bed-and-breakfast at all?'

'Mr Fox.' Isaacs spread his hands and stared at Fox with a plaintive expression. 'Just tell me what you want.'

'It's the same question, Morrie. Have you seen Gary Crombie in here recently? Or for that matter, was Billie Crombie ever in here . . . before his untimely death?'

Morrie Isaacs took out a large coloured handkerchief and mopped at his brow. Then with a flash of uncharacteristic courage, he leaned across and whispered. 'They wouldn't dare show their faces in here, Mr Fox,' he said.

Detective Sergeant Percy Fletcher, having been commissioned by Fox to get out and beat on the ground, used his knowledge of Soho and the surrounding district to good effect. There were not many clubs, dives, strip-joints, and massage parlours that Fletcher was not familiar with.

It was the seventeenth club he visited that produced some information. But then it was only a snippet.

He descended the area steps – the club was a subterranean one – and rapped on the door.

A wicket opened to reveal the blue chin of the resident bouncer. 'Yeah?'

Fletcher held up his warrant card. 'Come to inspect the justices' licence,' he said cheerfully.

The door opened, reluctantly. 'What's this all about then? Ain't had a copper look at the licence in years.'

'Life's full of little surprises, isn't it,' said Fletcher and walked through the internal door to the main part of the premises, knowing that the bouncer would already be on the house phone to the proprietor. Sure enough, before he reached the bar, which was only feet away, he was confronted by a bald-headed and overweight man with oily skin and a light grey double-breasted suit that would have got no marks from Fox in the sartorial stakes.

'Help you at all?'

'Unless I'm very much mistaken,' said Fletcher, 'you're Siggy Hoskins.'

'I have that honour. And who might you be?'

'Detective Sergeant Fletcher, Flying Squad.'

'Ah yes,' said Hoskins. 'You want to inspect the licence, I understand.'

'Inspect the licence? Whatever gave you that idea? No, Siggy, the Flying Squad are interested in crime.' Fletcher placed a certain ominous emphasis on the word.

'Well, my doorman said—'

'Doormen are notorious liars,' said Fletcher. 'At least that's my experience . . . particularly of that one.' He cocked a thumb in the direction of the entrance. 'On the contrary, Siggy, I've come to talk to you about Gina West . . . to say nothing of Tango Harris and the late Billie Crombie.'

'Never heard of any of them,' said Hoskins.

'That's unfortunate,' said Fletcher, gazing round the discreetly lit room. There were about twenty couples seated at tables. Some were clearly amateur adventurers, up west to see life in the raw. The others comprised, for the most part, tired-looking businessmen accompanied by young ladies – at least, they looked young in the half-light – who probably described themselves as escorts but who would undoubtedly take their clothes off and hop into bed if the price was right. 'In that case,' continued Fletcher, 'I'll just have to question one or two of your clientele. All regulars, are they?'

Fletcher stared hard at Hoskins's hand as it grasped his

sleeve. 'Sorry,' said Hoskins, leaving go immediately. 'P'raps you'd better come in the office. That's where I keep the licence,' he added a little more loudly, and waggled his head knowingly.

The office was a tip. An old desk stood across one corner, covered in papers, and next to it a filing cabinet on top of which was a bottle of whisky and some dirty glasses. Hoskins waved his hand towards a tired settee. 'Have a seat,' he said. 'Scotch?'

'Only if you've got a clean glass.'

'Of course, of course,' said Hoskins and opened a cupboard. He took out two fresh glasses and another bottle of Scotch and poured a stiff measure in each. 'It's malt. Only the best.'

Fletcher took a sip of whisky. 'Well, what d'you know about Gina West, Siggy?'

Hoskins sat down behind his desk. 'Is this confidential, Mr er—?'

'Fletcher.'

'Only I might have bent the rules a bit, see. I mean you take 'em on as hostesses and then you find out they're on the game, but . . . well it's very difficult.' Hoskins adopted an imploring expression.

'It's confidential.' Fletcher didn't bother to add that if Hoskins had anything important to say he would be the unhappy recipient of a subpoena to give evidence at the Central Criminal Court.

'She used to get in here. Quite often—'

'Did she work for you, or did she pick up clients in here?'

'Oh no, nothing like that, Mr Fletcher. No, she always come in with a punter. A couple of drinks before they went back to his hotel or wherever, I reckon.'

'When was the last time?'

Hoskins appeared to give the matter some thought. 'Must have been eight weeks ago, I s'pose. It was the night of the bust-up.'

'What bust-up?'

Hoskins lowered his voice, even though they were

alone in the office and the door was closed. 'Billie Crombie,' he said. 'She was one of his girls, see.'

'Yeah, I know,' said Fletcher. 'What was the argument about?'

'Well, Crombie come in here with his boy Gary and three of his friends.'

'Friends?' said Fletcher. 'You use the term loosely, I take it?'

Hoskins ignored the sarcasm. 'Well, Crombie – Billie, that is – had been drinking and they'd been doing the rounds, I should think. Collecting . . . if you know what I mean.'

'How much do they collect off you, Siggy?'

Hoskins forced a laugh. 'Not me, Mr Fletcher. This is a straight club.'

Fletcher laughed too and put his empty glass on the corner of Hoskins's desk. Hoskins promptly refilled it. 'Yeah, go on then.'

'Well, Gina was in here, with a mug, like, and Crombie went across to their table. He grabs this punter by the lapels and tells him to piss off. Some smarmy jessie from Birmingham, he was. Didn't look as though he was interested in birds. So, anyhow, he cleared off a bit sharpish, and then Crombie has a go at Gina. Tells her that she'd better come across with her payments, or she'd get a striping . . . or worse.'

'This was Billie Crombie doing all the talking, was it?'

'Yeah, that's right, Mr Fletcher.'

'What happened then?'

'He gives her a slap across the face and tells her to get working, that she hadn't got no time to go sitting round in clubs.'

'And after that? They go, did they?'

'No, they stopped and had a few drinks. Laughing and joking about it. And Billie Crombie says something to Gary about that's how he should run the business when he took over.'

'Anyone else in the club when all this happened?'

'It was early on. There was only two couples. Both regulars.'

'Names?' asked Fletcher brutally.

'Look, Mr Fletcher . . . please. You know the score. They was a couple of geezers what run with Tango Harris – only small fry, like – and a couple of scrubbers they must have picked up with.'

'Members of this club, are they?'

'Of course.'

'Then you'll know their names, won't you. On the other hand, I can seize the membership register and interview each and every one of them.' Fletcher was certain that none of them would have seen anything, but this was a way of persuading Hoskins to talk.

Hoskins looked extremely anguished. 'Danny Royce was one of them. The other was Tony Guerrini. I don't know the broads. They was guests, like.'

'Are you telling me, Siggy, that a couple of Tango's boys sat and watched this performance by Crombie and company, and didn't lift a finger? Didn't do or say anything?'

'Wouldn't have been very clever that, would it? I mean they was outnumbered.'

'Did Crombie know that they were Tango's soldiers?'

Hoskins shrugged. 'Maybe. I don't know. Might have been Crombie was showing a bit of muscle so's the word'd get back to Tango Harris. Your guess is as good as mine, Mr Fletcher.'

'So an unknown man and Gina West were assaulted and threats of GBH or worse made against Miss West. I reckon that amounts to an affray, Siggy. Very serious. Did you call the police to deal with this disorder on your premises?'

Hoskins had been pouring himself another drink and looked up quickly. But Fletcher was laughing.

'Danny Royce and Tony Guerrini appear to be two hooligans we should talk to, Jack . . . according to Percy Fletcher.' Fox stared down at the piece of paper in the centre of his blotter.

'Where do they fit in, guv?' asked Gilroy.

'Numbers Three and Four Cells at West End Central

for a start, I should think. Find them, Jack, there's a good fellow.'

Neither Royce nor Guerrini had protested when Gilroy and his Flying Squad team arrested them. It was not the first time they had been in police custody, of course, and were probably secure in the knowledge that their first telephone call would bring Tango Harris's solicitor hot-foot to the police station in Savile Row.

'One of my officers,' began Fox, 'tells me that you witnessed a serious assault, and a threat to murder.' He lit a cigarette and surveyed Danny Royce through the haze of smoke. He had left Guerrini on ice, having decided to interview the younger of the two prisoners first.

'Oh, yeah?'

'Yes, indeed. The incident took place some eight weeks ago at an insalubrious drinking club run by Siggy Hoskins and known, with startling lack of originality, as Siggy's Club.'

'Don't know nothing about no incident.' Royce lounged in the chair with an expression of veiled contempt on his face.

Fox had seen such expressions before . . . and knew how to remove them. But the time was not yet ripe. 'It involved Gina West, deceased, Billie Crombie, deceased, and one Gary Crombie – of doubtful parentage – as well as others as yet unnamed.'

'Oh yeah, I do remember that.' Royce leaned forward with an expression on his face that could have been mis-taken, by the naïve, for one of a desire to assist.

'Splendid,' said Fox. 'Tell me about it.'

'Nothing to it, really,' said Royce. 'Me and Tony was sitting having a couple of quiet drinks with two ladies . . .' Fox raised an eyebrow but otherwise let the description pass. 'And Crombie come in with his kid—'

'Gary, you mean?'

'Yeah, that's him, little tosser. And three other hoods. Well Crombie gets hold of this bird and gives her a slap-ping, and tells her to get going.'

'Gina West, would that have been?'

'Yeah, I think that's what she was called.'

'Did Crombie say anything about payment?'

If the painful expression on his face was any indication, Royce appeared to give that deep thought. 'Yeah, I think he did,' he said eventually. 'It was like he was her ponce and hadn't got paid.'

'And was he her ponce?'

'Well, word round the village reckoned he was.'

'By the village, you mean Soho, I take it?'

'Where else?' asked Royce, apparently mystified by the question.

'Then what happened?'

'Well, the bird cleared off, and Crombie and his mates stayed and had a few drinks. Then they buggered off an' all.'

'Interesting,' said Fox. 'And did Crombie threaten Miss West in any way?'

'Yeah, I think he promised her a striping. I couldn't hear proper, because he was holding her chin in his hand and talking close, like. But I reckon he must've threatened to top her. Leastways by the look on her face when she pissed off. Right scared she looked.'

'Tell me, how much does Tango Harris collect from Siggy Hoskins in protection money?'

'Tango Harris collecting protection money? You must be joking,' said Royce.

'True,' said Fox. 'I do have a curious sense of humour. But how much?'

'I don't know nothing about that,' said Royce.

Fox substituted Tony Guerrini for Royce in the interview room, but apart from that, nothing changed. Guerrini's answers were exactly the same as Royce's had been, down to the last full stop almost. And when Percy Fletcher listened to the tape, he confirmed that their account tallied with that given by Siggy Hoskins practically word for word.

'If ever I saw a set-up, it's this,' said Fox to Gilroy and Fletcher. 'First of all, Siggy Hoskins came across with the names of those two far too readily. And secondly, Tango

71

Harris will have heard that Royce and Guerrini had been nicked. You weren't exactly discreet when you pulled them, were you, Jack?'

'Well, you said—'

Fox held up a hand. 'No criticism, Jack. Precisely what I wanted. So, news having travelled rapidly to Chez Harris at Buckhurst Hill, what happens? Nothing is what happens. Now I would have expected one of Tango's extensive team of legal functionaries to have presented himself to the custody officer at West End Central within the hour. After all, we left it long enough, quite deliberately. But no protests, no mouthpiece, just uncharacteristic co-operation.' Fox spun the paper-knife in the centre of his blotter. 'I think that Tango Harris is trying to be clever in his old age. But,' he added, 'he's left it too late.'

'Do you want them held, guv?' asked Gilroy. 'Royce and Guerrini?'

'Good Heavens no, Jack. They're no earthly use to us in here. We shall let the hares run . . . in the vain hope that the hounds may come trotting after. Put Henry Findlater's team on it.'

'Well, Henry, what news have you?'

'We followed the suspects, sir . . .' Henry Findlater peered though his owl-like spectacles at his pocket-book.

Fox nodded amiably, accepting this as one of Findlater's little foibles. 'Good work, Henry.'

'And on leaving West End Central police station they travelled in a Saab motor car, index—'

'Henry, skip the details. Just tell me where they went.'

'They went to Tango Harris's place at Buckhurst Hill, sir.'

'Dear me,' said Fox, 'how extraordinarily careless of them. I wonder why they didn't telephone.'

'Probably thought we'd got an intercept on it, sir,' said Findlater.

'What a splendid idea, Henry. Now why didn't I think of that before?'

'Probably too busy, sir,' said Findlater innocently.

Fox shot him a suspicious glance. 'How long did this unsavoury pair remain at Tango Harris's ostentatious pad?'

Findlater glanced at his pocket-book once again. 'Just over the hour, sir. Then they went to Wandsworth.'

'Why Wandsworth, I wonder?' mused Fox.

'It's where they live, sir.'

Chapter Eight

Fox tapped out Tango Harris's telephone number and waited. An answering machine clicked and a recorded message started. Fox sighed audibly. 'Tango, this is Fox. I know you're there. Pick up the phone. Save me coming out.'

A female voice answered. 'Hallo?'

'Melody?'

'Yeah!'

'Fetch Tango to the phone.'

'I don't know if he's in.'

'Don't ponce about,' said Fox. 'Just get him.'

After some delay, a man's voice came on the line. 'Who's that?'

'You're a difficult man to get hold of, Tango—'

'What d'you want?'

'These fellows who you say can categorically row you out of the Gina West murder, Tango,' said Fox. 'The ones you were allegedly clubbing with on the night in question . . . as your mouthpiece so eloquently put it.'

'There's no "allegedly" about it.'

'Pleased to hear it. Who were they?'

'Why?'

'Because I intend to talk to them, Tango.'

'Be my guest. Terry Quincey and Des Nelson and their two birds . . . oh, and Melody, of course.'

'Of course,' murmured Fox.

'They'll tell you what I told you. And I'm getting fed up with being harassed.'

'Know the feeling,' said Fox, and put the phone down.

*

74

'Take Percy Fletcher with you, Jack, and do a bit of digging on these two layabouts that Tango Harris said were with him the night Gina West got topped. Then pick 'em off one by one. Lay hands on one when the other's not there. We'll give him a talking to and then grab the second one before we let the first go. Got it?'

'I'd better write that down,' said Gilroy with no trace of a smile. 'By the way, Mr Brace has sent us a copy of the handwriting expert's report, sir.'

'What are you talking about now, Jack?' asked Fox.

'The handwriting on the agreement form, sir. The solicitor in Richmond who drew up the agreement with John Phillips, who we think is Tango Harris, let Mr Brace have the original and he submitted it to the lab.'

'Let me get this straight, Jack. Phillips is the bloke whose credit-card voucher was found in the hotel room. Yes?'

'Yes, sir.'

'And the address went out to a flat in Richmond and from there back to Tango Harris's address at Buckhurst Hill. Right?'

'Right, sir,' said Gilroy patiently.

'Good,' said Fox. 'So what have you to tell me?'

'Nothing, sir.'

'Nothing?'

'Nothing, sir. The tests were inconclusive. The handwriting on the lease agreement was nothing like Tango Harris's, samples of which were seized when we nicked him—'

'Didn't nick him,' said Fox moodily. 'He volunteered to help us with our enquiries.'

'Well, whatever. The graphologist at the lab says in his report that it could have been Tango Harris's handwriting, but disguised. On the other hand, it might not be his at all.'

'Thank you, Jack,' said Fox. 'That's extremely helpful. Did he make any mention of Billie Crombie?'

'Same, sir.'

'What's that mean?'

75

'That the writing could have been Billie Crombie's, but he couldn't swear to it.'

'Terrific,' said Fox.

Fox, unable as usual to avoid interfering, went straight to West End Central police station the moment that Gilroy told him that Terry Quincey had been invited to come in and make a statement to support Harris's account of his movements the night Gina West was murdered.

'Friday the twelfth of October . . .' Fox began.

'What about it?'

'Where were you?'

'Had a night out with my bird,' said Quincey.

'Name?'

'Tracey Ogden. Why?'

'And who else?'

'Des Nelson and his bird.'

'What was her name?' asked Fox patiently.

'Cindy something.'

'Just the four of you, was it?' said Fox without hope that Quincey would agree.

'No. Tango Harris was with us, an' all. Oh, and his bird.'

'That would be Melody, would it?'

Quincey frowned. 'Yeah, I think that was her name. Me and Des call her Omega.'

'Omega? Why?'

'Lots of jewels and a lovely movement,' said Quincey with a grin.

Fox leaned across the table. 'Don't think of getting smart with me, Terence, dear boy. I have been known to get nasty.'

'It was only a joke,' said Quincey, moving back an inch or two.

'That's all right, then,' said Fox. 'I enjoy a joke. Particularly when I can see the funny side of it. So what time did this culture trip of yours begin?'

Quincey was alert to the danger of giving immediate answers. Policemen had, in the past, concluded that vil-

76

lains who had pat answers had probably made them up. Recollection of the truth, as any detective will tell you, takes a little longer. 'We met up down Tango's place. That's in Buckhurst Hill . . .'

'I know. What time?'

Quincey pondered the answer to that, too. 'Must have been about half four, I s'pose.'

'That's a bit early.'

'Yeah, well he invited us down to have a swim in his pool before we went up west. Very generous like that is Tango.'

'Then what?'

'We must have left there about half seven, I s'pose. Then we went for a meal up Morrie Isaacs's place.'

'The one that got burnt out four days later?'

'Yes, I heard about that,' said Quincey.

'What d'you know about it, as a matter of passing interest?' asked Fox.

'Me? Nothing.'

'Grapevine not working too well, Terence? Surely Tango must have said something about it.'

'Yeah, well he reckoned it was down to Billie Crombie. Said it was the sort of thing he would do.'

'I see. And did he say he was going to do anything about it?' Fox lit a cigarette and feigned a lack of interest in the reply.

But Quincey sensed the danger. 'No. Why should he? Nothing to do with him, was it?'

'So where did you go after you left Morrie's place?' Fox knew he wasn't going to get anywhere, but he had to go through the motions.

'Went round the clubs, then. Two or three places.'

'Including Siggy's?'

'Yeah, that's right. How d'you know that?'

'What time did you finish up?'

'Must have been about half-past one, I s'pose,' said Quincey immediately, having forgotten his self-imposed rule of appearing to consider the question.

'What did you all do then?'

'Split up, didn't we. I went off with my bird and Des went off with his.'

'And Tango?'

'Him an' all.'

'What d'you mean by that?'

'Well, he pushed off in his motor with Omega. Er, I mean Melody.'

'Well, that's that, then,' said Fox. 'We'll have all that taken down in writing and then you can go.'

'Oh, right. Cheers,' said Quincey.

'Yes,' said Fox.

Fox tossed the statement to one side. 'Not worth the paper it's written on,' he said. 'What about Des Nelson?'

'I interviewed him while you were talking to Quincey, sir,' said Gilroy.

'And?'

Gilroy laid another statement on Fox's desk. 'Word for word, guv. I reckoned they must have stayed up half the night rehearsing it. They could probably have carved out a marvellous career for themselves in the theatre.'

Fox pursed his lips. 'That's pitching it a bit high, Jack,' he said. 'Amateur dramatics at best, I should have thought.'

On Fox's instructions, Gilroy found the two women who Quincey and Nelson had said were with them – and Tango Harris – on the night of Gina West's murder. Tracey Ogden and Cindy Lewis were interviewed by Rosie Webster, but despite her talent for interrogation, Rosie was unable to extract anything more than a loose confirmation of what Quincey and Nelson had said. The one thing that the interviews did elicit, however, was that both women possessed incredibly poor memories. That they were nervous throughout was, in Fox's view, evidence that they were lying. But he knew that defence counsel would convince a jury that it was attributable to their fear of the draconian methods of police questioning.

'What about Melody, guv?' asked Gilroy.

'We'll leave her for the time being, Jack.' Fox pushed

78

the women's statements to one side. 'We've given Harris enough amusement for one week. And you know as well as I do that her story will match the others exactly. Her time will come, dear boy.'

'By the way, sir, Mr Brace has sent over a copy of the pathologist's report on Gina West.'

'Anything I should know about?'

'In brief, sir, she had been strangled.'

'Which comes as no surprise.'

'And she had sexual intercourse shortly before her death, sir.'

'Well, that's an astonishing revelation for a tom, Jack.' Fox yawned and stood up. 'I think I'll let you buy me a beer,' he said.

It was on the Wednesday following Billie Crombie's funeral that Fox got the phone call.

'Mr Fox?'

'Yes.'

'It's Sharon Scrope here. I've got to see you, urgent.'

'What about?'

'I ain't telling you over the phone, but it's important.'

'D'you want to come here to the Yard?'

'Not bleeding likely. Can't we meet some place?'

'Where are you now?'

'Waterloo East.'

'What are you doing there?'

'It's where I got off the train yesterday, like . . . from Catford. Mr Fox, I'm scared.'

'There's a pub in York Road,' said Fox, 'just by the footbridge that leads to the Shell Centre. I'll see you there in ten minutes.' And he dipped the receiver rest. 'I hope,' he added as he tapped out the number of the drivers' room.

Fox's driver, the mournful Swann, complained bitterly at having to leave a good poker hand and drove Fox and Rosie Webster to Waterloo, managing to arrive only two minutes later than Fox had promised.

Sharon Scrope was sitting at a table in the corner of

79

the pub, a gin and tonic in front of her. She was dressed in a tight-fitting short black skirt with a leather bomber jacket over a shocking pink T-shirt. Her face looked drawn and haggard and she wore very little make-up.

'Looks as though she's been dragged through a hedge backwards,' said Fox in an aside to Rosie as he bought the drinks.

'And some,' said Rosie.

They sat down opposite Sharon whose face immediately took on an expression of immense relief. 'Ta!' she said.

'What for?' Fox took a sip of his Scotch.

'For coming.'

'What is it you want, Sharon? What's all this urgent business that you're scared of?'

Sharon glanced round the pub as though frightened of being seen. Satisfied that she was apparently unobserved, she took a black book from her handbag and slid it across the table. 'It's that,' she said.

Fox thumbed through it. 'So? It's a diary. A five-year diary.'

'It's more than that, Mr Fox. It's everything Billie ever done.'

'You mean it's a record of his criminal activities?'

'Yeah!'

'Why? Why d'you suddenly want me to have this?'

'You was at the funeral, wasn't you?'

'Yes.'

'And you saw what happened. What that cow Arlene Fogg done.'

Fox nodded. 'I must say that your forearm smash was very professional.'

For the first time, Sharon smiled. 'Billie taught me that,' she said. 'In case I ever got into bother.'

'So you're giving me this' – Fox tapped the diary with his forefinger – 'because Arlene had a go at you at Billie's planting. Is that it?'

'There's more to it than that, Mr Fox. Yesterday, Gary

80

and Kenny come down my place in Catford. It was the flat what Billie give me, see. And they shoved me in their car and took me back to Billie's place—'

'That's in Catford, too, isn't it?'

'Yeah. Ain't far away. Anyhow, when we got there, that bitch Arlene was there.'

'She would be,' said Fox. 'She lives there. What was it all about, anyway?'

'Those two bastards dragged me up to Billie's bedroom and they raped me . . . on Billie's bed. Both of them. And Arlene was there all the time, laughing and shouting at them to do it again.' Sharon looked directly at Fox as she spoke, giving him the precise details of what had happened to her, but there were no tears, no emotion, just a straightforward account. 'Then when they'd finished, Arlene said as how that was a warning and that I'd better stay out of their way from now on or they'd have me cut . . . or worse.'

'Then what happened?'

'They threw me out and told me to walk home. And Arlene said I was to find some other place to live because the flat was Billie's and everything that was Billie's was hers now.'

'Did you go to the police?'

Sharon scoffed. 'Course not. What's the use of that?'

'You could bring a charge of rape against the two Crombie brothers . . . and Arlene for that matter.'

'Arlene? Don't be daft. She never raped me. How could she? And she ain't no dyke, neither.' Sharon stared at Fox as though he'd taken leave of his senses.

'She can be charged all right,' said Rosie quietly. 'This happened last night, you say?'

'Yeah.'

Rosie leaned forward and spoke softly. 'You should be medically examined, you know . . . even now.'

Sharon shook her head defiantly. 'Don't want none of that poncing around,' she said. 'Not having no doctors poking around in my privates.' She pointed at the diary. 'That's much better,' she continued. 'That'll do for all

81

three of them. That'll screw 'em for much longer than they'd get for screwing me.'

'So you don't intend to bring charges for rape?' Fox needed to be absolutely clear on that point.

'No. I said.'

'Did you go back to your place at Catford last night?'

'Not bloody likely. You think I'm mad or something? Well, leastways, just long enough to grab me things. Then I come here. Stayed in a hotel last night. Weren't much cop. That's where me things are now.' A sudden spasm of fear crossed Sharon's face. 'But I ain't staying there no more,' she said. 'Those bastards'll find me.'

'We'll come with you,' said Fox. 'We'll collect your things and put you somewhere safe.'

'But you don't know them, Mr Fox, they'll—'

'And you'll be under guard . . . until the trial.' Fox stood up and rubbed his hands. 'Things are looking up, Rosie,' he said. 'Things are definitely looking up.'

'Is that Detective Sergeant Jagger?' asked the voice on the telephone.

'Speaking.'

'This is Jason Morley. You came to see me the other day in Richmond. D'you remember?'

'Yes, I remember, Mr Morley.'

'I've found the letter I mentioned.'

'Good. Who's it addressed to?'

'Someone called Crombie.'

Jagger whistled quietly. 'Have you opened it?'

'No. D'you want me to?'

'No,' said Jagger hurriedly. 'Have you got any plastic bags? Clean ones. The sort you put food in when you put it in a freezer.'

'Yes, I think so.'

'Good. Put the letter in one of them and hang on to it. I'll get someone to collect it within about three quarters of an hour.'

Chapter Nine

It was a small house in Belgravia, not far from Gerald Road police station, which the police kept specifically for housing witnesses who were under threat. Usually, such people were what the Press calls supergrasses but Fox had little hope that Sharon Scrope would turn out to be one. He had been disappointed too many times in his long career of seeking out the unrighteous and was pessimistic about the outcome of this particular offer of information. But for once he was wrong.

Fox and Rosie Webster mounted the stairs to the sitting room at the back of the house. Despite there being four armed Flying Squad officers in the house, one of whom was a WDC, Fox considered it too risky to use the ground floor. Malcontents had been known to throw things through downstairs windows . . . like petrol bombs. 'Everything all right?' he asked.

'Yeah, ta,' said Sharon. 'Want some coffee?' Without waiting for an answer, she stood up and filled two more cups.

'How come,' said Fox, sitting down opposite the girl, 'that you have a record of everything that Billie Crombie got up to over the last five years? Did he know you'd written all this down?' He laid the diary on the coffee-table and lit a cigarette. The diary had been photocopied at the Yard and already teams of detectives were analysing its coded contents, but Fox wanted to hear Sharon's interpretation of her notes first-hand.

'It was Billie's idea,' said Sharon. 'He always reckoned that he'd get topped one day. That's what he used to say.

83

And he reckoned that if he did, Arlene'd be behind it. He never trusted her, you see, but she knew too much for him to dump her. Nor Gary and Kenny neither. They was too greedy. Always wanting more out of the firm.'

'But he trusted you, did he?'

'Yeah. He always said he could tell me anything and I wouldn't let on.' Sharon pointed at the diary. 'But he wanted me to keep all that, so's I could go to the police if ever anything happened to him.'

'Surely you don't think that Gary and Kenny killed their own father?'

Sharon shrugged. 'Search me,' she said. 'And who said he was their father? I reckon that's a tale what Arlene spun him all them years ago. They wasn't nothing like him to look at. And Billie reckoned she wasn't above going over the side a few years back.'

'Maybe so,' said Fox, 'but could they have topped Billie?'

'Not them personally, no. They was hanging round the house that night. Like, I mean they weren't down the dogs. But they could've got someone else to do it, couldn't they?' For a moment Sharon looked wistful. 'It's not bleedin' fair,' she said. 'I know he was at it, but he was a nice man. He was always good to me.'

'What did Arlene think of your relationship with Billie?'

'Weren't much she could do about it. Billie always protected me. Even when he weren't about, there was always a minder. I never went out on me own. But I know Arlene was just waiting. She weren't no good for him, not in bed nor nowhere, and she hated me for it. For giving him what he wanted. I should've split the minute I heard about him getting killed, I s'pose. But I was like numb when I heard. Should have known those bastards'd come after me. Shouldn't never have gone to the funeral neither, but I just wanted to say goodbye like.'

'That's all very touching, Sharon old love, but perhaps you'd get on with your spiel, eh?'

Sharon suddenly assumed a brisk and businesslike manner. 'All them lorry heists was down to Billie,' she said.

'Hold on a moment.' Fox held up a hand. 'We're going to record this, and then we'll have a statement typed up which I shall want you to sign. Is that all right?'

'Yeah. Course it is.'

'Right. How many lorry heists?'

Sharon picked up the diary and thumbed through it, searching for the entries. 'I think it was six,' she said. 'Should have been seven, except that Harris muscled in on the last one . . . and topped Frankie Carter.'

'Good gracious me,' said Fox. 'What an extraordinary revelation. And d'you know that for a fact?'

'Course I don't. But that's what Billie reckoned. He was hopping mad when it happened. Reckoned he was going to do for Tango Harris. Rang him up and told him so an' all. And he did.'

Fox's face still bore its usual sceptical expression. 'Did what?' he asked.

'Billie and the boys went up and threw a couple of petrol bombs in Morrie Isaacs's restaurant. To teach him a lesson, like. He never minded Tango milking Morrie – and one or two others, like Siggy Hoskins – but he reckoned that the lorry jobs was his.'

'So who was with him, the night he torched Morrie Isaacs's place?'

'Gary and Kenny. They was well at it.'

'Who else was on the lorry heist? The one when Frankie Carter was murdered?'

'Well there was Gary and Kenny for a start, and I think the other one was called—' Sharon broke off and skimmed through the diary. 'Harry Towler,' she said at length.

'And Wayne Parish, the driver, was the inside man.' Fox tried out another of his suspicions.

Sharon looked up in surprise. 'How did you know that?' she asked and then laughed. 'As a matter of fact, Parish got a bit arsey about it. Was straight on the blower whingeing about not getting his cut. Billie told him to piss off. He said that if he hadn't cocked it up, like, then Tango Harris wouldn't have had the gear away. Well that's like basically what he said.'

'And the other heists? Have you got the dates for those in that little book?'

Sharon looked up from the diary. 'D'you think I could have a drink, Mr Fox?'

'Why not,' said Fox. 'Look on it as a tax rebate. If you pay any tax,' he added thoughtfully. 'What d'you want?'

'Bacardi and Coke'd go down a treat.'

Fox nodded to Rosie who walked across to a cabinet and poured the drink.

'Yeah, here they are,' said Sharon. 'There was two before Christmas – one in November and one in December – and the rest was this year.' She raced through the diary reeling off dates.

Fox looked up sharply from the occasional notes he was making. 'Did you say the eighteenth of August?' he asked.

'Yeah.'

'And who took part in that job?'

'Like it always was. Gary and Kenny, Frankie Carter, and Harry Towler. Is that important then?'

Fox stood up. 'You don't know just how important, my flower of Catford,' he said. 'In fact, I think I'll have a drop of the Commissioner's Scotch.' He walked over to the drinks cabinet and poured himself a whisky. 'As a matter of interest, where was Billie that night?' he asked.

Sharon referred to the diary once more. Then she looked up and smiled. 'He was in bed with me. Why?'

'Was he now!' Fox gave the girl a sharp stare. 'And did you make a note of all the times you slept with him?'

'Not all of them. Just the good times.' Sharon smiled wistfully.

'What about the twelfth of October?'

Sharon bent to the diary again. 'Yeah, I was with him that night an' all.' She glanced up sharply. 'That was the night Gina was murdered.'

'Yes, I know. What d'you know about that?'

'Only that she was one of Billie's girls. She used to pay him.' Sharon shrugged. 'Know what I mean?'

'Yes,' said Fox, 'I know what you mean. Anything else of interest for the time being?'

Sharon sat back on the settee and took a sip of her drink. 'There's what Billie called an LF running down Twickenham. I never knew what that was, but I did know that Billie set it up, and Gary and Kenny are going to milk it for all they're worth. What's an LF, anyway?'

'It's a fraud,' said Fox. 'A long-firm fraud. The villains set up a shop, selling goods. They keep ordering stock and they keep paying for it. The order gets bigger each time, but they still pay. Then when they've got the confidence of the supplier and they're allowed credit, they put in a very big order and disappear overnight with the gear . . . without paying the bill, of course.'

Sharon nodded seriously. 'Yeah,' she said. 'That sounds about right for Billie. Very good at things like that, he was.'

'D'you still maintain that on the eighteenth of August you were in Siggy's Club and that during that evening Billie Crombie assaulted Gina West?' Fox studied Danny Royce with a mild expression on his face.

Unfortunately, having once been interviewed about the matter, Royce had assumed that to be the end of it and had forgotten his lines. 'If that's what I said, then that's it,' he said. But he sounded unconvincing.

'Very well. Daniel Royce, I am of a mind to charge you with conspiracy to murder Gina West and conspiracy to pervert the course of justice.'

'What?' Royce leapt to his feet. 'I never had nothing to do with that topping.'

'Oh, but you did, my son. In making a false statement to police, which in certain circumstances can amount to perjury, in which you accused Billie Crombie of a serious assault on Gina West, you have attempted to throw suspicion on him for her murder. And that, dear boy, could earn you a lot of porridge.'

'But I'm sure that—'

'And I can produce a reliable witness who is willing to say that Billie Crombie was several miles away at that time, and that Gary Crombie was actually engaged in a criminal enterprise in the depths of Kent. What d'you say to that?'

'I must have made a mistake.'

'Yes,' said Fox. 'I think you must. Who put you up to this? Tango Harris, was it?'

'I don't know what you mean.'

Fox nodded slowly. 'You're playing with fire, my son,' he said. 'But for now, you can make a statement repeating what you've just told me. Then you and your mate Guerrini, who's next door making a similar statement, can run back to Buckhurst Hill and tell Tango all about it.'

Royce looked relieved.

'But,' added Fox, 'you will be on police bail to reappear at this police station one month from now . . . or earlier if I decide to nick you.'

The interrogation of Sharon Scrope had gone on all day and half the next. By the time that Fox had the statement in front of him, he knew also that he was much closer to capturing Tango Harris, as well as Gary and Kenny Crombie, their mother Arlene, and sundry other villains.

'Denzil,' said Fox as DI Evans appeared in his office, 'I've got a special job for you.' He tapped the pages of statement on his desk. 'Don't cock it up, there's a good chap.'

Evans looked hurt. Whenever he was assigned to a task by Fox, the chief superintendent always had to throw in some cautionary instruction about doing it properly. But Evans was a good DI; he wouldn't have stayed on the Squad otherwise. 'What is it, guv?'

'Sharon Scrope tells me . . .' began Fox. It was to be the start of many directions to the Flying Squad over the next week or so. 'Sharon Scrope tells me that Billie Crombie financed the setting-up of an LF job down in Twickenham. Set up an obo on it and nick the principals thereof at the precise moment you can be sure of them going down. All right, dear boy?'

'Yes, sir,' said Evans despondently. 'Where in Twickenham?'

'Good heavens, Denzil, I don't know. But Twickenham's not a very big place. Put yourself about . . . but discreetly, mind.'

'Yes, sir,' said Evans flatly. Not for the first time, he wondered why he hadn't heeded his father's advice and become an accountant.

Evans's Flying Squad team consisted of two detective sergeants and nine detective constables. When they were told of the job that Fox had assigned them to, they muttered about long-firm frauds being the work of the Fraud Squad and nothing to do with the Flying Squad who went after real villains. A quick in-and-out job was what the Squad liked. But the truth of the matter was that Tango Harris was about to get his come-uppance, and they wanted to be a part of it. But as it happened, they were in at the kill anyway.

It didn't take long to identify the shop that was being used in Twickenham, even though the Squad didn't know precisely what they were looking for. But they knew the signs.

Roy Buckley, Evans's senior detective sergeant, went for a stroll around the commercial centre of Twickenham. It took him twenty minutes to find the shop and his view was that they deserved to be caught. The previous tenants, obviously victims of the recession, had been replaced by traders who hadn't even bothered to have a new fascia board made.

Buckley stopped and peered in. There were television sets and video recorders, most of them still in boxes, carelessly stacked everywhere and all marked down in price. It looked more like a warehouse than a shop.

Buckley crossed the road to another shop and bought a packet of peppermints. 'That's new,' he said to the man behind the counter, and pointed at the television shop.

'Been there about three months, I s'pose. Don't know how they do it. Shouldn't have thought they'd've got off the ground. Not these days. The UBR's a crippler for a start.'

'The what?'

'Uniform business rate,' said the shopkeeper. 'Still, they're the cheapest tellys I've come across. Something in that, I s'pose.'

'Much turnover, is there?' asked Buckley.

'Dunno, really. Never seen a delivery lorry, but there always seems to be blokes in there buying. There's a queue on Saturdays. What's it to you, anyway?'

'Trading standards,' said Buckley.

'Oh, right,' said the shopkeeper.

Evans received this information with some reservation. 'Might be the one, I suppose, Roy. Find out a bit more about them.'

'We're making progress, sir,' said Evans.

'I should hope so,' said Fox. 'And?'

'There are two of them at it, sir, names of Cliff Adams and Barry Baker.'

'Do we know them?'

'Both got previous for fraud . . . long-firm fraud,' said Evans triumphantly.

'Well there you are then,' said Fox as though possessed of divine insight.

'They keep their stock at a warehouse in Feltham. The suppliers deliver the goods there and Adams and Baker transfer it to the shop in Twickenham . . . usually at night.'

'Have you spoken to the suppliers, Denzil?'

'Yes, sir. They afforded them credit facilities four weeks ago and made a delivery. Our two paid the bill, but they've just put in an order twice the size of the last one and bigger than anything they've had before.' Evans was a much shrewder detective than Fox gave him credit for, and rather than waste time with fruitless surveillance he had approached the suppliers and told them what he

90

thought was about to happen. They had been more than happy to co-operate . . . provided, they said, they didn't lose any money.

'The chickens are coming home to roost, Denzil. They are definitely coming home.'

'Yes, sir,' said Evans, unsure what Fox meant.

'When is this mammoth delivery?'

'Tomorrow, sir. About four in the afternoon, according to the suppliers.'

'Splendid, Denzil. I shall be there to help you.'

'I knew that would happen,' said Evans. But he said it to Buckley . . . and not until he was back at his temporary headquarters at Twickenham police station.

The attack had been carefully planned.

Two of the Crombie brothers' accomplices had stolen the Ford Transit two or three weeks previously. Since then, in a lock-up garage under the arches of a railway line within easy distance of the Crombie residence in Catford, its chassis had been strengthened, its rear bumper reinforced, and false plates had been put on it.

During this time also, the Crombies had carried out several reconnaissances and made contingency arrangements.

The black Ford Transit drove slowly into the narrow Soho street. It was followed by a ten-year-old Vauxhall, but that apparently broke down just as it turned the corner and completely blocked the street. The driver got out, opened the bonnet and appeared to tinker with the engine.

The Ford Transit picked up speed and then braked hard before reversing sharply on to the pavement. There was a crash of breaking glass as the windows of the video shop were smashed in and the door, complete with door-frame, was pushed violently into the shop to be crushed and splintered beneath the wheels of the van.

Four men wearing stocking masks leaped from the back of the van. 'You'll piss off if you know what's good for you,' one of them shouted at the man behind the counter.

The man couldn't get out fast enough, crunching over broken glass in his desire to escape from what was clearly some sort of vendetta.

The gang started on a wholesale destruction of the shop and its contents before the leader took a bottle from the cab of the van and applied his lighter to the rag stuffed into the neck. 'Go!' he shouted as he threw the bottle into the cargo area of the van on to a bed of petrol-soaked rags.

There was a violent explosion as the bundles of waste ignited and great sheets of flame shot upwards and outwards as the men ran into the street. They jumped into the Vauxhall, now cured of its fictional ills and waiting with its engine running a yard or two on the safe side of the now fiercely burning video shop.

The driver skilfully negotiated a maze of back doubles until the car skidded to a standstill several streets away. Its occupants leaped out and into another waiting car, pausing only long enough to set fire to the Vauxhall.

Round the next corner and driving at a sedate speed the arsonists ripped off their masks.

'We're getting quite good at that,' said Gary Crombie. 'I reckon the old man would've been proud of us.'

'Pity that Tango Harris wasn't inside it,' said his brother Kenny.

'Never mind,' said Gary. 'We'll have the bastard yet, you see if we don't. But at least that'll have cost him a few grand.'

'Yeah!' Kenny Crombie laughed and lit a cigarette.

The warehouse was on an industrial estate. Evans's team had secured the co-operation of the manager of another warehouse opposite and several Flying Squad officers were now inside it, keeping observation on the suppliers' lorry that was unloading television sets and video recorders.

Fox, not believing in wasting time, was a mile or so away, in a pub with Gilroy. Outside, the complaining

Swann was listening to the radio, waiting for the signal that would tell him – and Fox – that things were starting to happen.

At half-past seven, Swann sauntered into the pub and ambled across to where Fox and Gilroy were sitting. 'Up and running, guv,' he said mournfully. 'Mr Evans says they're loading.'

Unhurriedly, Fox finished his Scotch and followed his driver.

Ten minutes after the delivery had been completed a pantechnicon had arrived, and it was that which had excited Evans's interest. Flying Squad cars had immediately taken up station at all the entrances to the industrial estate so that there was no way the villains could escape with their loot.

Fox, flanked by Evans and Gilroy, strolled up to the large van and peered in. A man had just wheeled in a trolley stacked with videos. He dumped his load and turned to come out.

'Well, well,' said Fox. 'If it isn't Gary Crombie. You're a long way from Catford, my son.'

Crombie dropped the trolley and brought up his fists.

'Don't even think about it,' said Fox.

Being inside the van with three Flying Squad officers outside, Crombie realized that there was no escape and let his hands fall to his sides. Familiar with the ways of the Flying Squad, he knew that there would be more of them about. 'Hallo, Mr Fox,' he said with a sickly grin.

At that point, Kenny Crombie came out of the warehouse carrying a television set. He took one look at Fox and the combined teams of Gilroy and Evans – some twenty-five officers in all – and promptly let go of the set. It fell with a crash of splintering glass as the screen disintegrated.

'Hope that's insured,' said Fox. 'In the van, my son, there's a good chap.' Kenny Crombie climbed in beside his brother. Seconds later, two more men appeared. 'And you'll be Mr Adams and Mr Baker, I presume.' Fox was starting to enjoy himself. 'In the van, my lovely lads.'

'Who the bleedin' hell are you?' Adams looked apprehensively at the circle of detectives. But he knew the answer.

'Thomas Fox . . . of the Flying Squad. And you're nicked. Official.'

Chapter Ten

'They won't say anything, Denzil,' said Fox, surveying the four prisoners now sitting disconsolately on a bench in the custody area of Twickenham police station. 'Just do the business and put them on the sheet.'

'But what about the fire-bombing of Morrie Isaacs's place, guv?' asked Evans. He couldn't believe that Fox wasn't going to bother about the murder of the barman.

Fox shrugged. 'We've only the word of some little tart from Catford that it's down to the Crombie brothers, Denzil, dear boy,' he said and lit a cigarette. He smiled at the custody sergeant, whose only censure of a chief superintendent smoking in the administrative part of a police station could be to frown slightly. 'We'll let them think we don't know anything about that. Makes them over-confident, you see. It'll fall into place, dear boy. Never fear. In the mean time, Jack and I will go and interview Mr Siegfried Hoskins in our constant seeking after truth.'

'What are you going to see him for, guv?'

'To rattle his bars a bit, Denzil. And possibly to close down a certain insalubrious establishment known to everyone but the Inland Revenue as Siggy's Club.'

As Fox had predicted, Siggy Hoskins was not at all pleased to receive a visit from the head of the Flying Squad. Over the years, many of the *habitués* of his club had related stories of Fox's activities, and nothing that Siggy had heard made him want to be the subject of a personal Fox interview. So far, he had avoided such a confrontation, but his luck finally ran out at about half-past ten on the evening of the Crombie brothers' arrest.

The same blue-chinned bouncer who had admitted Fletcher the previous week responded to Fox's sharp rap on the door and opened the wicket. The aperture was filled with a warrant card. The bouncer opened the door. 'Can I help you?' he enquired.

'When were you last nicked?' asked Fox conversationally.

'Dunno what you mean,' said the bouncer, taking several paces backwards.

'Be so good as winkle out your Mr Hoskins, dear boy,' said Fox.

Within seconds, the perspiring figure of Siggy Hoskins appeared in the entrance hall nervously wringing his hands. 'Welcome, gentlemen,' he said.

'Oh, I'm sorry,' said Fox, nodding at Hoskins's anxious hands, 'I didn't realize you were having a wash. You have an office, I presume?'

'Of course, gentlemen. Please come this way.' And Hoskins led them into the same dowdy office in which he had been interviewed by Fletcher. With an elaborate gesture, Hoskins indicated the worn settee.

Fox looked closely at it and remained standing. 'One of my sergeants spoke to you recently,' he began.

'Yes, indeed. A Mr Fletcher. Very nice gentleman.'

'Really?' said Fox. 'Must have been one of his off-days. Probably a bug of some sort.' He turned to Gilroy. 'Would you not think so, Jack?'

'Yes, sir,' said Gilroy. 'Lot of bugs about at this time of year.'

'Yes,' said Fox, switching his gaze back to Hoskins and staring hard.

'Perhaps I may offer you a drink, gentlemen.' Hoskins hovered near his drinks cupboard.

'Good gracious me, no,' said Fox. 'That would be most improper. But don't let me stop you.'

Hurriedly, Hoskins poured himself a large whisky and took a gulp. 'How can I help you, gentlemen?' he enquired.

'I am Thomas Fox . . . of the Flying Squad.'

'So I believe.'

'You'd better,' said Fox. 'Now then . . .' He changed his mind and sat down. 'My sergeant tells me that you gave him a graphic account of an assault that occurred on your premises some weeks ago involving a Miss Gina West and Billie Crombie. He went on to say that Billie Crombie was accompanied by his son Gary and three other undesirables.'

'Yes, that's right.' Hoskins fidgeted with his whisky glass.

'And when did this fracas take place?'

'The eighteenth of August,' said Hoskins promptly.

'Interesting,' said Fox and leaned back slightly as if carefully considering Hoskins's reply.

'Is there a problem?' asked Hoskins nervously.

'Only for you. I have to say, Siggy, that I am not greatly enamoured of little schlemiels like you who go about telling wicked lies to policemen.'

'P'raps I got the date wrong.'

'Yes, I think you probably did, Siggy.' Fox smiled at Hoskins. It was unnerving. 'But what I think is probably nearer the truth is that you made the whole thing up.'

'It's not true, Mr Fox.' Hoskins started to sound desperate.

'I just said that, but on second thoughts, I think that Tango Harris made it up. Then he passed you the script and you learnt it. In exactly the same way as Mr Daniel Royce and Mr Anthony Guerrini learned it. In case you've forgotten, they're the two nasty pieces of work you propped to Sergeant Fletcher as reliable witnesses.'

Gilroy, who had been leaning on the filing cabinet throughout this exchange, now shifted his position.

Fox held up a hand. 'No, Jack,' he said. 'Don't hit him . . . not yet.'

Hoskins took another slurp of Scotch and sat down heavily in the chair behind his desk. 'I'm in the middle here, Mr Fox,' he said.

'Indeed you are, dear boy. Indeed, you are. However,

I shall do my level best to assist you in extricating yourself from that difficult position.'

'How?'

'By persuading you to tell the truth. Furthermore, I shall start you off. Now then, you pay exorbitant sums of money to Tango Harris in order that he protects you from the scum that not infrequently enters this establishment for no better purpose than to cause you grief and aggravation. Am I right?' Hoskins remained silent. 'Good. I can see we're going to get on famously,' continued Fox. 'And in view of the fact that the alleged assault never took place, you will, I'm sure, readily agree with me that your story was a complete fabrication. Yes?'

'Yes,' said Hoskins miserably.

'There is another factor as well.'

'There is?'

'Oh yes. You say that Royce and Guerrini were in here that night and that they too witnessed this outrage. So that, in turn, can't be true, can it?'

'I s'pose not,' said Hoskins.

'And in fact, they weren't in here at all, were they?'

'No.'

'But they usually were. So how come they were missing that night?'

Hoskins was looking increasingly anguished. 'This could get me topped, Mr Fox. It's serious.'

'Where were they?' growled Fox.

'They was doing a job and they wanted me to alibi them . . . but I don't know nothing about the job, so help me.'

'Excellent.' Fox smiled. 'Now let us turn to the twelfth of October.'

'What about it?' Hoskins was stunned by Fox's rapid change of direction.

'Mr Thomas Walter Harris, aforesaid, better known as Tango, maintains, as do two other low-lifes, that he was here on that date.'

Hoskins spread his hands. 'I don't know,' he said. It was all getting too much for him. 'I can't remember everyone who comes in here.'

'Must be a problem. But this is easy. Tango Harris claims to have been accompanied by Terry Quincey and Des Nelson. Now they run with Tango and are probably members of your club. But it's unlikely that the two slags who were with them, namely Tracey Ogden and Cindy Lewis, are members. With me, so far?'

'I don't know what this is all about, Mr Fox, honest.'

'Therefore, Siggy, given the stringent regulations covering the sale of alcohol in this country, their names will appear in the records as guests of the said member or members.' Fox was far from certain that he was right. He was the first to admit that he hadn't quoted licensing law for years and was probably hopelessly out of date, but he was also pretty certain that Hoskins wouldn't know either.

'Oh my Gawd!' said Hoskins.

Fox turned to Gilroy. 'I take that as a definite maybe, Jack,' he said. He realigned his gaze on the unfortunate Hoskins. 'I wouldn't want you to get into any sort of trouble here, Siggy,' he continued. 'But the problem is that Miss Gina West was murdered on that night, and if Tango Harris was here he will doubtless require you to appear in Number One Court at the Old Bailey and give evidence. You know how to get to the Old Bailey, do you? Under your own steam, I mean.'

Hoskins lurched towards the filing cabinet and started an intensive search of its contents. Eventually, he produced a book. 'Visitors' Book,' he said triumphantly. Quickly he riffled through its pages until he found the entries for the twelfth of October. 'There's nothing here,' he said. There was a panic-stricken look on his face.

'That's all right then,' said Fox. 'So instead you'll be able to appear for the prosecution and swear that according to your records, Miss Ogden and Miss Lewis were not in the club that night, and to the best of your recollection, nor were Tango Harris, Terry Quincey, and Des Nelson. And just so that you don't forget it all again, my inspector here will take a statement to that effect. Oh, and if I were you, I wouldn't mention this little conversation to anyone. They might get cross. Of course, if you feel vulnerable, I could arrange to have a policeman in here at all times to guard you.'

'Oh my Gawd!' said Hoskins again.

'Religion's a great comfort at times like this,' said Fox.

'It's got to have been those bastard Crombies, Alfie. Can't have been no one else. They're bloody hooligans.' Tango Harris was marching up and down the side of his pool with savage intensity, hands thrust into the pockets of the terry robe he wore over his swimming trunks. 'D'you mean they just drove a bloody van into one of my video shops and set fire to it? In broad bloody daylight. I mean, what are the police doing, Alfie, eh?'

'It was quite dark actually, Mr Harris,' said Alfie Penrose.

Harris stopped his restless pacing to stare angrily at Penrose. 'Don't get bloody clever with me,' he said. 'You know what I mean.'

'Well, I don't reckon they'd have had time, like.'

'Why not? What else have they been doing, then?'

'They've been nicked, Mr Harris. The day after the fire as a matter of fact.'

'What for? For torching my bloody shop?'

'No. They got captured for a long-firm fraud down Twickenham.'

Harris broke into a cackling laugh. 'Oh dear me, Alfie. They're bloody amateurs, those lads. Who nicked 'em?'

'Tommy Fox and half the bleeding Sweeney.'

Harris stopped laughing. 'Oh, did he. That bastard's getting too close for comfort.'

'No skin off our nose, Mr Harris, is it? I mean all the time he's having a pop at the Crombies, he's leaving us well alone.' A note of doubt crept into Penrose's voice. 'Isn't he?'

'You stupid sod, Alfie. Can't you see what he's up to? Once he's got the Crombies bang to rights, he's going to turn all his bloody artillery on us. And I do mean artillery.'

'Yeah,' said Penrose. 'I hadn't thought of that.'

100

'Well you'd better start thinking . . . right now,' said Harris. 'Who's that tosser that used to be Billie Crombie's right hand?'

'Kevin Rix?'

'That's him. What's he up to now, now that poor dear Billie's gone and got hisself topped?' Harris grinned.

'Still in there. In fact, he's got alongside Arlene and the pair of 'em are trying to take over. Wouldn't mind betting she shopped Gary and Kenny to the Old Bill over the LF job.'

'Could be down to them, then,' said Harris thoughtfully. 'Got a little job for you then, Alfie. Listen carefully.'

After a few minutes of intensive briefing, Penrose walked away across the lawn towards his car, and Harris sat down on a sun-lounger and picked up the *Daily Telegraph*.

'Tango?'

'What?' Harris dropped his newspaper to look at Melody, now emerging from the pool.

'I do wish you'd tell me when people are coming in here.'

'Why? What's it got to do with you?'

'I've got nothing on, Tango. You're always doing it to me these days.'

'Yeah, well, these is trying times, babe,' said Harris.

'Just imagine,' said Fox, 'that I have one or two large fish, and a number of tiddlers, confined in a rather small tank.' He gazed round at Brace, Dorman, and Blunt, the three detective superintendents who between them were investigating the murders of Gina West, Harry Dodge, Frankie Carter, and Billie Crombie. 'And that I can reach in and take any one of them whenever I want to.'

The superintendents waited patiently. They had been summoned to Fox's office at New Scotland Yard for a briefing, only to be given a homely chat about fish tanks. But they knew enough of Fox to know that he would get to the point of it all sooner or later.

'What I want you to do,' continued Fox, 'is nothing.'

'Nothing, sir?' Nick Dorman, the youngest of the superintendents, had met Fox for the first time at the beginning of the Carter murder enquiry and didn't know his ways as well as the other two.

'Well, not quite nothing.' Fox smoothed the cloth of his trousers over his knees. 'Get all your case-papers together and make sure that the scientific evidence is collated, so that we're ready to go when we have a body.'

'And when's that likely to be, sir?' asked Brace.

'Won't be long,' said Fox airily. 'The murders of West, Carter, and Crombie are all down to Tango Harris's little team. The murder of . . .' Fox paused. 'Who was the barman at Morrie Isaacs's place, Gavin? Harry something, wasn't it?'

'Harry Dodge, guv.'

'That's the fellow. Are you doing that one as well?'

'Yes, sir.'

'Good. That one's down to the late Billie Crombie and his two naughty boys, Gary and Kenny. But I don't want any enquiries made. All that will happen is that potential witnesses will go shtum, Tango and the brothers Crombie will get to hear that we're after them, and it'll be much harder to screw the bastards.'

'What about the Romford hijacking, sir?' asked Dorman.

'Glad you mentioned it,' said Fox. 'That's Tango Harris's as well. How's the guard going on Wayne Parish?'

'We're managing, sir . . . just.'

'Knew you would. It won't be for long. I'm just trying to make up my mind when to nick him.'

'What for?' asked Dorman.

'He was Crombie's inside man, Nick.'

'How the hell did you find that out, sir?'

'Informants,' said Fox mysteriously. 'You should get some. They're very useful at times.'

'Morrie, dear boy, you don't look at all pleased to see me.' Fox stood in the refurbished entrance bar to Morrie

102

Isaacs's restaurant and gazed approvingly at the new decor.

'Every time I look up there's a policeman in here, Mr Fox,' said Isaacs.

'That's what happens when you carelessly allow your barman to get murdered, Morrie.'

'It wasn't my fault, Mr Fox.'

Fox put an arm round Isaacs's shoulder and steered him towards a table in the corner of the restaurant. 'That, Morrie, is a matter of opinion. You see, I have reason to believe that you've been paying protection money to Tango Harris for some considerable time now. But because there's a bit of a war between Tango and the firm that used to be run by the late and unlamented Billie Crombie, you were picked out for a bit of a singeing. Unfortunately, Harry Dodge got fried. Unfortunate for Harry, that is. Then along comes a representative of Crombie Inc. and suggests that in future you'd be much better off paying the Crombies instead of Tango Harris.'

'I don't know anything about that, Mr Fox, I swear.'

'Witnesses for the prosecution will appear in a forthcoming attraction at the Central Criminal Court and testify to this astonishing set of circumstances, Morrie. And you will be joining them . . . on our side.'

'Mr Fox, there's no way—'

'On the other hand,' continued Fox relentlessly, 'you could join the lads in the dock.'

'But, Mr Fox—'

Fox held up a hand. 'I haven't finished yet. Tango Harris and five others claimed that they had a meal here on Friday the twelfth of October, at about seven thirty.'

'I don't know. Perhaps they did.'

'I'm sure they didn't, Morrie. And I'll tell you why. You see, Tango – or perhaps one of his little friends – came here, probably on the Saturday following, to impress upon you that Tango had been here the night before. Now you must remember that, because I'm sure that they promised you violence if you forgot. But he wasn't here that night, was he?'

'He'll kill me,' said Isaacs.

'Quite probably, but I have foreseen that, Morrie.'

'You have?'

'Oh yes. And in order to avoid that unfortunate situation arising, Morrie, I'm arresting you.'

'What for?' Isaacs paled and started picking at the edge of the tablecloth.

'Shall we say conspiracy to pervert the course of justice?'

'That'll never stick.'

'Possibly . . . but something will, Morrie.'

'It's all highly irregular, Mr Fox,' said the Crown Prosecution Service solicitor. 'And I'm not sure that we'll be able to manage it anyway.'

Fox lit a cigarette and blew smoke round the office to the obvious displeasure of the young lawyer. 'I'm not asking for much,' he said. 'The Crombies, Adams, and Baker are up before the beak tomorrow – first remand – and I can see no reason why they can't be committed for trial at the Crown Court straight away. Then I can get on with frying my bigger fish. Oh, and no bail, of course.'

'But there are no grounds for opposing bail, Mr Fox.'

'Yes there are,' said Fox. 'They're villains and may interfere with witnesses. Apart from which, other more serious charges may follow,' he added ominously.

'Such as?'

'How does murder grab you?'

The solicitor shook his head. 'I don't know,' he said. 'The defence are bound to ask for more time to prepare their case.'

Fox scoffed. 'Defence? They haven't got one. We nicked them bang to rights.'

The CPS solicitor winced.

104

Chapter Eleven

Fox's plan to catch his fish one by one started with his decision to put a twenty-four-hour surveillance on the four villains known to be members of Tango Harris's gang. It was demanding of manpower, but the result would, in Fox's opinion, be well worthwhile.

Now that Billie Crombie was dead and his two sons were in custody, Harris believed he had a clear run at the lorry-hijacking business. But he had calculated without the Flying Squad, doubtless encouraged by the fact that Fox had appeared unable to make a charge of murdering Gina West stick. In other words, he had become cocky . . . which was exactly how Fox had planned it. Consequently, teams of detectives kept watch on Royce, Guerrini, Quincey, and Nelson, waiting for them to strike.

It took two weeks.

Tango Harris didn't know for certain that Fox had obtained permission to place an intercept on his telephone line, but he wasn't prepared to chance it, and he drove from his house to a nearby telephone box. He knew that would be safe. The watching detectives, to whom he had the audacity to wave, couldn't tell who he was calling, obviously . . . but they had a damned good idea. Fox hadn't hoped to learn anything from watching Harris, of course, and had mounted that blatantly overt observation just to annoy him.

Two days later, at ten o'clock at night, Fox's strategy was rewarded when Harris's four villains assembled at a warehouse in Greenwich. Ten minutes later a Ford

Granada drove out, followed by a Vauxhall Carlton, and the registration numbers of each were quickly checked on the police national computer. The Ford's number was allocated to a motorcycle in Exeter, and the Vauxhall should have been a motor-mower owned by the Department of the Environment for use in the Royal Parks.

'Those bastards don't deserve to succeed, Joe,' said DS Buckley. 'They obviously don't know anything about computers.'

'They're getting cocky, skip,' said DC Bellenger.

The two cars, travelling within the speed limit, made for Shooters Hill Road and then turned south on to the Rochester Way.

'You know what this team's up to, don't you, Joe?'

'Yeah. Nicking lorries.'

Buckley grinned in the dark interior of the car. 'It's the method, Joe. The idea is that if they pick off a lorry making for the Dover ferry, no one will notice it's gone until it doesn't get there . . . if you see what I mean. Gives them time to get to the slaughter, unload, and make tracks.'

Numbers Three and Four teams of the Flying Squad – Gilroy's and Evans's – had been alerted by radio to the movement and were rapidly closing on the two cars containing the four robbers. About half a mile past Falconwood railway station, the Granada and the Carlton fell in behind an articulated lorry clearly heading for Dover. The leading car – the Granada – flashed its headlights three times and the lorry pulled into a lay-by, to be followed by the Granada and the Carlton.

'The driver's in on it,' said Buckley. 'They're not tooled up.'

Sure enough, the four villains had alighted from their cars without any weapons.

Within seconds, eight Flying Squad cars had stopped, completely blocking the carriageway, and more than thirty detectives – and their drivers – had leaped out and surrounded the lorry.

Too late, the robbers realized their error. One of them,

Guerrini, raced back to the Granada and was in the act of pulling out a sawn-off shot-gun when DC Bellenger hit him across the back of the neck with his truncheon. The remaining three, seeing that they were surrounded by a seemingly vast number of police officers, some of whom were holding pistols in an extremely menacing fashion, raised their hands.

'You're nicked, the lot of you,' said Denzil Evans. 'Attempted robbery.'

There are very few operations in the annals of the Criminal Investigation Department where there has not been a monumental cock-up of some description. And it was now that the latest one occurred. The driver of the artic, appreciating that something nasty was afoot, put his lorry into gear and pulled out of the lay-by, secure in the knowledge that any attempt by a Flying Squad car to stop him forcefully would be doomed to failure.

'Attempting to rob what?' asked Danny Royce, and laughed.

'Jesus Christ!' said Evans, which seemed to sum up the thoughts of all the Flying Squad officers present. His anguish was not alleviated when Danny Royce laughed again. 'You just watch your bloody self, Royce,' Evans shouted, his Welsh accent suddenly very pronounced. He turned to Buckley. 'Why wasn't there a car blocking that lorry?' he demanded, adopting the usual police ploy of thrashing about for someone else to blame.

'Wouldn't have done much good, guv,' said Buckley.

'Well don't stand there,' screamed Evans. 'Get on the bloody radio and get the damned thing stopped. Tell Kent as well, in case he makes it over the border.'

In fact, the articulated lorry was stopped two miles down the road by a resourceful Traffic Division officer who had picked up the All Cars message. He overtook the vehicle in the Range Rover, tucked in front of it and then reduced speed, finally forcing the artic driver to slow right down and stop. His wireless operator advised the Flying Squad and the traffic men were soon joined by three Squad cars, one of which contained the irate Evans.

Evans leaped from his car and ran to the driver's cab. 'Come out of there, you bastard,' he shouted.

The lorry driver dismounted. 'What's up, guv?' he asked innocently.

'Well, well,' said Evans, recovering his composure. 'Wayne Parish. What a coincidence.'

By now, DS Buckley, with the aid of the traffic officers, had opened up the back of the lorry. 'Not bad,' he said. 'Stacked full of personal computers.'

'I thought you said they knew nothing about computers, skip,' said Bellenger.

'They were obviously hoping to learn,' said Buckley.

Fox, who for once had decided not to interfere with the actual operation, could not resist joining in the interrogation. He had been delighted when he heard that Royce, Guerrini, Quincey, and Nelson had been arrested, along with Parish, and the following morning he made his way to Rochester Row police station in Westminster where the five prisoners were being held in the high-security accommodation there.

'There's one thing that puzzles me, guv,' said Evans.

'Only the one, Denzil?' said Fox.

'If Mr Dorman had got Parish under protective surveillance, how come there was nobody watching him when he got pulled with the lot we nicked?'

'Simple,' said Fox. 'I told Mr Dorman to take it off. Sharon Scrope told me that Parish had worked as the inside man on the job where Frankie Carter was topped, but that might have taken a bit of proving. I therefore assumed, following that cock-up, that he had almost certainly been recruited by Tango Harris and I thought that we would wait until we caught him at it. And we did.'

'Bit risky, though, guv, him having his lorry blagged twice.'

'Yes, indeed,' said Fox. 'But not risky for Tango. Only for Parish. He'll very likely get the sack,' he added and walked through to the interview room.

Wayne Parish looked up when Fox entered. 'I've got nothing to say,' he said.

108

'I have,' said Fox. It was not going to be a long interview and he didn't bother to sit down. 'Apart from last night's little fiasco, Wayne, dear boy, you are going on the sheet for conspiracy to murder one Frankie Carter who, you may recall, got nastily shot the last time your lorry got hijacked.'

Parish sat bolt upright. 'That was nothing to do with me.'

'Then why, I have repeatedly asked myself, did you say nothing about it when you were first interviewed? You may remember that I had to drag it out of you. Anyway, it'll be something for you to dwell on in the confines of your flowery dell, won't it.' Fox strode to the door and paused. 'On the other hand, you may feel inclined to tell me all you know about the activities of Tango Harris.'

'That's bloody duress,' said Parish, by now thoroughly alarmed.

'Yes,' said Fox, 'I do believe it is.'

Fox did not interrogate the four principals who had been involved in the great computer hijacking. He assembled them in the interview room and made them an offer. 'Tango Harris is not best pleased with you lot,' he began.

'Who?' they chorused.

'Oh dear,' said Fox. 'He'd have done better employing the string quartet that used to play in Lyons Corner House.'

'Nothing to say,' said Guerrini, who had apparently appointed himself spokesman.

'The situation is this, gentlemen . . .' Fox beamed at the prisoners. 'Tango Harris is sitting in his luxurious drum at Buckhurst Hall, laughing like a drain. And if you think that he will send one of his best lawyers down here to defend you – which would be a waste of money anyway – you can think again. As things stand, I am mindful to charge you all with the murder of Gina West, Frankie Carter, and Billie Crombie. Mr Harris, of course, claims he had nothing to do with any of them.'

All four started talking at once, but Fox held up his

hand. 'You do not have to say anything unless you wish to do so,' he intoned, 'but what you say may be given in evidence.'

Detective Inspector Gilroy entered the warehouse at Greenwich and gazed around. 'They've been well at it,' he said.

'Looks like Aladdin's cave,' said Fletcher.

'Right, lads,' said Gilroy to his team. 'Get to it.'

One detective seated himself at a table and started to list the property which the warehouse contained. There were television sets and video recorders in profusion. There were cases of whisky, cartons of cigarettes, and a vast array of electrical goods. And a substantial amount of uncut cocaine. By the time they had finished, Gilroy reckoned that there must be close to half a million pounds' worth of goods . . . and that didn't include the drugs.

'D'you know what, guv?' said Fletcher, laughing. 'I reckon this was Billie Crombie's slaughter and they just took it over when they topped him.'

'Could be right, Perce, but it's not all that funny.'

'Oh, but it is, guv. I can't wait to see the Crombie brothers' faces when we pop into Brixton and tell them.'

'OK to banjo this, guv?' DS Crabtree, Gilroy's other sergeant, was standing by a metal cupboard secured with a large padlock.

Gilroy walked across and pulled at the padlock. 'Yeah, give it a go, Ernie. Got the tools?'

'Never go anywhere without them, guv.' Crabtree walked out to the boot of his car and returned, seconds later, with a long case-opener. 'That ought to do it,' he said. Placing the tip of the jemmy in the hasp of the padlock, he wrenched hard. The padlock flew off and clattered on to the concrete floor.

Being careful to open it by its edge, Gilroy swung the door wide open. 'Now there's a sight for sore eyes,' he said. Inside the cupboard was an arsenal of weapons. Several hand-guns were laid out neatly on a shelf above a row of shot-guns, the barrels of which had been shortened to an illegal length. But next to the shot-guns was a rifle with a telescopic sight. 'That,' said Gilroy, under-stating his find, 'might be just what we're looking for.'

The ballistics expert at the Metropolitan Police Forensic Science Laboratory was in no doubt. 'That,' he said, 'is the weapon which was used to kill Billie Crombie.'

The sixteen-stone figure of Kevin Rix was tied securely to a chair in Tango Harris's warehouse in Wanstead. He had put up a good fight when Alfie Penrose and a few other members of Harris's gang had seized him outside a pub in Dulwich. But they had eventually subdued him and bundled him into the back of their van.

Now, looking both desperate and terrified, Rix strained against his bonds, all the time mouthing obscenities at his captors. His self-esteem was not helped by the fact that Penrose and company had divested him of all his clothes.

'You wanna watch your mouth,' said Penrose. 'There'll be a lady here in a minute.'

Rix's only answer was a further string of profanities. Penrose laughed.

There was a sudden noisy commotion from immedi-ately outside the warehouse before the door was opened to admit a further four members of Harris's team carrying the struggling and gagged figure of Arlene Fogg. With obvious relief they tied her securely into a chair facing Rix, but on the other side of the warehouse.

'If you bastards lay a finger on her—' began Rix.

'You'll what?' Tango Harris sauntered slowly out of the small office in one corner of the warehouse, drawing on a pair of leather gloves as he walked. 'You and your boys have been damaging my property, Kevin,' he said. He glanced over his shoulder. 'You and the beautiful Arlene, that is. Done one of me video shops, ain't you? Drove a bleedin' van into it and set fire to it. Now I don't call that friendly, Kev. Not at all friendly.'

There was a loud groaning noise as Arlene tried to shout through the sticking plaster over her mouth.

Harris ignored her. 'Now I don't like that sort of thing,

Kevin,' he continued. 'And I don't like Tommy Fox and the bleeding Heavy Mob breathing down my neck because someone's topped one of Billie's bloody toms, neither. Specially when they try to put it down to me.'

'That video job wasn't down to me,' said Rix. 'And Billie never topped the tom.'

'No? Well, who was it down to, then?'

'Haven't a clue,' said Rix.

Harris turned to Penrose and nodded. Penrose struggled across the warehouse with a small portable generator and taped two bare wires from it to Rix's genitals. At a further signal from Harris, he started to wind the handle.

Rix let out a scream and arched in his chair. 'Bastards!' he yelled from between his clenched teeth.

Harris gestured for the torture to stop. 'Who torched my video shop, Kev?' he asked.

'I don't know.'

Harris nodded and the power began to flow again, Penrose winding the handle more vigorously.

'All right, all right,' shouted Rix, the sweat rolling down his face. 'It was Gary and Kenny and a couple of others.'

There was a further loud groaning from Arlene that sounded very like a protest of some sort. Harris grinned at her and then turned back to Rix. 'Was it really? Well, that's very satisfactory, Kevin. So glad you were able to help.'

'You bastards.'

Harris walked across to Arlene. 'If I have any more bother from your little firm,' he said, 'you'll be the one getting that treatment next time. So be warned. But just to show that we're into equal opportunities here, we'll give you a little something to take home.' Harris walked across to the corner of the warehouse and picked up a hose. 'Stand her up,' he said. Then turning the water on full, he saturated Billie Crombie's common-law widow from head to foot.

Harris threw down the hose with a laugh. 'Take the

lady home,' he said and watched as Arlene was dragged out to the van that had brought her to Wanstead from Catford. Then he walked across to Rix and stared at him for a moment or two. 'Randy,' he said without looking away.

'Yes, Mr Harris.' Randy Steel, a tall, gangling black man, detached himself from the wall he had been leaning on and strolled over.

'Kill him,' said Harris and peeled off his gloves.

'The situation is this,' said Fox, gazing round the conference room. 'So far, we've nicked the two Crombie brothers, together with Adams and Baker. They can have the LF job, at the very least. But I'll be disappointed if we can't find evidence of further wrongdoing on their part. We also have Morrie Isaacs in custody, more for his own good than ours. And we have the computer cowboys, Messrs Royce, Guerrini, Quincey, Nelson, and Parish.' He perched on the table at the front of the room and lit a cigarette. 'The ballistics man has tied in the rifle that Jack Gilroy found with the murder of Billie Crombie. But there's a snag there. It seems likely that the slaughter where it was found could have been Billie Crombie's. And that means that either the Crombie brothers could have blown their old man away, or Tango Harris's mob did so after they'd taken it over. Or at least, put the rifle there after they took it over. Either out of carelessness . . . or to fit up Gary and Kenny Crombie.'

'Or Arlene,' said Crabtree with a grin.

For a moment or two, Fox stared at Crabtree. 'You may have a point there, Ernie,' he said. 'Although she doesn't strike me as the Annie Oakley of Catford Bridge somehow . . . but you never know your luck.'

'What's next, guv?' asked Gilroy.

'Next,' said Fox, 'we wait and see what the Falconwood Five have to say. I've suggested that they'll all go on the sheet for the murder of Frankie Carter. That ought to stir 'em up a bit. I shall now inform them that I am considering further counts . . . like the topping of Billie

113

Crombie. That should make them run for the lifeboats.'

'Anything else, guv?' asked Fletcher.

'Ah, Perce! Glad you're here. Given that Gina West was one of Billie Crombie's girls and that he was into big-time vice, there are doubtless other young ladies about the West End who may well have a tale to tell. Get out and beat on the ground, there's a good fellow.'

'They're not likely to talk, guv,' said Fletcher.

'We have got the Crombies in custody, Perce.'

'Yes, sir, but not Tango Harris.'

Fox nodded slowly. 'You're quite right, Perce. I knew there was something else I had to do.'

But Fox decided to leave Tango Harris at liberty for a while longer. Apart from the fact that he rather enjoyed picking Harris's soldiers off one by one and leaving him more and more isolated, he wanted to make absolutely certain that when eventually he ascended the steps at the Old Bailey, Harris would be facing an indictment about the size of the *Encyclopaedia Britannica*.

Chapter Twelve

Detective Superintendent Brace's enquiries into the murder of Gina West had confirmed that she had been a high-class call-girl. And Sharon Scrope had said that Billie Crombie had been Gina's ponce.

But those sparse facts made Detective Sergeant Fletcher's excursion into the vice centre of London no easier.

Girls in the Gina West class of prostitute would not be found loitering in the darkened doorways around Soho. Among London's network of hotel hall porters, head waiters, taxi drivers, and night-club doormen there would be many willing to provide a prospective client with the telephone number of a prostitute . . . but only when they were asked, of course. The mug, as he is known, would then ring the girl concerned and arrange for her to come to his hotel room, or even his private apartment, there to provide him with her specialized services.

The select quality and attractiveness of the women ensured that a price of at least five hundred pounds would not seem excessive. But her ponce got a considerable slice of the take and there was, of course, a commission to be paid to whoever had made the introduction.

And it was a risky business. From time to time, such girls were murdered, and it was not unknown for them to be attacked and even tortured by sexual deviants.

The only factor in Fletcher's favour was that when a murder had occurred, as in the case of Gina West, these women felt more than usually vulnerable all the while that the murderer was on the loose, and there was a greater willingness on their part to give information. Sometimes.

Fletcher took a seat at the bar of a well-known West End restaurant whose proprietor would have been horrified to learn that his head waiter acted as a contact man for prostitutes. But Fletcher had no intention of advising the proprietor of this fact because he knew that the head waiter would get the sack. And that would cut off a very useful source of information. And right now, information was what he wanted. Which was why he was sitting at the bar with a whisky and water, watching the lunch-time clientele and waiting patiently until he caught the head waiter's eye.

'Hallo, Mr Fletcher.' The head waiter glanced around briefly. 'You lunching here today?'

'On my pay, Albert? You must be joking.'

Albert, who was better known to the patrons by a French name, dropped his voice. 'I can always lose the bill, Mr Fletcher.'

'I'm afraid those days are gone, Albert,' said Fletcher. 'For all I know, my Commissioner might use this place.'

'You're entitled to eat where you like, surely?'

'Oh, sure,' said Fletcher. 'But the Commissioner knows I couldn't afford to eat here. Therefore, I'm on the take, or getting a freebie. Either way I'm out of a job.'

Albert shrugged. 'What can I do for you then, Mr Fletcher?'

'You've heard about Gina West's murder, I suppose.'

'Who hasn't? Are you working on that one?'

'Sort of. What I want, Albert, is the name of another girl . . . preferably from the same stable.'

Albert looked apologetic. 'I'm sorry, Mr Fletcher,' he said, conscious that he might be overheard by others in the bar. 'More than my life's worth. You know what things are like . . . especially at the moment. I'd love to help, but if I'm seen giving information to the police . . .' He shrugged and, signalling to the barman, pointed at Fletcher's glass. 'Guest of the house,' he said. Moving

116

his head nearer Fletcher's ear, he whispered, 'I won't tell the Commissioner,' and moved away to greet two patrons who had just entered the restaurant.

Fletcher finished his drink and took his coat from the doorman. In the pocket was a printed card. And on the card was a name and a telephone number. There was no address, but then prostitutes of Gina West's calibre don't work like that.

It had taken Fletcher only ten minutes to ring the Yard from West End Central police station and get a subscriber check on the telephone number of the girl who called herself Cheryl. According to British Telecom records, her real name was Jean Rogers and she lived in a flat in Clarges Street.

It was two o'clock in the afternoon and it was unlikely that Cheryl would be working. Fletcher pressed the buzzer on the intercom beside her front door.

'Yes?' A woman's voice crackled out of the metal box.

'Miss Rogers?'

'Yes.'

'I'm a police officer,' said Fletcher.

The door opened an inch or two on the chain. 'How do I know?'

The girl carefully scrutinized Fletcher's warrant card and then admitted him.

It was an elegant flat, richly furnished, with a view across Green Park to Buckingham Palace. Jean Rogers was elegant too. About thirty years of age, she was tall and slim with long black hair. 'What is this all about?' she asked with the sort of haughtiness that men often find attractive. With a movement of her hand, she invited Fletcher to sit down on a settee, and then sat down herself, opposite him.

'Did you know Gina West?' asked Fletcher.

'No. Should I have done?'

Fletcher held up the card which had been left in his pocket by Albert, the head waiter. 'I thought you might have done,' he said.

'Oh, I see,' said the girl.

'She was murdered last month in a hotel room near here.'

'Yes, I know. But what has that to do with me? Incidentally, how did you know where I lived, if that card was all you had?'

'I'm a detective,' said Fletcher. 'Let's stop beating about the bush, Miss Rogers, shall we? I know what you do for a living.'

For the first time since his arrival, Jean Rogers smiled. 'Are you here on business or pleasure?' she asked.

'Business. Mine, not yours.'

The girl glanced at her watch, a Baume and Mercier. 'I have an appointment in about half an hour's time,' she said.

'That's early.'

'It's never too early for sex, but I doubt that you've come here to discuss my working practices.'

'Who's your ponce?' asked Fletcher.

Jean Rogers raised her eyebrows. 'I don't know what you mean.'

'Miss Rogers, I'm not looking to do someone on an immoral earnings charge. Frankly, I couldn't care less how you make your money, but, without wishing to alarm you, Miss West was murdered by someone who wanted to take over what they saw as a very lucrative empire. It was a message from one ponce to another that he was muscling in. Taking over. Do I make myself clear?'

'Crystal.' The haughtiness had returned.

'Let me mention two names,' said Fletcher. 'Tango Harris and Billie Crombie.' Jean Rogers ran her hand nervously through her hair. 'I can see that they register,' he went on.

'You're not seriously suggesting that I know anything about either of them, are you, Sergeant?'

'Yes, I am. But let me tell you what's happened so far. Billie Crombie is dead. Murdered. And his two sons, Gary and Kenny, are on remand in Brixton Prison awaiting trial.'

'That really makes no difference to me.'

'So your ponce is Tango Harris, then.'

Jean Rogers had started to look quite agitated. 'I didn't say that.' She stood up. 'Look, I really must get ready,' she said.

Fletcher stood up, too. 'Is it Tango Harris?' he demanded.

'Yes.' The girl whispered the answer. 'Now leave me alone,' she added.

'Miss Rogers, we are going to nail Tango Harris. For too long, he has been running rings round the law, pleasing himself what he does. He has murdered people, taken huge profits out of prostitution, drugs, armed robbery, and a host of other illegal ventures that I won't weary you with.'

Jean Rogers sat down again, quite suddenly. 'I don't think you know what you're asking,' she said. 'Like an actress, my face is my fortune, to say nothing of other parts of my anatomy. If Harris sends some of his people to see me, I shall never work again. If I live. I've got nothing to say, to you or anyone else.'

Fletcher sighed. 'Supposing we lock Harris up?'

The girl laughed and ran a hand through her hair once more. 'And when's that going to happen? You're not the first policeman who's promised that, you know.'

'We've got six or seven of his associates in custody already,' said Fletcher, 'and Harris's turn will come.'

'Yes, maybe. I'll make a deal with you, Sergeant. When you come here and tell me that Harris has just been put away for thirty years, I might have something to say.'

Fletcher shrugged. He knew that was the best he was going to get. It was always the same. Harris, and to a lesser extent, Crombie, had succeeded in terrifying potential witnesses by the threat of violence. And it was violence that they wouldn't hesitate to use. And had used. Over and over again. 'We could provide you with protection.'

'That would do wonders for my business, wouldn't it?

A policeman on the door while I'm ministering to the needs of a tired businessman.'

When Percy Fletcher got back to the Yard, he found Fox's office empty. Knowing the way Tango Harris worked, he was concerned that Jean Rogers might be in some danger. If Harris found out that the girl had been visited by police, he would assume that she had given them information. 'Seen the guv'nor?' he asked a DC who was walking down the corridor.

'In the Squad room, skip. Bit of a thrash going on.'

The Flying Squad office was full of people. In the centre stood Tommy Fox, a glass in his hand.

Fletcher stopped next to Jack Gilroy. 'What's going on, guv? Harris been nicked?'

'No, Perce. Rosie's promotion's come through.'

'Oh, bloody hell,' said Fletcher. 'That means she'll be posted. Or will the guv'nor try and hang on to her?'

Gilroy shrugged. 'Don't see how he can stop it. Not these days. There was a time in this job, Perce, when crime was considered to be the most important thing the job had to cope with. Now it's five-a-side football and the Metropolitan Police Band. If I had my time over again, I'd become a bandsman.'

'I doubt it, guv,' said Fletcher. 'They're all civvies now.' He pushed his way through to where Rose Webster was talking to Fox. 'Rosie,' he said. 'I just heard. Congratulations.'

Rosie Webster poured a glass of Scotch and handed it to Fletcher with a smile. 'Thanks . . . Perce,' she said.

Fletcher took a sip of whisky and looked around. 'Can we have a quiet word somewhere, guv?' he said to Fox. It was not that he didn't trust the other officers, it was just that the hubbub of conversation made it impossible to talk seriously.

Fox moved out into the corridor. 'What is it?'

Fletcher explained how he had tracked down Jean Rogers, and then went on to summarize his interview with her. 'It looks very likely that she was one of the

120

Crombie harem that got taken over by Harris, guv,' he continued. 'If I'd known, I wouldn't have gone in cold. It was unfortunate really. A shot in the dark.'

Fox looked thoughtful. 'Splendid, Perce.'

'It is, guv?'

'Yes, dear boy. You've just given me an excellent reason for preventing those prats in Personnel and Training from posting Rosie to Hampstead.'

'Is that where she's going, sir?'

'Not any more, Perce,' said Fox. 'Not any more.'

'That bastard Harris is well informed, guv'nor,' said Gilroy.

'So they tell me, Jack. About what in particular?'

'One of the lads on the intercept rang in to say that one of Harris's bloody snouts has just been on the phone, telling him that Percy Fletcher went to see Jean Rogers, alias Cheryl, yesterday afternoon.'

Fox stood up. 'How long ago was this, Jack?'

Gilroy glanced at his watch. 'No more than ten minutes, sir.'

'Excellent.'

'It is, sir?' Gilroy looked puzzled.

'We shall go and visit Miss Rogers.'

'Do we know where she is, guv?'

'At home, Jack,' said Fox. 'At least, she should be,' he added mysteriously.

'Good afternoon, Miss Rogers. I'm Thomas Fox . . . of the Flying Squad. May we come in?'

'I suppose so.' Jean Rogers opened the door wide and then led the way into her sitting room.

'This is Detective Sergeant Webster,' said Fox, indicating Rosie.

'Really?' Jean Rogers sounded uninterested.

'I'm here, Miss Rogers, because we have reason to believe that your life is in danger,' said Fox.

Jean Rogers looked alarmed. 'How? In what way?'

'We don't know precisely, but we intend to guard you from now on.'

121

'It's all because that policeman came to see me yesterday afternoon, isn't it?'

'That's only partly the reason,' said Fox. 'The real reason is that you've got Tango Harris for a ponce.'

Gilroy, Fletcher, Bellenger, and Rosie Webster were with Jean Rogers in her flat in Clarges Street. Forty-eight hours had elapsed since Fox's visit and the imposition of a strong guard. Other officers, in cars and on foot, were in Clarges Street and were the first to see the two men approach.

Inside the flat, Gilroy was informed of the sighting on his personal radio. Jean Rogers was ushered into her bedroom and Rosie, dressed in shirt and jeans, slipped off her earrings and prepared to answer the door.

The buzzer sounded and Rosie lifted the handset of the intercom. 'Hallo.'

'Miss Rogers?'

'Yes.'

'It's the police here. Can we come in?'

Rose opened the door an inch or two and stepped back.

The first man through the door was stocky, but slightly shorter than Rosie, and with a full head of black hair. As he moved forward, he released the blade of the flick-knife in his hand. But he was totally unprepared for what happened next.

Rosie grabbed his hair with both hands, suddenly forcing his head downwards. At the same time, she brought her knee up and smashed it into the man's nose. Keeping her grip on his hair, she pulled him forward and then threw him past her so that he hit the floor with a satisfying thud. The second man's mouth opened in astonishment at the ferocity of the attack on his partner, and that left him vulnerable. Rosie took a pace forward, grabbing his shoulders and bringing her knee up at the same time . . . straight between his legs. The man screamed in agony and fell backwards into the hallway outside the front door.

Detective Sergeant Ernie Crabtree had followed the

two men up the stairs and now looked down at the writhing figure at his feet. 'Oh dear,' he said. 'What a very distressed gentleman.'

When the call came into the Flying Squad office, Fox shouted for Swann and raced to Clarges Street. But by the time he arrived, an ambulance was already drawn up outside Jean Rogers's block of flats.

Inside the flat, the two would-be attackers were being placed in stretcher-chairs by the ambulance attendants, watched by a group of Flying Squad officers.

'Well,' said Fox. 'That looks like two more of Tango's jolly helpers that we've picked off. I suppose they're down to you, Rosie.'

'No problem, sir,' said Rosie. 'They refused to fight.'

Fox sighed. 'Bloody promotion's gone to your head, I suppose,' he said.

'I'm afraid there's blood on the carpet, sir,' said Rosie, aware of the forms that had to be completed in connection with damage to property.

Jean Rogers appeared from the bedroom. 'Don't worry about the carpet,' she said. 'I have a little man in every so often to clean it.' She walked to the cocktail cabinet and took out a bottle of gin. 'I don't know about you,' she said, addressing Fox and his officers, 'but I could do with a drink.'

'Good result, guv,' said Gilroy, 'but there are still some more of Tango's soldiers out there.'

'I think there probably are, Jack,' said Fox.

'Well, for one there's the snout who telephoned Harris and tipped him off about Percy Fletcher's visit to Jean Rogers.'

'Oh, that's easy, Jack,' said Fox. 'That was me.'

Chapter Thirteen

It is the practice at the Central Criminal Court to list defendants alphabetically on the indictment and that is the order in which the counts are put to them when they are arraigned.

On the list outside the public entrance to the court, only the name of the first accused appears followed by the phrase '& others'.

Thus the brothers Crombie, Barry Baker, and Cliff Adams were listed as 'Adams & others'. Which would have done nothing whatever for the self-esteem of the Crombie brothers if they had seen it. However, not being prisoners on bail, they were privileged to have their own personal entrance to Number Four Court at the Old Bailey.

'Put up Adams, Baker and the Crombies,' cried an elderly screw. And the four were ushered quickly up the steps and into the dock.

Once the traditional flummery had been completed and the business of dispensing justice had begun, the associate put the counts concerning the long-firm fraud to each of the prisoners in turn and noted their pleas. When the name of Kenneth Christie Crombie was read out, the judge looked up. 'Were you named after Dame Agatha,' he asked, 'or the Rillington Place murderer?' and received a dutiful laugh from the public gallery.

Adams pleaded guilty and was put down to await sentence. The same thing happened with Baker. But Gary and Kenny Crombie, having originally intimated that they would follow suit, changed their minds and a plea of Not

Guilty was entered. The judge was not amused. He was now faced with a full trial when all he had anticipated were pleas in mitigation and sentencing. And defence counsel made a note of the judge's remark about the Rillington Place murderer as constituting possible grounds for an appeal if the necessity arose.

The trial dragged on, but the crux of it was the appearance of the Crombie brothers in the witness box to give evidence on their own behalf.

By the time that their testimony was over, and despite a valiant effort by prosecuting counsel in cross-examination, the Crombies' counsel had elicited enough to make a useful closing speech. 'There is no evidence,' he said, 'that Gary and Kenneth Crombie were aware of the unlawful implications of their actions. By offering to assist their friends in what they firmly believed to be an innocent act of kindness, they suddenly found themselves in a police station and charged with a serious crime. Imagine, ladies and gentlemen, your own reaction if, having undertaken to help some friends to load their lorry, you next found yourself appearing in the dock at the Old Bailey. And for what? For helping someone out. I cannot impress upon you too much, ladies and gentlemen, the anguish that these young men have suffered, to say nothing of their recently widowed mother, who was relying upon them for aid and comfort.'

There was an audible sob from Arlene Fogg, who was sitting in the front row of the public gallery.

'I put it to you, ladies and gentlemen,' continued defence counsel, 'that these young men have been the victims of circumstance. Neither will it have escaped your notice that my clients were unashamedly taken advantage of. Their testimony that Adams and Baker, while in custody, had privately admitted to my clients that they had deceived them and then laughed about it afterwards, should be enough to convince you of my clients' innocence.'

And it did. Thirty minutes after retiring, the jury returned a Not Guilty verdict in respect of all the counts against the Crombie brothers.

'Well if that doesn't beat cock-fighting,' said Denzil Evans, 'I don't know what does.'

When Adams and Baker were brought back into court for sentencing, the judge, who like the jury had been misled by the bogus testimony of the Crombies, rebuked them sternly on the matter of taking advantage of friends who offered them assistance. Then he sentenced each of them to five years' imprisonment.

'Excellent,' said Fox.

'What's good about that, guv?' asked the mystified Evans. He had expected Fox to explode at the verdict.

'Once Messrs Adams and Baker have settled in, Denzil – unpacked and that sort of thing – we shall visit them, and talk to them in kindly tones. In the mean time, we shall set Rosie Webster to interrogating Jean Rogers, alias Cheryl, a resting whore.'

'Those bastards have had us over, Mr Fox,' said Adams.

'Yes, but they're criminals, dear boy, and criminals tend to do that sort of thing.' Fox pushed his cigarette case across the table.

'It's a bloody con, that's what it is.' Adams lit a cigarette and leaned forward in his chair, resting his arms on the table. 'Me and Barry's doing a bloody five-stretch now, and it was their scam.'

'What did you get out of it . . . apart from five years in the nick?' asked Fox.

'Bugger all,' said Adams.

Fox nodded sympathetically. 'You have fallen among thieves,' he said, which Adams would have recognized as a truism . . . if he had known what a truism was.

'Gary and Kenny said they was going to plead, the bastards. And we was all going to throw ourselves on the mercy of the court.'

'Very unwise,' murmured Fox.

'But when it comes to it, they put it all down to us. If we'd done what was agreed, we'd've scored eighteen months at worst.'

'It's a funny old world that we live in,' mused Fox,

apropos of nothing in particular, 'but with your record that is the most optimistic statement I've heard in years. However, I have not given up on the Crombies. And as you have nothing to lose but your chains, I suggest that you tell me all about their activities.'

'That'd take a bloody week, Mr Fox, and no mistake.'

'When it comes to screwing the Crombies,' said Fox, 'I am a man of infinite patience.'

'In that case, Mr Fox,' said Adams, 'you'd better get your clerk in. I've got a lot of talking to do.'

Denzil Evans spent two or three days interrogating both Adams and Baker in some depth. When he had finished, each of the disgruntled prisoners had dictated statements which ran into several dozen sheets of paper.

Fox read through the statements twice and then looked up. 'Added to what Sharon Scrope has given us, Denzil, dear boy,' he said, 'there is enough evidence there to arrest the Crombie brothers and Arlene Fogg for a start. Cff you go and get warrants.' He laid the statements down and placed a hand on them as if fearing they might escape. 'I do love it when thieves fall out,' he added.

There was a small and exclusive gathering at the Crombie house when the police arrived. Although it was several days since their acquittal, the Crombie brothers had prudently decided to wait until now to celebrate their escape from the clutches of the head of the Flying Squad. It was a mistake.

Arlene Fogg opened the door. Obviously refusing to recognize that she would never see fifty again, she had adorned herself in a silver lamé blouse, cut so wide at the neck that it failed to cover her black bra straps. Her legs were encased in a pair of light-green stretch-polyester trousers, the bottoms of which stopped above her ankles and were only held down by straps under her feet. This unedifying picture was completed by a pair of carpet slippers with pink bobbles on the front.

'Good evening, madam,' said Fox. 'We are the police.'

127

'I know who you bleedin' are,' said Arlene. 'What d'you want?'

'You for a start, Arlene . . . and your two dear sons.'

Arlene turned suddenly and shouted down the long hallway. 'Gary, it's the law. Scarper!'

'Other officers,' said Fox, blithely ignoring Arlene's outburst, 'are stationed in your garden with a view to arresting any fleeing felons who happen to spill out of your rear windows.'

Arlene turned to face Fox once more, her arms akimbo in an attitude of defiance. 'Then I hope you've got a brief,' she said.

'Of course,' murmured Fox, withdrawing the warrant from his pocket. 'Rarely go anywhere without one these days.' He pushed past the protesting Arlene and marched purposefully down the hallway followed by DI Evans.

The room at the back of the house which Fox now entered was occupied by Gary and Kenny Crombie and two young women each dressed in Catford uniform: a revealing white blouse and tight black leather skirt which stopped just below her backside. The elder of the brothers was in the act of wrenching back the curtains only to find that a grinning DC Bellenger was standing on the other side of the window.

Reclining in a black plastic-upholstered armchair was a muscular man in his early thirties, wearing jeans and a T-shirt. His hair was dyed blond and he wore a chunky medallion round his neck.

'Good grief,' said Fox as his gaze travelled round the room. One wall was covered in pine cladding on which were three brightly coloured ducks in tight formation, and a print of an Asian woman. A cocktail bar stood in one corner behind which were optics and an inset aquarium. A fluorescent light shone down from above. On the opposite wall was a simulated log fire, beneath a shelf crowded with ornaments that vied with each other for lack of taste. Among other equally awful items, there were a brass carriage-clock with a pendulum of revolving balls, a ship in a bottle, a model of a horse and cart, and an electric light that contained some sort of constantly

128

moving ectoplasm. 'I wouldn't mind betting, Denzil,' said Fox, 'that they have a pine lavatory seat as well.'

'What's this all about, squire?' asked the sprawling muscles.

'Who are you?' asked Fox.

'Harry Towler. I'm her feller. What's it to you, anyway?'

'Splendid,' said Fox. 'I've been looking for you.' He turned to Arlene. 'You didn't let Billie get too cold before importing a fancy-man, did you, Arlene?' he said. 'Now then . . .' He addressed the assembled company. 'I have a warrant for the arrest of Gary and Kenneth Crombie . . . and Muzz Arlene Fogg.'

'I think we'd better be going, Gary,' said one of the girls. 'Can you call us a minicab?'

Gary Crombie had taken but one pace towards a Mickey Mouse telephone that stood on a table in the corner, when Fox spoke again.

'Don't bother. We've got plenty of transport outside.'

'Oh, ta,' said the girl. 'We live in Forest Hill.'

'Quite possibly,' said Fox, 'but you're going to Catford police station, along with the three stars of this little show . . . and you,' he added, nodding at Towler.

'I ain't done nothing,' said Towler. 'What's this all about, anyhow?'

'How do lorry heists grab you?' asked Fox. 'I can give you dates if you want to be awkward.'

'Oh!' said Towler.

'Who is the owner of this property?' Fox looked round.

'I am,' said Gary Crombie and Arlene in unison.

'No you bleedin' ain't,' said Arlene. 'Billie left it to me in his will.'

'We don't know that for sure yet, Ma.'

'Oh yes we do.' Arlene took a pace towards her son. 'I've seen the bleedin' will, so don't you go arguing with your elders and betters.'

Fox stepped between them. 'Right,' he said. 'Gary Crombie will stay. Denzil, remove the rest to the nick before war breaks out.'

'What's coming off here then?' asked Arlene.

129

'We are going to search these premises,' said Fox, 'in the presence of the householder who, for the purposes of the Police and Criminal Evidence Act, I deem to be Gary Crombie.'

'Well that's bloody right, that is,' said Arlene.

'Couldn't have put it better myself, madam,' said Fox.

The attack on Jean Rogers which had been frustrated by her police guard, ably led by Rosie Webster, had convinced the call-girl of two things. Firstly, that she was in danger from Tango Harris, and secondly, that the police were able to protect her from him. If she did not now make a statement telling all she knew of Harris's activities, she thought the police might lose interest in her and possibly withdraw the officers who were looking after her. But Tango Harris wouldn't know that she hadn't made a statement. Would, in fact, have convinced himself that she had. And just to be on the safe side he might be tempted to silence her permanently.

With a sigh, and a characteristic pushing at her hair, she sat down opposite Rosie Webster and started to talk.

As Rosie Webster settled down to listen to Jean Rogers's enlightening tales of Tango Harris, Detective Inspector Gilroy finished taking a statement from Wayne Parish admitting that he had been a willing accomplice in the attempt by Quincey, Nelson, Royce, and Guerrini to hijack Parish's lorry-load of computers.

The five of them had now been in custody for some time, but despite frantic phone calls, Tango Harris's lawyer still hadn't appeared to help them out of their predicament.

They didn't know, however, that Harris, feeling more and more vulnerable as a result of Fox's relentless attack on his empire, was trying desperately to distance himself from the criminal activities of his accomplices.

Consequently, the four robbers had reluctantly concluded that they had been abandoned, and started to sing like a quartet of highly tuned canaries.

Interviewed independently they had each made a lengthy statement which had started, as is usual in such cases, by accusing the other three of being the prime movers in the robbery for which all four had been arrested. But then they had almost fallen over themselves to provide details of killings, savage beatings, robberies, protection rackets, vice rings, and a host of other less serious, but none the less illegal, enterprises.

And they had implicated Tango Harris in each and every crime they mentioned.

When they had finished, the statements joined the ever increasing pile of damning evidence that Fox hoped would take Harris out of circulation for a long time.

'Well, Jack?'

Gilroy sat down in the chair opposite Fox's desk. 'They made separate statements about the Carter job, sir, but Quincey, Nelson, Royce, and Parish each put Frankie Carter's murder down to Guerrini.'

'And what does Mr Guerrini have to say about it?'

'He puts it down to Royce, sir.'

'Looks as though Guerrini wins on points then.'

'Yes, sir, but the evidence of one co-conspirator against—'

'Jack, dear boy, *please*.' Fox held up his hand. 'What we have to do now is find some positive evidence that Guerrini was the one who pulled the trigger . . . and more to the point, find the trigger that he pulled.'

'Easy, sir,' said Gilroy with a grin. 'One of the shooters we found in the warehouse at Greenwich matches the round taken out of Carter's head.'

Fox nodded gloomily. 'That doesn't surprise me, Jack. That doesn't surprise me at all. But, given that all four probably had access to the said shooter, how do we tie the weapon in with Guerrini?'

'I think we might be in with a chance there, guv. Ever fired a Walther?'

'Can't say that I have, Jack.'

'Well, when it's fired, the recoil carries the slide back. If you've got it in a double-handed grip but you let your

131

left thumb stray upwards, the slide'll take a chunk out of it.'

Fox leaned forward. 'And?'

'It's a slim chance, guv, but the lab found slight traces of dried blood on the underside of the slide. DNA testing might just tie it in with Guerrini . . . once we get a blood sample from him. If we can.'

'Still doesn't prove that he killed Carter, Jack. If he injured himself, he might have done it on another occasion.'

'The prison doctor has examined Guerrini and found two parallel scars at the base of his left thumb compatible with such an injury, and is willing to testify that the scar is about the right age for the injury to have occurred at the same time as the murder.' Gilroy laid a couple of statements on Fox's desk. 'That's the prison doctor's report, sir,' he said. 'And the other one is the ballistics report. If it's not down to him, guv'nor, he's going to have a lot of fun talking his way out of it.'

Fox lit a cigarette and walked across to his drinks cabinet. 'D'you know, Jack,' he said, handing Gilroy a glass of whisky, 'I think you'd do quite well in the CID. Ever thought of making a career of it?'

Chapter Fourteen

'Mr Adams and Mr Baker are very cross with you,' said Fox.

'Oh yeah?' Gary Crombie affected a look of gross indifference.

'You will recall that they were convicted of running a long-firm fraud in Twickenham. A long-firm fraud which, incidentally, they seem to think you profited from . . . in more ways than one. Furthermore, they seem to think that you dropped them in it by pleading not guilty and putting it down to them.'

'Well, we wasn't, was we?'

'Weren't what?'

'Guilty.'

'Of course not, Gary, dear boy.' Fox lit a cigarette and studied the elder Crombie from the far side of the interview room.

'What?' Fox's unexpected reply jarred Gary Crombie's cockiness and put him off balance.

'You see,' continued Fox, setting off on another stroll around the room, 'I have the greatest faith in British justice. And if a good old British jury says you're not guilty, then clearly that's it.'

'What's your bloody game, Mr Fox?' Gary Crombie swivelled round in his chair so that he could keep Fox in sight.

'Oh, it's not a game,' said Fox. 'It's called letting bygones be bygones.' He finally tired of walking about and sat down opposite Crombie. 'It's the future that interests me, Gary, dear boy. Cigarette?' He pushed his case across the table.

'Ta!' Crombie took a cigarette and waited for Fox to produce his lighter. 'There's something coming off here,' he said.

'Indeed there is,' said Fox. 'What is coming off is that you are going down for a very long time, together with your brother Kenny.'

'You must be joking.' Crombie scoffed and blew smoke into the air. 'There wasn't nothing in my drum . . . and you know it.'

'There certainly wasn't anything of value there, dear boy. Unfortunately, bad taste is not yet a criminal offence. No, I am talking of the information given me by Messrs Adams and Baker aforementioned.' Fox casually threw two bundles of paper on the table.

'What's them?'

'Those, dear boy,' said Fox, 'are copies of statements made by Cliff Adams and Barry Baker, and in view of the fact that they contain serious allegations against you, you are entitled to copies.'

Crombie fingered the edge of the pile of paper. 'That'll be a pack of bloody lies.'

Fox nodded sympathetically. 'I thought so too,' he said, 'but I shall investigate what they have to say with vigour. Of course they will be charged with conspiring with you and others to commit all manner of offences,' he said, but refrained from mentioning that the assistance of Adams and Baker would probably ensure them a minimal sentence, if not a reduction in the time they were already serving. 'Now this . . .' Fox threw another statement on the table. 'This is part of a statement made by Miss Sharon Scrope in which she gives details of all manner of villainy in which you and your brother Kenny were involved.'

Gary Crombie sat up sharply. 'What's that little cow been saying?'

'Enough to put you and Kenny down for a long time . . . to say nothing of your own dear mother.'

'She's only trying to get her own back because Kenny and me—' Crombie stopped, suddenly realizing that what he was about to say was not at all clever.

'If you were going to claim that she only made that statement because you and Kenny raped her under Arlene's supervision, you can forget it,' said Fox. 'You see, she refused to lay charges and if your smart brief mentions it in court, she will deny that it ever took place. Clever that, don't you think?'

'The little bitch,' said Crombie.

'Mind you,' continued Fox, 'by the time I get around to looking into it all, Tango Harris will have taken much of it over, I suppose. In fact, he's probably done so already.'

At last Crombie got the drift of what Fox was driving at. 'You want to know about Tango Harris, Mr Fox?' he asked.

'That would be extremely useful, dear boy.'

Crombie's eyes narrowed. 'What's it worth?'

'To you, at the going rate, about twenty years I should think. Each!'

'What d'you mean . . . each?'

'You, Kenny, and Arlene.'

'Ma never had nothing to do with it.' Gary Crombie sat up sharply. 'It was all down to my old man.'

'Ah!' said Fox, 'the Oedipus complex.'

'Do what?'

'Never mind. You wouldn't understand. Might be worth mentioning to your counsel, though.'

'Look, Mr Fox, supposing we was to grass up Tango Harris.'

'Yes . . .' Fox drew the word out doubtfully.

'Well, I mean would it help like?'

'It would certainly help me.'

'Yeah, I know. But would it help me?'

'Oh, I see. Well, Gary, that would be a matter for the Crown Prosecution Service. But I might put in a word. If you came across with some good stuff. But you must understand that I can't make any promises.'

Gary Crombie ignored that. He was firmly convinced that Fox could fix anything. 'How about me and Kenny having a get-together with our mouthpiece . . . and Ma. I mean we could have a bit of a chat and see what we could come up with. Know what I mean?'

'What a good idea,' said Fox. 'But don't be too long about it.'

'Kenny and Ma might not agree, though, Mr Fox.' Crombie obviously thought it prudent to hedge his bets.

'I can imagine. Particularly Arlene. Quite cantankerous when the mood takes her, I should think. But look at it this way. I've got more than enough to put you three away, but at the moment I am not at all sure of securing a conviction against Tango Harris. And all the while you're picking oakum, or whatever they do in the nick these days, Tango will be out there enjoying the fruits of your labour.'

'Not if I can bloody help it,' said Crombie with feeling.

Fox was quite out of breath by the time he reached the second floor of Gerald Road police station in Belgravia. 'This is a poxy nick,' he said as he reached the doorway of the chief superintendent's office. 'Why haven't you got a lift?'

'Got to be fit to be in the Uniform Branch,' said the chief superintendent, a youthful man called Miskin. 'Who are you?'

'Detective Chief Superintendent Thomas Fox . . . of the Flying Squad.'

'Oh!' Miskin stood up and shook hands. 'This sounds like trouble.'

Fox closed the door and sat down uninvited. 'There are three massage parlours on your ground,' he began. 'And they're all run by Tango Harris who recently acquired them from the late Billie Crombie . . . following a takeover bid.'

'Who?'

'Oh, God!' said Fox. 'Let me explain.'

'What d'you want me to do?' asked Miskin when Fox had finished his summary of Harris's activities.

136

'To put it simply,' said Fox, 'raid them and secure sufficient evidence of Harris's complicity to enable me to arrest him.'

Miskin looked appalled. 'I haven't got the men for that,' he said. 'Might be able to do one of them . . .' He turned in his chair and looked at a calendar. 'Next Tuesday at the earliest.'

Fox shook his head. 'This evening. And all three at once.'

Miskin laughed. 'We can't just go in at a moment's notice,' he began. 'There's nothing unlawful about a massage parlour . . . if massage is all they're doing.'

'Oh, do leave off,' said Fox.

'We have to mount observations, otherwise we've got no evidence and—'

'I have.'

'But there are warrants to be obtained and I'll have to find the extra men.' Miskin didn't like being rushed and was fighting a desperate rearguard action.

'Warrants!' said Fox dropping a sheaf of papers on Miskin's desk. 'The Commander Operations has assigned the territorial support group to assist and I've got twelve Flying Squad officers standing by . . . downstairs. And that's another thing,' he added. 'You haven't got a car park.'

Miskin stared at Fox with a helpless expression on his face. 'I know,' he said. 'Anyway, what's the hurry? I can't just make the arrangements—'

'You don't have to,' said Fox. 'You can come along for the ride, if you like, seeing as it's on your ground, but don't keep on about arrangements. I've had some before,' he added unkindly, 'and I don't want some lairy PC getting on the blower and advising the said massage parlours of police interest so that everything is squared away by the time we go charging in.'

Miskin bridled at that. 'I hope you're not suggesting that any of my men would—'

'Yes I am,' said Fox brutally. 'And so would mine, given half the chance. You see, most policemen don't attach too much importance to massage parlours. Come to that, neither do I. If some pillock wants to pay a poxed-up whore an exorbitant sum of money for a quickie, why should we worry? Both willing partners, aren't they? And it's not exactly the crime of the century. But right now, Mr Miskin, it's Tango Harris I want. And if one of his massage parlours turns out to be a brothel then I shall capture him for it.'

'Well, I suppose you know your own business best.'

Fox grinned. 'D'you know,' he said, 'it's a long time since I've heard a Uniform Branch man say that about a CID officer.'

The canoeist was a hardy soul. Every morning he paddled from Hammersmith to Battersea, reckoning that, even in winter, it was a better way to travel than crushed into a stifling, overcrowded train.

It was as he was approaching Putney Bridge that he spotted a dark shape floating in the water. He back-paddled briefly and steered his canoe towards it. Then he made vigorously for the bank, beached his craft, and ran to the telephone box in Lower Richmond Road.

As the police car came towards him, the canoeist took off his woolly hat and waved it.

The wireless operator wound down his window. 'You the bloke who put up the call about a body floating in the river, mate?'

'You can just see it over there.' The canoeist pointed.

The two policemen got out of their car and walked to the river bank. 'Job for Thames Division.' The driver put his hands in his pockets and surveyed the broad sweep of the river. 'Get on the set, Charlie, and do the business, will you.'

The operator turned away towards the car and the driver reluctantly took an incident report book from his pocket.

Signs advertising the hire and sale of adult videos and magazines and another advising of the availability of qualified masseuses were plastered over the blacked-out

138

windows of the shop. Over the door another sign forbade entry to persons under the age of eighteen.

'That's a nice touch,' said Fox. He had decided to lead one of the raids himself. Teams raiding the other two massage parlours were under the command of DIs Gilroy and Evans. Rosie Webster was with Fox.

'Help you?' A seedy-looking individual reading a magazine about motorcycling was seated behind the counter.

'Shouldn't think so,' said Fox as he parted a screen consisting of plastic strips and disappeared into the rear of the premises.

''Ere, 'old on.' The motorcycle enthusiast leaped to his feet but suddenly gave a convincing impersonation of suspended animation as he saw the uniformed inspector standing in the doorway of the shop.

'Are you the owner of this establishment?' asked the inspector who had been designated to take care of the administrative niceties of the operation.

'Manager,' said the seedy one. 'What's going on?'

'You're being raided, that's what's going on,' said the inspector and, accompanied by several uniformed PCs and a number of Flying Squad officers, followed Fox.

'Well I'm blessed,' said Fox. He had entered a dimly lit room off a corridor. On a high couch lay a naked man whose sexual needs were being attended to by a naked woman. Naked, that is, apart from a white boilersuit around her ankles.

The woman – she was about forty and had brassy blonde hair – was not in the least abashed by Fox's sudden entry. 'You'll have to wait your turn,' she said, glancing over her shoulder. 'Waiting room's down the corridor.'

'Oh, right.' Fox detailed a constable to take particulars of the consenting adults involved and moved on. In the next room, much like the first he had entered, Fox was treated to the rare sight of a man tied hand and foot to a leather couch from which the stuffing was trying to escape. Riding him vigorously was yet another naked woman. Both were oblivious to Fox's arrival until the flash of the police photographer's camera alerted them.

'What the bloody hell . . . ?' the woman yelled, and stopped her physical exertions.

'Photo-finish,' said Fox. 'And you can untie him and bring him into the paddock.' He nodded towards the man whose panic-stricken face indicated quite clearly that he wished he was somewhere else.

'That,' said Fox, 'seems to have been a successful operation.' He surveyed the assembled Flying Squad officers gathered in the conference room. 'What did your manager have to say, Rosie?' Fox had last seen Rosie Webster leaning over the manager of the massage parlour-cum-adult-video shop in a most threatening manner.

'Couldn't wait to get out from under, guv,' said Rosie.

'Rather like the bloke we found in Room Four,' said Fox and acknowledged the laughter with a nod. 'Has he said what we want to hear?'

'Got a DC taking a lengthy statement from him right now, sir. Falling over himself to tell us that he was only one of Tango Harris's employees and didn't know what was going on in the back room. Came as an awful shock to him to discover that the qualified masseuses wore nothing under their white boiler suits . . . just in case.'

'Just in case?'

'There's a sliding scale for massage apparently, sir. Fully dressed, it's thirty quid. Topless, it's fifty, and boiler suit round the ankles costs seventy.'

'And what do they get for that?'

'Just a massage,' said Rosie. 'Oh, and a shower.'

'Cheapskates,' said Fox. 'And what about the "personal services" we saw?'

'I gather those are privately negotiated, sir,' said Rosie. 'But you-know-who gets a rake-off.'

'How did you get on, Jack?' Fox turned to Gilroy.

'More of the same, sir. A brothel disguised as a massage parlour. There's ample evidence to support charges, and the manager gave us a quick cough that it had been run by the Crombies until recently when it was taken over by Tango Harris.'

'Denzil?'

'We're all right, too, sir,' said Evans. 'Only one slight complication, though.'

'What?'

'One of the customers was an MP.' Evans looked sympathetic.

'Which party?'

'He was a Tory, sir.'

'Oh well,' said Fox, 'I dare say they'll be pleased to hear he's normal. Incidentally, what's happening about all the obscene videos . . . assuming they are obscene?' The expression on his face implied that they couldn't possibly be anything else.

'All seized, sir,' said Rosie. 'Some poor uniformed inspector has been assigned to view them and make notes.'

'How many were there?'

'About four hundred out of the three raids, guv. Give or take.' Rosie grinned.

'Good grief,' said Fox. 'The poor sod.'

During the next three days, Fox instituted raids on a further fourteen massage parlours in and around the West End of London. In eleven cases, his officers found enough evidence to prosecute the owner for keeping a brothel, publishing obscene material, and living on immoral earnings. The managers of nine of the establishments were only too keen to tell the authorities that the owner in question was Tango Harris. The other five were part of the disintegrating Crombie empire. By engineering what he called a confluence of legislation, Fox was able to ensure that the premises were closed down and the stocks of videos and magazines seized pending a court order for destruction.

'The river police have just found Kevin Rix in the Thames near Putney Bridge,' said Gilroy.

'Really?' Fox stirred absently at his cup of coffee. 'Making sure of a good place for the boat race, was he?'

'That's not till next April, sir,' said Gilroy, attempting to match Fox's cynicism.

'Billie Crombie's right hand, wasn't he?'

'Yes, sir.'

'Careless, leaving him floating about like that,' said Fox. 'Tango's usual style is a motorway bridge. Still,' he added, 'I suppose they're difficult to find these days, what with the recession and cut-backs and all that sort of thing.'

'We don't know that it's down to Tango Harris, guv.'

Fox scoffed. 'You got a better front-runner then, Jack? What's the SP?'

'He'd been shot. Twice in the head,' said Gilroy reading from a message flimsy. 'And the local CID reckon the body had been weighted, but broke loose.'

'Do they indeed? Well I'm not having them mucking about with it. I'll get the DAC to give it to Gavin Brace.'

Gilroy looked surprised. 'It's not on his area, sir, and anyway, he's a bit tucked up.'

'Really?' Fox pretended to look surprised. 'He's practically tied up the Gina West job, and the murder of Morrie Isaacs's barman is down to the brothers Crombie. No, Jack, he'll be bored to death. Much better if I give him something to do.'

'He was hoping to go on leave, sir.'

'Leave,' said Fox. 'What's that?'

Chapter Fifteen

Still persisting in going out and interfering when, according to his superiors, he should have been behind his desk dealing with the paperwork, Fox wound down the window of his Ford Granada and peered across the rain-swept street at the building opposite. 'Is that it?' he asked.

'That's it, sir,' said Gilroy.

'Where are the feet?' Fox always used that disparaging term to describe the Uniform Branch.

'Holed up in carriers round the corner, sir. Complete TSG. One, two, and twenty.'

'Better call 'em up then.' Fox had decided that the territorial support group, consisting of one inspector, two sergeants and twenty PCs would be adequate for the job. He intended that they should be there for a show of uniforms, but not otherwise to interfere. 'Where's my umbrella, Swann?'

'In the boot, guv.' The lugubrious Swann made no attempt to move.

'Well do the decent thing, there's a good fellow.' Fox sighed at the inadequacy of his driver's initiative.

Swann undid his seat belt and, mumbling some inaudible complaint, got out of the car and ambled round to its rear.

'Can't get the staff, Jack, that's the trouble with the job today, you know.' Fox stepped out into the roadway and took his umbrella from Swann. 'This is supposed to be a near-beer joint, isn't it?'

'Supposed to be, sir. But our information is that there's

143

a full range of alcoholic refreshment available . . . apart from a few other entertainments.'

'Splendid.' Fox paused long enough to observe three police Transit vehicles moving slowly into the street before striding across to the entrance of the premises he was about to raid. 'Seems to me, Jack,' he said, 'that we're doing a hell of a lot of the feet's work for them these days.' He stopped at the doorway. 'I mean to say, they're the chaps who are supposed to deal with brothels and infractions of the licensing law, aren't they?'

'Yes, sir.' Gilroy assumed that Fox was in one of his waspish moods.

There was no indication on the outside of the building that any sort of business, nefarious or otherwise, was being carried on within, but then Fox didn't expect an illegal drinking den to advertise itself too overtly. He knocked at the door. An unsavoury-looking individual opened it an inch or two. Fox kicked the door wide and in doing so, propelled the minder half across the hallway to collide with a shabby table.

''Ere, what's the game. You looking for trouble?'

'Strange to relate, dear boy, it's what I'm paid for,' said Fox. 'And we've come to enjoy ourselves.'

'If you're from Crombie, you can tell him that he'll be mixing it with Tango Harris from now on.'

'As a matter of fact,' said Fox, 'we're from the Flying Squad and right now, mixing it with Tango Harris is our full-time occupation.' He glanced over his shoulder as the territorial support group started to come through the door. 'And if your dainty little forefinger goes anywhere near that alarm button, my son, you'll be sleeping at the local nick tonight . . . until we can fix you up with a bed-sit in Brixton.'

The doorman, who had heard that the Flying Squad were frequently armed when they went out on raids, promptly placed both hands in the air and stood stock-still. 'There's nothing wrong here, guv'nor,' he said, his whining voice indicating that he was very quick to grasp that the odds were overwhelming.

144

'Pleased to hear it,' said Fox, 'but you won't mind if we satisfy ourselves as to that alleged state of affairs, will you?'

The main room of the club contained about fifteen tables, each with a red-shaded lamp on it. In one corner of the room was a bar presided over by a black man in a red jacket whose job in life was to serve the three leggy waitresses who bustled between there and the tables.

For a few moments, Fox stood and took in the scene. But he was in no hurry. He had arranged for the uniformed inspector in charge of the TSG to place a few of his men at the rear of the premises where the fire exit gave on to a labyrinth of passageways leading eventually to another street.

The men sitting at the tables were a mixture, but consisted mainly of a few Arabs and a leavening of tired businessmen. Each man was accompanied by a woman. Fox knew instinctively that the glasses in front of these so-called hostesses would contain nothing stronger than fruit juice, and although their 'guests' had paid vast sums for their own refreshment, they too would not easily get drunk. Unless they were willing to pay much more for the privilege. Fox, though, knew that they weren't there for the alcohol alone – they could buy that at standard prices at the pub down the road – but for the entertainment. Such as it was.

The uniformed officers filed in and started on the routine task of taking names and addresses.

Fox walked across to the bar. 'Who's running this place?' he enquired.

'Who's asking?' The barman, a surly expression on his face, wiped the top of the counter with a sponge cloth. Obviously aware that the presence of a large number of uniformed policemen spelled trouble anyway, he was determined to be as awkward as possible.

But Fox was not in the mood to play games. He leaned across the bar until his face was within inches of the barman's. 'You're nicked,' he said. And turning to a PC said, 'Put him in the van, lad.'

'What's the charge, sir?'

'Obstructing police in the execution of their duty,' said Fox. 'For a start.'

Thanks to the fact that the doorman had been effectively immobilized by the constant presence of one PC, it was some minutes before the putative owner of the club was aware of the presence of police. By then it was too late. Emerging from his office in the far corner of the bar, he stopped and waved his hands distressfully in front of his body. 'What's happening?' he asked of no one in particular.

A comely redhead in a very short flared skirt placed her tray of dubious-looking drinks on a side table. 'We've been busted, Mickey, that's what,' she said. 'What d'you want me to do?'

'Cover yourself up, for Christ's sake,' said the owner, nodding at the girl's naked breasts. 'They'll have you for that.'

'Wouldn't be the first,' said the redhead drily. She was worldly wise enough to know that there wasn't much chance of the police prosecuting a waitress for being topless. Not these days, anyway.

'You, I take it, are Mr Michael Finn?' Fox smiled politely.

'Yes. There's no trouble here, officer, I assure you,' said Finn anxiously. 'Just a few friends having a few drinks. There's no money changing hands.'

'Leave it out,' said Fox, leaning heavily on his umbrella. 'Several of my officers have already elicited from your customers that they have paid for intoxicating liquor.'

'But it's not intoxicating liquor, Officer,' said Finn with a smirk. 'It's just that they think it is.'

'Oh, splendid,' said Fox. 'In that case I shall do you for theft. As well. You will have ample opportunity, at a later stage, to explain what those optics contain . . . the ones labelled whisky and gin and brandy and vodka . . .' Fox waved his umbrella towards the bar. 'And now,' he went on, as if dismissing that minor problem, 'where are the peep-shows?'

146

Even in the dimly lit room, it was apparent that Finn's face went much paler. 'Nothing like that goes on here, Officer.' He paused, peering closely at Fox's face. 'You must be new around here,' he added.

'I suppose you could say that,' said Fox. 'I'm the head of the Flying Squad.'

'Oh, Christ!' Finn sank into a chair which fortunately was quite close by.

'Tell me, Mickey,' said Fox, adopting a conversational tone, 'how much a week does Tango Harris take out of this dodgy enterprise?'

'I've never heard of him.' Even Finn realized that he sounded unconvincing.

'Strange thing, that,' said Fox. 'The bonehead on the front door mentioned him in the very first sentence he uttered.'

'I'll sack him,' said Finn, an edge of malice in his voice.

'Could run up against the employment laws there,' said Fox. 'Very difficult to get rid of staff these days.'

'Found it, sir.' Gilroy appeared at Fox's elbow.

'Found what?'

'Upstairs, sir. Two or three booths where privileged clients can peer through a window into a bedroom and watch a tired-looking jessie screwing a bird who's old enough to be his mother. To the accompaniment of music.'

'What sort of music, Jack?'

' "Ride of the Valkyries", I think, sir,' said Gilroy.

'How appropriate,' said Fox. He turned to Finn. 'And I don't suppose for one moment that you've paid a fee to the Performing Rights Society, Mickey.'

It was Detective Sergeant Fletcher's fate, or so it seemed to Detective Sergeant Fletcher, always to be on the fringe of Fox's enquiries. But not only on the fringe. Apart from obeying Fox's frequent injunctions to get out and beat on the ground, Fletcher often found himself doing the less attractive tasks. Today's job was to put the fear of God – and Tommy Fox – into the prostitute population of central London. This he did by the simple expedient of mentioning to a few policemen at two or three police stations that Tommy Fox was launching an offensive. Fletcher knew, deep down, that it was the quickest way of sending his message to the ladies of the town.

'You're asking a lot, you know,' said Jean Rogers, the call-girl known professionally as Cheryl.

'So's Tango Harris,' said Detective Sergeant Rosie Webster. 'And all the while that he's allowed to roam free, girls like you are going to be in danger.'

'I've told you all I know about him.' Jean Rogers had not worked since the day of the attempted attack on her, and had remained in her Clarges Street flat under police guard. When Rosie Webster had last interviewed her, she had made a long statement setting out all that she knew about the vice business in London. And Tango Harris's involvement in it. 'You'll never stamp out prostitution, you know,' she said.

Rosie laughed. 'We're not trying to,' she said. 'It would take more than the resources of the Metropolitan Police to eradicate something that's been going on since the beginning of time. But we don't like the Tango Harrises of this world leaning on people. Even less do we like girls like you being murdered because you won't play ball.'

'Unfortunate choice of phrase,' said Jean Rogers drily.

For a moment or two, Rosie studied the prostitute seated opposite her. 'You're an elegant, well-educated girl,' she said. 'Why in hell's name did you get involved in this business?'

'Money . . . that's all. It might surprise you to know that I was educated in a convent. I've even got some A-levels. But I wanted a bit more out of life than working in some dreary office from nine till five every day. I wanted somewhere decent to live, and a car, and designer clothes.'

'Well, now you've got it, was it worth it?'

For a moment or two, Jean Rogers looked sad. 'I don't know any more,' she said. She stood up and walked across the room to a secretaire. When she turned to face Rosie

148

again, she was holding a card in her hand. 'I still don't know if I'm doing the right thing,' she said, 'but I've known this girl for about four years. Billie Crombie was her ponce until she got a visit . . . as I did. Then, like me, she was forced into working for Harris. There was no argument. It was made very plain that if we didn't co-operate, we'd get a beating.' She handed the card to Rosie. 'A beating that would disfigure us for life.'

'You should have gone to the police,' said Rosie.

Jean Rogers scoffed. 'You're joking,' she said. 'What good would that have done? What were we supposed to do? Walk into Savile Row and tell the desk sergeant that we didn't like our new working arrangements? He'd probably have referred us to an industrial tribunal. When he'd stopped laughing.'

Rosie Webster shook her head. 'He wouldn't, you know. It's this very wall of silence that stops us getting at people like Harris . . . or Crombie for that matter. Or the people who'll take their places once we've locked them up.'

Jean Rogers nodded towards the card she had handed Rosie. 'What'll happen to her?'

'Nothing.'

'Then what—'

'It's better you don't know, Jean, but believe me, the mere fact that Harris is her ponce will give us the leverage we want. Trust me.'

Jean Rogers ran her hand through her long black hair and smiled. 'I never thought I'd see the day when I had to ask the police to help me run my business,' she said.

'This card . . .' Rosie Webster glanced at the paste-board in her hand. 'Fay. Is that her real name?'

'No, of course not. Her real name's Dorothy Roberts.'

'Where does she live?'

'St James's somewhere, I think. But you can find out surely? Her phone number's on the card.'

'How come you know her?'

Jean Rogers hesitated for a moment. 'There are one or two punters,' she said, 'who like two girls together, and they like a bit of a show to start with. It turns them on. If ever I got one of those, I'd give Dorothy a call . . . and vice versa.' She sighed. 'If you're going to make it with another woman, you like to know her.' It all sounded very matter-of-fact.

'Was Gina West approached by Harris, d'you know?'

'Yes.' There was no hesitation in Jean Rogers's reply. 'She was one of Billie Crombie's girls and I think that she, like us, finished up in the middle. She told me that two of Harris's people visited her one day and told her that Harris had taken over from Crombie. And that their cut had gone up to seventy per cent. It was exactly the same as the visit I had. They also said that they'd be watching us to make sure that we didn't cheat them.'

'Did she go along with it?'

Jean Rogers shook her head. 'The suggestion is that she refused to work for Harris and got murdered as a result.'

'By Harris . . . or some of his people?'

'It would hardly be anyone else, would it? I got the impression that Harris was set to take over everything that Crombie was running. Strip joints, massage parlours, clubs. The lot.'

'How did you hear that?'

'Oh, come on,' said Jean Rogers. 'You're a police-woman. In my trade you get to hear all sorts of things. I even know of one or two girls on the game who regularly feed titbits to MI5. Didn't you know that we make the best spies?'

'Yes,' said Rosie. 'That's why I'm talking to you.'

Chapter Sixteen

The stooped, loping figure of Spider Walsh fought briefly with the velvet curtain over the door and emerged blinking into the saloon bar.

'Over here,' said Fox, who was languishing in a seat in the far corner.

'Hallo, Mr Fox.' Walsh, who fancied himself as Fox's favourite informant, surveyed the clientele of the pub suspiciously and then eased himself into the seat beside Fox.

'I hope you're not wasting my time, Spider.' Fox placed a five-pound note on the table. 'Get yourself a drink . . . and don't forget to bring me the change.'

Walsh snatched at the money and stood up again. 'Would I do a thing like that, Mr Fox?' He looked reproachfully at the detective.

'Yes,' said Fox. 'Get a bloody move on.'

A few minutes later, Walsh returned and sat down again. He took the head off his glass of Guinness and sighed audibly. 'Cheers, Mr Fox.'

'I haven't come here just to fill you up with stout, Spider. What have you got?'

'It's not much, Mr Fox.'

'Is it ever,' murmured Fox.

'But I've heard a whisper.'

'Good grief,' said Fox. 'You want to be careful.'

'I think it might be worth a bit.' Walsh shot a sideways glance at Fox.

'That depends, Spider. What is it?'

'I've heard that there's this swish club—'

'Where?'

'Down Dagenham, Mr Fox.'

Fox scoffed. 'Don't be ridiculous, Spider. It can't be swish and be in Dagenham. Swish and Dagenham do not go together.'

'Well, anyhow . . .' Walsh pressed on, completely impervious to Fox's sarcasm. 'Seems Billie Crombie had a finger in running it, like. But then Tango Harris give him the big E.' Walsh looked round furtively, as if afraid that the mere mention of Tango Harris's name would get him into serious trouble.

'I have to say,' said Fox, 'that this hot information of yours comes as no surprise.'

'Ah, but there's more, Mr Fox.'

'Your generosity knows no bounds, Spider. What more could there possibly be?'

'There's another finger operating down Dagenham, name of—'

'Tinsel Walters,' said Fox. 'I know. So what?'

'Oh! You know then?'

'There is little that goes on among the criminal fraternity to which I am not privy, Spider, but what do you know of Tinsel Walters and his activities?'

'Well, he reckons that Dagenham's his territory, and that he is going to teach Tango Harris not to go poking his nose in down there.'

'Interesting.'

'Word is that he's going to give this club a sorting out.'

'Is he now. Date, time, and place been whispered in your shell-like by any chance, Spider?'

'Nothing pacific, like, Mr Fox.'

'The word is "specific", Spider. Not that you'd know what it meant anyway.' Fox paused. 'Then again you could well be right.'

'Perce.'

'Yes, guv,' said DS Fletcher.

'Tinsel Walters. Seems to think he's the king of Dagenham. Get out and beat on the ground, Perce. See what comes up, there's a good fellow.'

152

'Right, guv.' Fletcher sighed inwardly. Here we go again, he thought.

Dorothy Roberts, known to her clients as Fay, walked swiftly through the lobby of the hotel, looking neither to the left nor to the right. She wore a black suit with a white blouse and black court shoes. There was a leather bag over one shoulder and she carried an expensive brief-case which undoubtedly contained a credit-card machine. It was five o'clock in the evening and she looked the epitome of the successful young businesswoman. Which, in a sense, she was. The hall porter took the envelope she dropped on his counter and swept it into a drawer, making no other acknowledgement of her arrival. She walked across to the lift and rode to the second floor.

It had been an easy task for Detective Sergeants Buckley and Rosie Webster to follow the call-girl from her flat in St James's. She wasn't expecting to be followed and hadn't noticed them.

The man who opened the door of the second-floor room was about thirty-five years of age. His suit would have cost at least two thousand dollars in New York and he probably paid ten times what the man in the street would pay for a haircut. But money was no object to him. He was in London on business and fully intended to combine that business with a certain amount of pleasure. And right now, that pleasure took the shapely form of Dorothy Roberts. After all, he could afford it. The sweat of his late father's brow had made sure of that.

He ushered the girl towards the settee in his sitting room – he had a suite, of course – and opened a bottle of champagne.

At eight o'clock the American admitted the floor waiter who wheeled in dinner for two. At half-past ten Dorothy Roberts went home.

At twenty minutes to eleven, Roy Buckley and Rosie Webster knocked at the door of the American's suite.

'Good evening, sir. We're police officers.' Buckley displayed his warrant card. 'I wonder if you could spare us a moment of your time.'

'Of course,' said the American, tightening the belt of his robe and casting an appreciative eye over Rosie's figure. 'Do come in, officers. What seems to be the problem?'

Buckley affected a flat and slightly nasal tone, giving the impression that he was very much the stylised policeman. 'It's about the prostitute who just left your apartment, sir,' he began.

'What in hell are you talking about?' The American immediately bristled. 'I resent that. Resent the implication that I would . . . Anyway, that's a slur on the young lady in question. If it's any of your concern, she's a business associate of mine and we were conducting important discussions over dinner. It's more private in here than in the restaurant and—'

'Sir!' Buckley held up a hand, interrupting the American's unconvincing flow of excuses. 'You're a visitor to London, I believe, sir.'

'I'm an American.'

'Well, it's no offence against our laws here, sir, to entertain a young lady in your hotel room . . . even if you pay for it—'

'Now look here, officer—'

'Let me finish, sir,' said Buckley, quite enjoying his role as a dim policeman. 'We are hoping to enlist your help.'

That appeared to mollify the American and he mellowed slightly. 'Oh, I see. How can I help, then?'

'We know these things go on, sir.' Buckley briefly closed one eye. 'But it's the people behind them that cause us the grief and aggravation, as you might say.' He paused. 'I think you'd probably call them the Mafia in America, sir.'

'Fer Chrissakes!' said the American, thoroughly alarmed by this throw-away line. Then he glanced at Rosie. 'Begging your pardon, ma'am.'

'If you could just see your way clear to letting us have a statement, telling us how you contacted this young woman – Fay, I think she's called – and what you paid her—'

'That's enough.' The American strode towards the door. 'I'm sticking to my story that she's a business associate. I don't know anything about her being a hooker, or anything about the goddam Mafia. I'm sorry, but I can't help you. Good night, officers.' The American closed the door and walked across to the telephone. 'Get me the hall porter,' he yelled into the mouthpiece.

The hall porter had just replaced the receiver of his telephone following a rather unpleasant and one-sided conversation with the American as Buckley and Rosie walked through the lobby.

'And that's going to happen to all the toms who work for Tango Harris,' said Buckley quietly to the hall porter as they passed his desk.

'Lovely fellow, the American in two-oh-four,' said Rosie, and winked.

Buckley and Rosie Webster did it six or seven more times, working from the list that Sharon Scrope had provided. And that, combined with Percy Fletcher's message, did it. Suddenly, Tango Harris's string of fillies found they weren't under starter's orders any more.

'Tinsel Walters, guv.'

'Yes,' said Fox. 'What about him?'

'Handled some of the loot from a silver bullion job about eight years ago, hence the name Tinsel. Collected a five-stretch down the Bailey.'

'I remember that job,' said Fox. 'Warehouse at Gatwick, wasn't it?'

'That's the one, guv. Since then, he's been trying to convince everyone that he's going straight.'

'Oh, really?' Fox looked faintly amused. 'Had any success with that fairy tale, has he?'

'Well, he hasn't been nicked again, guv, if that's what you mean. But he's putting himself about in Dagenham and Gants Hill. The usual.'

'The usual what?'

'Two or three massage-parlours-cum-knocking-shops, a betting shop or two, and a bit of leaning on certain

155

local traders who'd rather not get into bother with his little team of heavies.'

'Protection, you mean?'

'In a word, guv, yes.'

'How was it that he tolerated Billie Crombie in his midst then?'

'He didn't really, guv, but he wasn't prepared to do anything about it. But when Billie got his come-uppance, he swore that Tango Harris wasn't going to muscle in. Tango was strictly a West End operator, so Tinsel reckoned. The word is that Dagenham's his.'

'Is that a fact?' said Fox. 'Well, I've got news for him. Any whispers about when this show-down is likely to occur, Perce?'

'Word is that it's one of next Saturday's attractions, guv,' said Fletcher.

Despite Fox's conviction that there couldn't possibly be any swish night-clubs in Dagenham, the one that Spider Walsh had mentioned was none the less above par for the area. The waiters wore bow ties and there was a live band. It looked to be a well-regulated establishment.

The operations commander for the area was a hard-nosed Uniform Branch officer who had spent much of his service at police stations in the East End of London and he greeted Fox's news of a possible punch-up with enthusiasm. 'I've laid on two TSGs, Mr Fox,' he said, 'just to be on the safe side. And I've dug out the local superintendent to take charge. That'll give you nearly fifty officers all up. What about riot gear?'

'Oh, I don't think that'll be necessary.'

'I was only joking,' said the commander with a grin.

'But I think we ought to have a unit from SO19 on stand-by.'

'What?' The commander looked shocked. 'Firearms Branch?'

'These blokes aren't pussy-footing about, guv'nor,' said Fox. 'They kill people, and if they find themselves sur-rounded by your TSGs, they won't hesitate to shoot their way out.' Fox actually thought that to be a bit unlikely,

156

but he didn't much care for the Uniform Branch complacency that applied the same strategy to a raid of this sort as it did to a demonstration of environmentalists in Trafalgar Square. It was better to have more than less. That way the message would get through to both Tinsel Walters and Tango Harris that the police meant business. 'So long as we don't frighten them off.'

'No problem there, Mr Fox. We'll hide them up. All of them. We can give them a shout when we need them.'

' "We", sir?'

The commander grinned. 'I'm not going to miss this,' he said. 'Don't want to get in the way, of course, but—'

'No, that's fine,' said Fox. 'I'm going in with a WDS and we'll just hang around until the fun begins.'

'Smashing!' said the commander. 'Mind if I join you?'

'Be my guest, sir,' said Fox.

'I'm glad you said that. CID are paying for the drinks, are they?'

'Of course,' said Fox. 'See you on Saturday . . . provided you come in plain clothes,' he added, determined to get the last word.

Fox grabbed at the telephone and tapped out a number. 'This is Detective Chief Superintendent Thomas Fox . . . of the Flying Squad,' he said.

'Morning, Mr Fox,' said the head of Press Bureau at New Scotland Yard, pushing his glasses back on to the bridge of his nose.

'I wish to deny Press reports that the Gina West murder enquiry is being run down,' said Fox.

'But there are no Press reports to that effect, Mr Fox.'

'I know that,' said Fox, 'but I want to deny it just the same. Get them to say something like: "Police have denied that the Gina West murder enquiry is being run down. In fact, an early arrest is anticipated." Got that?'

'Yes, Mr Fox,' said the head of Press Bureau, thoroughly mystified.

'Good,' said Fox and put the phone down.

'What d'you bloody mean, they're not working?' Tango

Harris stood aggressively by his swimming pool, legs apart and hands thrust deep into the pockets of his terry robe. He glanced across at Melody as she emerged from the pool. 'Go and put some clothes on, you silly cow,' he said.

'Like I said, Mr Harris, Tommy Fox has put the frighteners on them.' Alfie Penrose looked apologetic.

'How?'

'His Heavy Mob have been following the girls around, waiting till they leave, and then talking to the mugs. And he's put the fear of Christ up the contacts, an' all. Most of them don't want to know any more.'

'They will if they know what's good for them,' growled Harris.

'Apparently he's been telling them you've got Mafia connections, Mr Harris.'

A brief smile flitted across Harris's face. 'I'm beginning to wish I had, Alfie. Things are getting a bit uncomfortable.'

'And there's another thing, Mr Harris,' said Penrose hesitantly.

'What?'

'Tinsel Walters is getting all arsey about the Dagenham set-up.'

'Let him,' said Harris. 'He'll have to be teached.'

'Word is, Mr Harris, that he's going to do the place over . . . just to teach the present owner who's boss.'

'Is that a fact? Well, what have you done about it?'

'Nothing, Mr Harris. That's why I'm here. Well, one of the reasons. See what you thought, like.'

'Well, you just get a little team together, Alfie, and get down there. They're paying for protection, and they're entitled—'

'But they ain't, Mr Harris.'

'What d'you mean, they ain't?'

'Tinsel Walters is trying to collect. The gaffer down there told Lenny to piss off last time he went, and one or two of Tinsel's hoods showed him the door . . . in a manner of speaking. Frankly, I think he's playing both ends against the middle.'

158

'Really?' Harris spat the word out, low and menacing. 'Well, he'll have to be teached as well. Any motorways being built near Dagenham, Alfie?'

Penrose grinned. 'Probably find one, Mr Harris.'

'You do that, Alfie. We could even put a plaque on it. The Tinsel Walters Memorial Motorway Bridge.'

Penrose laughed nervously. 'I like the sound of that. Can I use your dog-and-bone?'

'No,' said Harris. 'That bastard Fox has got the phone tapped as well.'

Chapter Seventeen

Fox had not underestimated the power of either Tango Harris or Tinsel Walters, and if they wheeled out their heavies, the arena of the dance floor – at present filled with gyrating couples – could turn into a battlefield. Consequently, he had selected a table in the corner near the service exit so that he and Rosie were in a position to effect an escape if the necessity arose. The area Operations Commander had reluctantly agreed to station himself on the other side of the room. Reluctantly, because at first he thought that it was a Fox ploy to avoid buying him drinks.

'Who's the blonde girl with the commander?' asked Fox. 'She surely can't be his wife.'

'No, sir. She's a uniformed inspector from Dagenham nick. We were at training school together. She's very good at self-defence.'

Fox chuckled. 'Does the commander know that, I wonder?' he said. He glanced casually round the room. 'So far, I've spotted Alfie Penrose and Lenny Lovell. No doubt there's a few more of Tango's foot-soldiers about.'

'Isn't that Randy Steel, over there near the band?' asked Rosie. 'The black fellow with the frizzy-haired brunette. Used to run with Joey Watkins.'

Fox peered across the room. 'I do believe it is,' he said. 'Didn't know he was out. Wonder who he's running with now?'

'He's a Wanstead villain,' said Rosie. 'Perhaps he's just a spectator.'

Fox scoffed. 'There's no chance of that,' he said.

The battle, when it came, was short and fierce. At about nine o'clock, Rosie suddenly pressed at her left ear. Fox had instructed her to wear the personal radio on the grounds that the earpiece, covered by her hair, was less likely to be spotted by the inquisitive than if Fox had worn it . . . and have everyone shout at him because they thought he was deaf.

'Roy Buckley reports that there's a dodgy-looking Transit drawn up outside, sir,' said Rosie. 'Mr Gilroy's calling up the cavalry.'

'Splendid,' said Fox. 'I was beginning to get bored.'

There was a sudden yell and a crash as a waiter was toppled so violently that he and his trayful of drinks slid across the dance floor. Leaving a trail of broken glasses, he collided forcibly with the tight knot of shuffling dancers and, with an involuntary rugby tackle, brought down a plump young lady. Her partner, unaware of the cause of the accident and believing the waiter to be some sort of foot-fetishist, kicked him in the ribs.

A loud explosion sent dancers and diners shouting and screaming for cover, some diving beneath tables, others running for the exits, as a man in a dark sweater and jeans, and wearing a ski mask, let fly into the ceiling with two rounds from a sawn-off shot-gun, creating a minor blizzard of falling plaster. In his panic, one man ran into the ladies' toilets and got his face slapped.

The white-jacketed barman threw himself under the counter as another hoodlum, dressed like the first, took careful aim at the bar. Both barrels of his sawn-off shot-gun swept away optics, bottles, and glasses, and shattered the mirrors behind into a hailstorm of tiny fragments.

'I'll bet he's a wizard at clay-pigeon shooting,' said Fox mildly. 'Still, they do a lot of it in Essex.' He lit a cigarette and leaned back in his chair.

From the fringe of the tiny dance floor came the swelling sounds of fractured furniture and splintering glass as four more men, all in ski masks, embarked on a deliberate foray of destruction, kicking over tables and chairs, smashing bottles and glasses, and firing shot-guns

161

indiscriminately into the air, now white with falling plaster. The pungent smell of nitro powder from the shotguns mingled with the overpowering odour of alcohol coming mainly from the bar area. That, together with the swirling plaster dust, caused several outbreaks of coughing and spluttering from among those patrons not still shouting and screaming or attempting to escape.

The large mirrored ball in the centre of the ceiling was among the last victims of the attack. Struck by the full force of two twelve-bore cartridges, it detached itself from the ceiling and, disintegrating into a million pieces, spread across the dance floor to join the carpet of broken glass that lay there. Not to be outdone, its severed electrical supply erupted into tiny sparking blue flames.

The band, clearly not descendants of those brave souls who played when the *Titanic* went down, having come to an earlier abrupt and discordant stop, dropped their instruments and lay flat on the floor, encouraged, no doubt, by a sweep of shot that removed the front skin of the base drum, rendered the high-hat totally beyond repair, and created a flurry of shredded sheet music.

'I have to say that I don't disagree with that,' said Fox. 'Quite the worst band I've heard in ages.' He yawned. 'The feet are taking their time,' he added and waved at the commander.

Lenny Lovell made to tackle one of the invaders and was promptly felled with the butt of a shot-gun that smashed his jaw. Randy Steel and Alfie Penrose wisely decided that the opposition was overwhelming and ran for different exits on opposite sides of the room. Penrose was foolhardy enough to make for the door nearest to Fox's table. Fox withdrew his short detective stave from an inside pocket and leaning to one side, struck a devastating blow at Penrose's kneecap as Harris's henchman passed the table. With a scream, Penrose crashed to the floor, clutching his leg. If any other members of Tango Harris's task force were present, they obviously decided that unashamed cowardice should be substituted for valour and abandoned any ideas of participating in the unseemly brawl.

Having driven the clientele literally to the walls, the six members of Tinsel Walters's gang now found themselves isolated at the bandstand end of the large room. It was a tactical error that gave them no opportunity to take hostages.

'Armed police! Drop your weapons.' The sergeant's voice was like a whiplash and the villainous octet suddenly realized that they were faced by a row of very offensive-looking men in navy-blue flame-proof overalls and blue berets which were slowly gathering a sheen of white plaster dust. Each member of the police firearms unit, crouched in a threatening 'triangle' stance, was pointing a menacing Smith and Wesson revolver at Walters's gang in a double-handed grip. There was a clatter as sawn-off shot-guns hit the floor, and hands made desperate attempts to touch what was left of the ceiling.

The seventh member of the gang, unarmed, had been cut off from the rest of his platoon and was outside the ring of armed police. He decided to make a run for it. The blonde inspector, who had been seated at the commander's table, leaped at him. With a speed that created a frightening blur of her movements, she seized him and tossed him through the air so expertly that he landed violently on his back, winding him and jarring his spine so severely that he would probably be plagued by a slipped disc for the rest of his life.

'Nice one,' said Fox. 'Your blonde mate has just captured Tinsel Walters.'

After it was all over, some fourteen prisoners had been detained at Dagenham police station. A harassed custody sergeant, pencil behind his ear and surrounded by piles of paper, tried to make administrative sense of the evening's events.

Fox surveyed the sorrowful collection and turned to Gilroy. 'Well, Jack, not a bad night's trawl. And that's another branch we've lopped off Tango Harris's tree.'

'How so, guv? We only nicked two of his lot. Alfie Penrose and Lenny Lovell.'

163

'Alfie Penrose is his right-hand man, Jack. Anyway, it was three we nicked. Don't forget Randy Steel.'

'Is he one of Tango's soldiers, then?'

'Let me put it this way, Jack. I am prepared to give him the benefit of the doubt. That is to say, I doubt that he was an innocent bystander. Therefore he's one of Tango's men. Unless he can convince me that he's not.'

'Things are progressing nicely, gentlemen.' Fox smiled benevolently at the police officers who faced him in the conference room. In the front row were the three detective superintendents investigating the five murders that had occurred so far, three of which Fox was firmly convinced had been committed by Tango Harris. Or, at the very least, on his behalf.

'Where are we with the Gina West job, Gavin?'

Gavin Brace flipped open a file that was resting on his knees. 'Struggling, sir,' he said with a wry smile.

'Good gracious,' said Fox, and then nodded slowly as though he had fully expected Brace's reply. 'If it's down to Billie Crombie, I suppose that's it.'

'Jagger's obtained the application form from the credit-card people. There's an outside hope that we might get something from that,' said Brace. 'But I shouldn't hold your breath, sir.'

'What about the sample?'

'It's been confirmed that there was semen in Gina West's vagina, guv'nor, but of course we've not been able to take any intimate samples as yet. If we can get those, we can put them up for DNA comparison.'

'Bit late to get one from Billie Crombie's body. But does a DNA test work on a post-mortem sample?'

Brace shrugged. 'I don't know sir, but I've asked the lab to look into it. I suppose the best we can hope for is a clear-up. But it would mean an exhumation.'

'Anything else?'

'No, sir. None of the staff at the hotel can make a positive ID. The receptionist had the best view of Mr Phillips, but her description would fit Tango Harris, Billie

Crombie, and the BBC Symphony Orchestra . . . all of them. The fingerprint on the dressing table was a blow-out, and those on Gina West's briefcase and in her flat at St John's Wood are all hers.'

'Don't know what you've been doing,' muttered Fox. 'Nick?'

Nick Dorman glanced at his notes. 'As good as wrapped up, sir. I'm willing to give Tony Guerrini a run for the murder of Carter.'

'Refresh my memory, Nick,' said Fox, lighting a cigarette and leaning back in his chair.

'Jack Gilroy found a shooter in the slaughter at Greenwich which the ballistics people say was the one used to murder Frankie Carter. There were traces of blood on the underneath of the breech slide, and Guerrini had an injury compatible with having got his thumb in the way of it. I'm willing to put him up on that and let him try and talk his way out.'

'Have you been able to obtain a blood sample from him?' asked Fox.

'Yes, sir. Gave it quite willingly, but then he didn't have the benefit of one of Harris's high-powered lawyers.'

'Has he said anything?'

'Only that if he goes down, he'll take Tango Harris with him, guv.'

'Excellent,' said Fox. 'We'll have to see if we can't help him.' He glanced across at David Blunt. 'And how's the great Catford Stadium outrage getting on, Dave?'

'We drew a blank on the buildings near the stadium, sir. The main one's a school and was locked up at the time. There was no sign of a breaking.'

'That's unusual for Catford,' murmured Fox.

'But we do have a witness . . . of sorts.'

'Oh?'

'There's a railway line on each side of the dog track. But the one on the right as you go in has two footbridges over it from Doggett Road. One at each end of the stand. And it's opposite the stand where Crombie was when he was shot.'

165

'You're not going to tell me he was hit from a passing train, I hope,' said Fox.

Blunt grinned. 'Doubt it,' he said. 'But we have a witness who saw a man run down from one of the footbridges and leap into a car. He said he thought he was carrying a snooker cue. And believe it or not, sir, he got the number of the car. It was nicked at Dulwich and abandoned in Hither Green. Enquiries are continuing.' Blunt grinned again.

'Ye Gods!' said Fox.

'The interesting thing is that the footbridge where chummy was seen is closed off. It doesn't lead anywhere.'

'Not even to a billiard hall?' asked Fox and got a laugh.

'No, sir,' said Blunt, 'but then you don't expect people to play snooker wearing a ski mask.'

'Depends on the climate,' said Fox drily, and got another laugh.

'But the pathologists and the ballistics officer both say that the shot that killed Crombie could well have come from the footbridge.'

Fox nodded slowly. He knew that the evidence that Blunt had collected so far did not get them very much closer to finding the killer. 'These experts didn't tell you who pulled the trigger, I suppose, Dave?'

'No, guv,' said Blunt, 'but I'm working on it.'

'Right,' said Fox, suddenly standing up. 'I think I shall now talk to Alfie Penrose regarding the dastardly murder of Billie Crombie.'

The weaselly figure of Alfie Penrose limped into the interview room shepherded by a large constable.

'Nasty limp you've got there, Alfred,' said Fox.

'I s'pose you think that's funny,' said Penrose, lowering himself painfully into the chair opposite the chief superintendent. 'I've got a complaint.'

'I can see that,' said Fox. 'Still, I'm sure that a successful businessman like you has got private medical insurance.'

'I'm talking about you hitting me on the knee.'

166

'You always did have a vivid imagination, Alfie. I, and three other officers, saw you trip and fall in your haste to escape from that nasty scene last night. As a matter of interest, what were you doing there? Long way from home, weren't you?'

'Entitled to go out and enjoy myself, ain't I?' Penrose glared churlishly at Fox.

'You were there, dear boy, for the sole purpose of repelling boarders. Except that you didn't anticipate that Tinsel Walters's lot would be tooled up. You underestimated them, you see. Tinsel Walters is coming up in the world. Least he was. As a matter of fact, the last time I saw him, he was coming down, very hard, thanks to a charming young policewoman who was trying to teach him the cha-cha-cha. I don't suppose Tango Harris is very pleased with you, Alfie.'

'It weren't nothing to do with me,' said Penrose. 'I was just having a quiet drink with me bird when them hooligans come in busting the place up.'

Fox paused and looked expectant. 'Ah!' he said eventually. 'I thought for one moment you were going to ask where the police were when you needed them. But, of course, you know the answer to that, don't you?'

'I want to know why I've been nicked,' said Penrose.

'Oh dear,' said Fox. 'Didn't the officer tell you? How remiss of him. I shall have to have a word. You have been arrested, Alfred, for the common-law offence of conducting yourself in a noisy, disorderly, and turbulent manner to the annoyance of firm and courageous citizens.'

'What are you going on about?'

'I distinctly saw you rolling about on the floor, shouting and screaming and thereby disturbing the peace.'

'Course I was. You'd just hit me with your truncheon. Anyway, I won't be joining the lifers in Parkhurst for that, will I?' Penrose smirked and lit himself a dog-end which he withdrew from the recesses of his East End suit.

'Not for that, no,' said Fox. 'But . . .'

Penrose sat up. 'What d'you mean by that?'

'I have it in mind to charge you with the murder of Billie Crombie at Catford Stadium, Alfie.'

Penrose's face went white and he gripped the edges of the table. 'That's not down to me,' he gasped.

'Oh yes it is.'

'You ain't got no evidence.'

'Yes I have.' Fox took out his cigarette case and opened it. Carefully selecting a cigarette, he lit it and blew smoke into the air.

'You can't have. I wasn't there.'

'Wayne Parish says you were.'

'That little tosser. He's only been with the firm five—' Penrose suddenly stopped, realizing that he had said too much. 'Anyway, his word's—'

Fox held up his hand. 'Don't presume to give me a lecture about the evidence of one co-conspirator against another, Alfie.'

'Well it's true. My brief told me that the last time—'

'Because,' interrupted Fox, 'Parish will not be charged on the same indictment as you. Therefore, he's not a co-conspirator. Clever that, isn't it?'

'I swear I never had nothing to do with Billie Crombie's topping.' Penrose was starting to sound desperate now. Desperate but unconvincing.

'Well who did then?'

At last Penrose saw Fox's ploy. 'Are we talking a trade-off here?' he asked.

'Trade-off?' Fox contrived to sound appalled. 'Perish the thought. No, Alfie, it's quite simple. I put you on the sheet for Crombie's murder and I put Parish in the box. He tells a sorrowful tale, does our Wayne. How he was press-ganged into working for Tango Harris, made to take part in all sorts of villainy. Dear me, he'll have the jury crying their eyes out. He's very convincing, you know.' It was all untrue, of course. Fox hadn't yet got around to suggesting to Parish that he might benefit from telling police what he knew of Tango Harris's activities.

'You don't know what you're asking, Mr Fox.' At last it came. The whingeing, respectful tone, and the realization that the police held all the cards, and that Penrose's only hope was to try offering them something they wanted . . . in exchange for his liberty.

'Well?'

For a moment or two, Penrose lapsed into deep thought, his chin sunk on his chest. Then he looked up. 'He'll bloody kill me, Mr Fox.'

'Who will?'

'Tango. He's a vicious bastard and if I grass him up, he'll have me.'

'Won't get the chance,' said Fox, 'because the minute I've finished talking to you, I'm going out to Buckhurst Hill to nick him. And this time it'll stick . . . all of it.'

Penrose stared at Fox with baleful, unbelieving eyes. 'What will?'

'Murder, conspiracy to murder, robbery, conspiracy to commit robbery, living on immoral earnings.' Fox paused. 'Well, that'll do for a start,' he added.

'Billie Crombie's murder was down to Randy Steel.' Penrose spoke slowly and distinctly.

Fox scoffed. 'You're joking. I never had Randy Steel down for a marksman.'

'Don't have to be with the weapon he used. Telescopic night-sight an' all.'

'Mmm! Lucky I've got him banged up next door. But tell me, Alfred . . .' Fox leaned across and stubbed out his cigarette. 'He didn't just take Billie Crombie out because he was bored, surely?'

'Course he never. Tango set it up. He reckoned Billie Crombie was overreaching hisself. Had to be taken out. Then he was going to take over Billie's empire.'

'What about Gary and Kenny Crombie . . . and Arlene Fogg?'

For the first time in the interview, Penrose laughed, a grating cackle. 'Those two wankers couldn't run a whelk stall down Southend,' he said. 'And as for Arlene, the old bag, she's well past it. All wind and piss.'

'Doesn't sound too promising,' said Fox. 'All I've got so far is your word that Randy Steel was the hit man.'

169

For a long time, Penrose remained silent, staring down at the table and picking at the wooden surface with a grubby fingernail. Then he looked up. 'If I give you the SP, Mr Fox, will I get some consideration?'

'You know better than to ask that, Alfie,' said Fox, 'but if it's worth it, I'll see what can be done. But it'd better be good.'

'What if I turned Queen's Evidence?'

'I have to warn you about that, Alfie,' said Fox. 'If you make admissions to the court and offer to give evidence against your accomplices and the court doesn't believe you, you'll go down anyway.'

'Don't you worry about that, Mr Fox. They'll believe me. I've got chapter and verse. I know it was Randy Steel, because I drove the motor. I parked up in Doggett Road alongside Catford Stadium and kept the engine running. Randy nipped up the steps of the footbridge – the one that's shut off – done the job and away.'

'Whose car was it?'

'Nicked,' said Penrose. 'And we dumped it down Hither Green.'

'What's Steel's alibi?'

'Dunno.' Penrose shrugged. 'You'll have to ask him that.'

'And what happened to the rifle?' asked Fox.

'We give it a couple of days, then we went down Greenwich and bunged it in Billie Crombie's slaughter. Well, Tango reckoned it was his by then anyway.'

'I'll have to put this up to the Crown Prosecution Service, Alfie,' said Fox. 'If you're prepared to take the chance.'

'That's not all, Mr Fox.'

'Oh?'

'Kevin Rix's murder . . .'

'What about it?'

'That was down to Randy Steel an' all. I was there, along with Tango Harris. An' it was Tango what give the order.'

170

'Well, well,' said Fox. 'Any more?'

Penrose looked at Fox with a lopsided grin on his face. 'Yeah,' he said. 'I can tell you something about the topping of Gina West, an' all.'

Chapter Eighteen

'They tell me that Billie Crombie's two lads are after your blood, Randy,' said Fox.

'I'm worried sick.' The tall, lithe figure of Randy Steel was sprawled on the bunk in his cell.

'But there's worse. Arlene Fogg's very upset . . . to the point that she might do something quite nasty. I should take to wearing a cricket box if I were you, just in case you bump into her.' As all three were in custody, Fox knew that there was little chance of such a confrontation, but he couldn't resist piling on the agony.

'I don't know nothing about Billie Crombie. So if you're thinking of fitting me up with that job, I should just have another think.' Steel's long, bony finger traced the spaces between the brickwork on the wall near his head.

'Well if that's the case, you won't mind telling me where you were on the evening of Billie Crombie's murder, will you?'

'I was down my local boozer, having a drink with the lads.' Steel stared up at the ceiling and yawned, a contemptuous look on his face.

'That's all right then.'

It was only when he heard the cell door slam shut that Steel realized Fox had gone.

'One Randolph Steel is in custody at Dagenham police station,' said Fox.

'Is that a fact?' The licensee of the pub placed the

Scotch that Fox had ordered on the bar and turned to the till.

'He says that he spent the whole of the evening of Friday the nineteenth of October in here.'

'If that's what he said, then that's right.' The licensee banged Fox's change down on the bar.

'And that he left at closing time.'

'That's right.'

'And you can give me exact details of times? What time he arrived and what time he left? And who else was here?'

'Yes, I can. He came in here at just after six.' The licensee gave the middle distance a reflective stare. 'He played the one-armed bandit for about a quarter of an hour. Pulled a jackpot, too. Then he had a few games of bar-billiards.'

'Bring his own cue, did he?' Fox asked mischievously.

'Are you joking?' asked the licensee. 'It's not the world championships, you know. Not in here.'

'And he was here until closing time, was he?'

'One of the last to leave, but he was out by twenty past. We're very careful to observe the law here, you know.'

'Are you absolutely certain that it was Friday the nineteenth?'

'Absolutely.'

'But he wasn't in here on Saturday. Is that right?'

The licensee pondered that question for only a moment. 'If he said he wasn't, then he wasn't.'

'Yes, but are you certain that he wasn't in here on the Saturday?'

'I'm bloody positive, mister. What d'you want me to do, swear an affidavit?'

'Not yet,' said Fox, 'but in the mean time, I take it you're willing to make a statement to that effect?'

'Yes.'

'Good,' said Fox.

'How are we going to break that alibi, sir?' asked Rosie Webster in the car on the way back to the Yard.

173

'Don't have to,' said Fox. 'Billie Crombie was murdered on the Saturday, not the Friday. But our friendly neighbourhood licensee back there was so busy remembering what he was supposed to say that he didn't notice I'd got the dates wrong. Very careless of me, really.'

'That's not playing the game, sir,' said Rosie with a grin.

'Neither's killing people,' said Fox. 'Even people like Billie Crombie.'

The time had come. Tommy Fox, accompanied by Three and Four Teams led by Detective Inspectors Gilroy and Evans respectively, drove out to Buckhurst Hill.

Back at Scotland Yard there were piles of statements cataloguing Tango Harris's criminal activities in full. Teams of Flying Squad officers had spent hours patiently interrogating prisoners and chronicling Harris's wrongdoings over the past five years. There were details of his nefarious business enterprises, the crimes he had committed, or had arranged to have committed, and lists of establishments and prostitutes who paid large sums of money for protection they rarely, if ever, received. There were horrifying details of the brutal treatment he had meted out to those who didn't want to co-operate: beatings, electric-shock treatment, savage torture, and gangland killings that were reminiscent of the 1960s.

Harris's former associates who, one by one, had been arrested by Fox and his men, were suddenly anxious to have Harris put away . . . ideally for a very long time.

It was not the same security guard who had been on duty at the time of their last visit, but Fox persuaded him that unless he wished to be the first of the day's prisoners, he would admit the police without advising Tango Harris beforehand. The security guard, quick to grasp the basic principles of self-preservation, swung the gates wide.

Having deployed his officers so that the large house was surrounded, Fox made his way to the swimming pool, convinced that Harris spent most of his time there. He pushed open the sliding doors just as Melody emerged

174

from the pool. She put her hand to her mouth and emitted a tiny scream. Obviously embarrassed by the seemingly constant flow of unannounced visitors over the preceding weeks, she had covered her usual nakedness with a black and yellow striped one-piece swimsuit.

'Good gracious!' said Fox. 'You look like a Colorado beetle. Where's Tango?'

'Gone.' The girl walked across to one of the sun-loungers and picked up a towel.

'Gone where?'

'I don't know.'

'Well he must have said something.'

'He just said he was going away on business.'

'When did this happen?'

'The day before yesterday.'

'Did he say when he would be coming back?' Fox was annoyed with himself. He had lifted the surveillance that he had put in place merely to annoy Harris, but even if he hadn't, he had to admit that it would have been easy for Harris to escape from his mansion at Buckhurst Hill by any one of a number of ruses.

'No. I think he's gone to London.'

'Whereabouts in London?'

The girl shrugged and clasped the towel round herself. 'I really don't know. He never lets on. But he said he'd be back soon.' She didn't sound too hopeful about that.

Evans appeared in the doorway behind Fox. 'Searched the house, sir.'

'And?'

'Just the butler, sir. Leastways, that's what he calls himself.' Evans looked round the pool. 'Where's Tango Harris, sir?'

'Legged it,' said Fox shortly.

Evans nodded towards the girl. 'But Melody lingers on, eh, sir?'

Fox gave his DI a withering glance. 'Don't ever think of becoming a stand-up comic, Denzil,' he said. 'You'd fall flat on your face. You'd better fetch this so-called butler down here.'

175

'I don't think he'll be much help, guv,' said Evans with a smirk and retraced his steps to the house.

'D'you mean to say that he didn't leave a telephone number or an address in case some business cropped up?' Fox took a pace or two nearer Harris's girl-friend.

Melody leaned her head to one side as she towelled her wet hair. 'No, nothing,' she said.

'Has he ever gone away like this before?'

The girl appeared to give that some thought. 'Not while I've been living here, no.'

'And how long's that?'

'About six months.'

'Very helpful,' said Fox and turned as Harris's butler entered the pool house. He was dressed in a conventional black suit and stood with his feet together and his shoulders slightly bowed while clasping his hands nervously. 'Good afternoon, sir. I'm Trevor, the butler, sir. I understand you were seeking Mr Harris, sir.'

'Where is he?'

'I regret to say, sir, that the master left no details of his movements, beyond assuring me that he would return shortly.' The butler dropped his voice to a whisper and with a limp-wristed movement pointed a forefinger in the direction of Harris's bed-mate. 'Have you enquired of Miss Melody, sir?'

'Yes I have enquired of Miss Melody, dear boy, and she appears to know as much as you do. Did Harris take his car with him?'

The butler winced slightly at the omission of a prefix to his employer's name. 'One of them, sir, yes.'

'One of them! How many's he got then?'

'Just the three now, sir. He sold the Bentley quite recently.'

'Which one did he take?'

'I believe it was the Porsche, sir.'

'Thank you, Trevor,' said Fox. 'You're very kind.'

The butler bowed slightly. 'Will that be all, sir?' he asked.

176

'For the moment, Trevor. Thank you so much.'

'Thank you, sir.' The butler turned and made his way back to the house.

'Camp as a row of pink tents,' muttered Fox. He turned to Evans. 'Have you got the number of Harris's Porsche, Denzil?'

Evans flipped open his pocket-book. 'Yes, sir.'

'Circulate it,' said Fox.

'Harris's car has been found in the long-term car park at Gatwick Airport, sir,' said Gilroy.

'That was quick,' said Fox.

'Bit of luck really, sir. There was a bomb scare and the local Old Bill checked all the registrations in that section of the car park. And up came Harris's Porsche.'

'So where's the bugger gone?' asked Fox.

Gilroy shrugged. 'No idea at this stage, sir, but he made a call to Melody last night.'

'Where from?'

'We couldn't tell, sir, but we've got British Telecom laying on a trace in case he rings again. If his car was at Gatwick, though, it's an odds-on chance he's gone abroad.'

'That's a skilful bit of detective work, Jack,' said Fox acidly. 'Get hold of Ron Crozier for me, will you. On the double.'

Detective Sergeant Ron Crozier had two girls – one still at university – and a wife who did a part-time job in the travel business. He had started out his adult life as an actor, but after three years resting more than he was working, he decided to become a policeman . . . just until something better turned up. After two years on the beat at Marylebone Lane police station, and twenty-two years in the CID, nothing had. The one mistake he had made was to tell Fox, in a careless moment, of his previous occupation. From then on, when any job cropped up that required what Fox perceived as acting skills, the name of DS Crozier sprang automatically to his mind.

'Ron, dear boy, how d'you fancy being an estate agent?'

Crozier remained impassive in front of Fox's desk. 'Never really thought about it, sir. I've still got another six years to do for pension.'

Fox raised an eyebrow. 'What a droll fellow you are, Ron,' he said. 'Sit down and listen. I've got a little job for you.'

Crozier took a seat and sighed inwardly. He knew all about Fox's 'little jobs'.

Wearing a dark suit and carrying a briefcase, Crozier arrived at the gates of Tango Harris's impressive dwelling at Buckhurst Hill. He presented the security guard with a business card, hastily but professionally produced by the Yard's printers, on which was an address of a non-existent estate agent and the telephone number of a line which was kept permanently linked to a Metropolitan Police establishment as cover. Just in case anyone felt like checking credentials.

The security guard returned from his cabin and handed the card back to Crozier. 'You're to go up to the house, Mr Collins,' he said and opened the gate.

Crozier was admitted by Trevor, the butler, and conducted into a sitting room. Melody, doing her lady-of-the-house bit, rose gracefully from a chair. 'What's all this about, Mr Collins?' she asked.

'I've come to take details of the house, madam,' said Crozier in his best estate-agent voice. 'And to give a valuation, of course.'

'But what for?' Melody appeared genuinely mystified by Crozier's arrival.

'Ah!' said Crozier thoughtfully. 'Perhaps Mr Harris didn't tell you. He's placing the house on the market.'

'He's what?' Melody was unable to keep the rage out of her voice.

'If it's not convenient, madam, I could come back another day.'

'I think you'd better,' said Melody. 'When Mr Harris is here.'

'Oh dear!' Crozier adjusted the horn-rimmed glasses with the plain lenses that he was wearing and looked sympathetic. 'I was given to understand that Mr Harris would not be returning, madam. I believe that mention was made of auctioning the contents. My partner is dealing with that side of things, of course.'

'Well I'm telling you, here and now, that nothing's happening until I've spoken to Mr Harris.' Melody marched across to the drinks table and poured herself a large vodka to which she added a mere hint of tonic water. 'And when I speak to him, I shall give him a piece of my mind.'

Crozier smiled inwardly. He could hardly wait to read the transcript of the next conversation between the girl and Tango Harris. 'Of course, madam,' he said. 'I'll give you a ring in a couple of days' time, if you wish.'

'Don't bother,' said Melody. 'The deal's off.' She took a gulp of vodka and tonic and banged the glass down so violently that liquid spilt over on to the polished surface of the table.

'How did it go, Ron?'

'I reckon she's about to do her Congreve bit, guv'nor,' said Crozier.

'What the devil's that supposed to mean?' asked Fox.

' "Nor Hell a fury, like a woman scorn'd" . . . sir.'

'Bloody actors,' said Fox. 'Get out.'

'She telephoned Tango Harris last night, sir,' said DI Henry Findlater who, among his other duties, had been made responsible for overseeing the intercept on Harris's Buckhurst Hill telephone.

'So the little cow knew all along where he was.'

'So it would seem, sir.' Findlater glanced down at the sheaf of papers in his hand. 'The number goes out to a hotel in New York.'

'New York!'

'Yes, sir. That's in America, sir.'

'I know where bloody New York is, Henry. What's been done about it?'

179

'Nothing as yet, sir. I thought you'd want to speak to Joe Daly yourself.'

'Too right,' said Fox angrily. Joe Daly, the legal attaché at the American Embassy in Grosvenor Square, was in reality the senior resident FBI agent in London. 'What did she have to say to the bold Tango?'

'Well, after he'd torn into her for calling him at that number, she shredded him, sir. Led off alarming about him putting the house on the market without telling her.'

'And what was his reaction to that?' asked Fox.

'He denied it, sir, and that made it worse because she swore that he was deliberately deceiving her. In short, she didn't believe him.'

'Anything else?'

'Overall it was a pretty acrimonious conversation, sir. And it wasn't helped by the fact that Harris asked who this estate agent was.'

'What did she say to that?'

Findlater permitted himself a smile. 'She said that she didn't know, sir. Told Tango that she had forgotten to ask for his card.'

'Dozy tart,' said Fox. 'Bet that pleased him.'

'On the contrary, sir,' said Findlater. 'He seemed quite upset about it.'

Chapter Nineteen

Denzil Evans had been dispatched, hot-foot, to Criminal Intelligence Branch in an effort to discover if there were any reasons why Tango Harris should have gone to New York in particular. Fox was more than familiar with the ways of the criminal fraternity, in which Harris saw himself as a leading light, and was certain that he would not just have stuck a pin in an atlas. He must have a contact.

Evans walked through the door reading a file. 'Ten years ago, sir,' he said.

'Oh, splendid,' said Fox and paused. 'What the hell are you talking about, Denzil?'

'A bloke called Pearson, guv'nor. Charlie "The Rat" Pearson.'

Fox sighed. 'Sit down and begin at the beginning, dear boy, will you.'

'About ten years ago, guv, there was an American called Charlie Pearson over here from New York. Attempting to muscle in on the drugs trade. Seems he was in touch with Tango Harris . . . among others. Well Tango had no interest in the drugs game at that time and tried to point Pearson in the right direction. Didn't see him as a threat, you see.' He glanced up. 'There's just a brief note on Harris's file about it, but it all came to nothing. Drugs Squad got word from the FBI and chased Pearson out. End of story.'

'How interesting,' said Fox and stood up. For some seconds he stared out of the window at the Victoria Street traffic. Then he turned. 'In that case, Denzil,' he continued, 'I reckon the Americans owe us one. Where did this Pearson come from?'

'New York, sir.'

'Yes, Denzil, you said that, but New York's a big place.'

Evans hurriedly consulted the file. 'Manhattan, sir,' he said at length.

'Excellent.' Fox sat down again. 'Find out which police station – or whatever they call them – takes this Manhattan and I'll give them a ring.'

'How do I do that, sir?' Evans closed the file, a plaintive look on his face.

'No idea,' said Fox cheerfully. 'But you're a detective. So detect.'

'I had the New York office check it out for you, Tommy.' Joe Daly turned from the side table with two cups of coffee and set one down in front of Fox.

'Any joy?' Although Fox had got some information from Harris's criminal intelligence file, he saw no harm in trying to elicit a little more from the archives of the FBI.

'They confirm it's a hotel in Manhattan and he's there. Must be costing him a bomb, I reckon.'

'Does it look as though he's stopping?'

Daly shrugged. 'Who's to tell. A guy can say he's going to stay in a hotel for a month and leave the next day . . . but he's booked in for two weeks, according to the special agent who did the enquiry.'

'Did your man see Harris . . . talk to him?'

'Nope. I asked the agent just to make a few enquiries and then leave it alone. I reckon that if we'd interviewed him, he'd have taken off straightaway.'

'And if he leaves, we've lost him.' Fox was furious that Harris had managed to slip through his fingers. He had thought that leaving him until last would make the gang leader think that he was untouchable. But obviously something – or someone – had alerted him to the fact that Fox was closing in. And ironically, the very phone call that had told the police where Harris was could be the cause of his moving on.

182

'I guess so. But we could arrest him now if you're prepared to start extradition proceedings.'

Fox scoffed. 'I want that bastard at the Old Bailey next month, not in five years' time, Joe. And with your legal system, he could spin it out for ever. Appeal after appeal after appeal. You never stop over there.'

Daly laughed. 'I don't see how you're going to get him back any other way.' And after a pause, added, 'We could start deportation proceedings. If what you say is true, he's an undesirable alien.'

'He's that all right,' said Fox. 'But from what I hear, deportation can take as long as extradition. Anyway, how long can he stay if you don't institute any proceedings? In the States, I mean.'

'Officially, ninety days. The New York office checked with Immigration and they confirmed that he came in as a tourist. That means he had to produce a return ticket, but . . .' Daly shrugged again. 'So what's a return ticket? With his record, he'd never have gotten a visa, but as a ninety-day tourist he didn't need one. Unfortunately, Tommy, the reality of the thing is that once he's there he can lose himself just by moving about.'

'Yeah,' said Fox. 'That's what I'm afraid of. Any information about associates . . . contacts?'

Daly shook his head. 'Nothing, Tommy. I'm sorry.'

For moment or two Fox remained silent, looking round Daly's office. He was determined not to let on to the American what he knew about Charlie 'The Rat' Pearson. 'I think I'll go and get the bastard,' he said at last.

'Now hold on, Tommy. I know how you feel about this scum-bucket, but you can't just go to New York and kidnap him.'

'Can you put me in touch with a hard-nosed detective at the local police station, Joe?' he asked, by no means certain that Denzil Evans would find a name to talk to.

'If you mean the precinct house that takes in the hotel,' said Daly with a smile, 'then they're all hard-nosed. Wouldn't survive else. And sure, I can put you in touch. I'll make a phone call and let you know.'

'Splendid chaps, you Americans,' said Fox. 'But first, I have to talk to a certain young lady from Buckhurst Hill.'

Fox decided not to waste time going to Buckhurst Hill himself and sent Gilroy and Rosie Webster to bring Melody and Trevor the butler to Rochester Row police station.

Melody was not happy. And some of Harris's aggressive influence had obviously rubbed off. 'I want to know why I've been brought here,' she began truculently. 'And secondly, I want Mr Harris's solicitor sent for . . . immediately.'

'You know that Tango's not coming back, I suppose,' said Rosie, ignoring Melody's tantrum.

'Of course he is.'

'Why did you lie to the police when you said that you didn't know where he was, Melody?'

'I didn't know and I don't know now.'

'He's in a hotel in New York, which you well know, because you telephoned him there the night before last and spoke to him. So how come you say you don't know where he is?'

Melody's eyes opened wide. 'How did you know that?' she asked.

Rosie ignored the question. If the girl was too dim to work it out for herself, Rosie wasn't going to help her. 'He's not coming back, you know.'

'I know that.'

'And you're quite happy to wave goodbye to him and this rich life you've been living, are you?'

'He's going to send for me. We're going to live in Florida.'

Rosie laughed. 'Oh, you poor innocent child,' she said. 'Tango's there on a ninety-day visit and there's no way he'd get a residency permit . . . not now we've given them details of his record. The New York police have been keeping him under observation for us. And he's already shacked up with some gorgeous American bimbo—' The last part wasn't true, of course, but Rosie didn't see why she shouldn't discomfit Melody a little bit more.

'I don't believe it.'

Rosie smiled sympathetically. 'He won't be sending for you, my love. The moment my guv'nor asks them, the New York police will lock him up pending extradition proceedings.'

'But I—' Suddenly the girl began to realize that her artificial life with Tango Harris was not as idyllic as she had at first thought. And that, apart from anything else, it had come to an abrupt end.

Rosie lit a cigarette. 'Face up to it, Melody, you've been used. And you're not the first. Tango Harris picked you up because he fancied your body and now he's discarded you – like he did Penny Sinclair – because you've become an encumbrance to him and his business. And he's found someone he likes better. You're history, my love. The next time you see him will be when you're in the dock at the Old Bailey . . . playing Ethel Le Neve to his Doctor Crippin.'

Melody's make-up failed to disguise that she had gone ashen white. 'What d'you mean? I haven't done anything.' Panic-stricken, her fingers started to intertwine nervously as the sheer enormity of her predicament set in. Until now, she had thought that being a gangster's moll was all romantic make-believe, like it was on the videos she spent much of her time watching, but slowly the fact that the police were not playing games began to sink in.

'On your own admission, you've been living with Tango Harris for the last six months, during which time he's been up to all sorts of villainy. He has murdered people, tortured them – women as well as men – and set fire to their property when he couldn't get his own way. You might just be next. And, my girl, there's no way you're going to walk away from that. You must have been involved, must have helped, aided and abetted.'

'I didn't. I didn't.' The full implications of living with

185

a villain like Tango Harris suddenly hit Melody. 'I didn't know what he was doing. I knew nothing about his business. I was just having a good time.'

'How old are you, Melody?'

'Twenty-three. Why?'

'Be a shame to spend the best years of your life in Holloway, wouldn't it?'

The girl burst into tears. 'I don't know anything,' she sobbed. 'Really I don't.'

'That's a pity,' said Rosie. 'Because it's just possible that if you helped us, you could be helping yourself.'

'I'll tell you anything,' said Melody, tears still coursing down her cheeks. 'Anything at all. What d'you want to know?'

'For a start,' said Rosie, 'you can tell me if you were out with Tango in the West End on the twelfth of October last. Harris claims that you, he, and four others, namely Terry Quincey and Des Nelson and their two girlfriends Tracey Ogden and Cindy Lewis, went out together that night.'

Melody stared at Rosie, wide-eyed. 'I've never even heard of them,' she said. 'And Tango never took me up the West End. Never.'

'You're in a bit of tricky situation, Trevor,' began Gilroy.

Harris's butler sat with his legs crossed and his hands folded neatly in his lap. 'I don't see why, sir,' he said.

'Well, Trevor, the fact of the matter is that your Mr Harris is probably the biggest villain at present outside one of Her Majesty's prisons, and right now I'm considering what part you played in all this.'

Trevor seemed unconcerned by Gilroy's statement. 'I think you must be mistaken, sir,' he said mildly, 'if you don't mind me saying so.'

Gilroy surveyed the man opposite him and wondered. Trevor was one of the most reserved and self-confident prisoners he had ever interviewed. Brought somewhat unceremoniously from Buckhurst Hill that morning, he had made no protest at all. He had asked Gilroy if he could lock up the house and set the burglar alarm, and then allowed himself to be escorted to the police car, all the time giving the impression that he was showing out an honoured guest, rather than being arrested. 'How many times did Randy Steel come to the house, Trevor?'

Trevor folded his arms and stared briefly at the ceiling. Then he looked back at Gilroy. 'Would that be the coloured gentleman, sir?' he asked.

'That's the fellow,' said Gilroy.

'Ah yes, I remember him. Mr Steel came to the house a couple of times, as a matter of fact.'

'Can you remember dates, by any chance?'

'Not from memory, sir, I'm afraid. If I could consult my household diary, then I would be able to tell you.'

'What's your household diary got to do with it?'

'I always recorded visitors in my diary, sir.'

'Why?'

Trevor looked slightly guilty. 'It's a question of wines and spirits, sir. I'm afraid that Mr Harris was a stickler for keeping check on the stocks and if there was a sudden rise in consumption, he would want to know why.' The butler paused. 'I'm sorry to have to say, sir, that Mr Harris was not above suggesting that the staff may have been helping themselves. They never did, of course,' he added hurriedly. 'I myself am a teetotaller.'

'Yes, but why the diary?'

'It was so that if Mr Harris raised the question, I could tell him that so-and-so was here that night and that several bottles of Scotch, or whatever, were consumed, sir.'

'Good God!' said Gilroy, surprised that a villain like Harris, who would help himself to anyone else's property without a qualm, would as readily accuse his butler of stealing. 'Did Harris know that you kept this diary?'

'Oh no, sir. A well-trained butler never reveals the secrets of his profession.'

'Quite,' said Gilroy with a chuckle. 'And I can imagine that your Mr Harris wouldn't have been too pleased to know of its existence. However, what I am going to do now, Trevor, is to send you back to Buckhurst Hill with

187

one of my officers to collect this diary of yours and bring it back here.'

'I don't know about that, sir.' Trevor looked doubtful. 'It is confidential, you see. What I mean is that Mr Harris would be most upset if he knew about it, particularly if he knew it had been shown to a third party.'

'Most commendable,' said Gilroy, trying not to laugh. 'But perhaps I should explain the machinery of the law to you. Either you collect it voluntarily, or I get a warrant from the Bow Street magistrate and go to Buckhurst Hill and seize it . . . along with anything else I can find.' Gilroy felt that it was unnecessary to tell Harris's butler that he was going to do that anyway, but Fox had insisted that the case against Randy Steel be sorted out first.

'Oh, well, sir, if you put it like that . . .' Trevor shrugged. 'I'm sure Mr Harris will understand my wishing to help the police. I think he would have wanted to do so himself if he had been here.'

'Yes,' said Gilroy, 'I'm sure he would.'

'Trevor turned out to be a bit of a gold mine, guv'nor.'

'You could have fooled me, Jack,' said Fox.

'The diary he kept shows that Randy Steel called at Buckhurst Hill on the evening of the nineteenth of October—'

'That reckons,' said Fox. 'That was the night he was supposed to have been in his favourite boozer.'

'Yes,' said Gilroy. 'Funny that. But the butler swears that Steel turned up at Buckhurst Hill, saw Harris, and left a while later carrying a rifle which he put in the boot of his car.'

'What the butler saw,' murmured Fox. 'Did he describe the weapon?'

'Only to say that it appeared to have a telescopic sight, sir. He did volunteer the information that Steel told him that he'd borrowed it to go rabbit shooting with.'

'Hope he knows more about Chablis than he does shooters,' said Fox. 'Shouldn't think there's much rabbit shooting in Wanstead,' he added. 'At least, not with telescopic night-sights.'

'Perhaps he was after the hare at Catford Stadium, guv,' said Gilroy, 'missed it and hit Crombie instead. Incidentally, there was one other thing of interest.'

'What?'

'An entry in Trevor's diary for the day of Gina West's murder.'

'What about it?'

'He had it off, sir.'

'Would you care to rephrase that, Jack,' said Fox and then shook his head slowly. 'No, that's too much. You're surely not trying to tell me the butler did it.'

'Never know your luck, guv,' said Gilroy with a slight grin.

'True,' said Fox thoughtfully. 'Get a photograph of the inimitable Trevor and ask Mr Brace to show it to the hotel staff. And to that solicitor fellow at Richmond . . . the one who drew up the lease for the flat down there that the mysterious Mr Phillips rented.'

'Right, sir,' said Gilroy. 'What about Melody? Any good?'

'Nothing of any value, Jack.' Fox tossed Melody's statement across the desk towards Gilroy and yawned. 'All she does is to list comings and goings, none of which comes as any surprise to us. Even the days when she says he was away on business – and we know what that means – are no great help because she says she doesn't know where he went. Obviously he wasn't a man to bring his work home.' Fox grinned. 'Oh, well, there's only one thing for it. I shall have to go and fetch the bastard myself.'

Detective Sergeant Jagger knocked on Fox's door and peered in hesitantly. 'Excuse me, sir.'

'Yes.'

'DS Jagger from West End Central, sir.'

'Well don't hover, dear boy. Come in.'

'Mr Brace asked me to come and see you, sir. *Re* the Gina West murder.'

'What news?' Fox looked expectant.

'I did a bit off my own bat, sir, and went back to the

chief security officer at the credit-card company. A Mr Sharp, sir.'

'Ron Sharp? Used to be a detective superintendent?'

'That's him, sir.'

'Well?'

'It was an outside chance, sir, but I got hold of the form that our mysterious Mr Phillips completed when he applied for the credit card.'

'Hold on, skip.' Fox held up a hand. 'I am sitting at the top of a very complex enquiry here. Just remind me. And you'd better sit down.'

'Thank you, sir.' Jagger perched himself on the edge of one of Fox's chairs. 'When the body of Gina West was found, sir, we also found a credit-card slip in her brief-case. It went out to a bloke called John Phillips, but enquiries seemed to trace it back to Tango Harris . . .'

'Yes?' Fox's eyes narrowed.

'But we thought he'd been set up by Billie Crombie.'

'Don't we still?'

'I don't think we do, sir. Not any more. I got Finger-print Branch to run a test on the application form.' Jagger laid the brief report on Fox's desk. 'They found a mark which gave them about seven points, sir. The only trouble is that seven points aren't enough.'

Fox rubbed his hands together. 'Might not be enough for you, skip,' he said, 'but it's more than enough for me.'

'But there's more, sir.' Jagger handed another report over. 'Jason Morley, the present occupant of the flat that John Phillip's credit card was sent to, received a letter some days after he moved in. It was addressed to Billie Crombie.'

'Aha!' said Fox.

'Morley didn't open it,' continued Jagger, 'but we did. It contained several blank sheets of paper on which were found fingerprints which have not only been identified, but which will stand up in court.' Jagger leaned forward and pointed to a name in the report. 'Reckon that's your man, sir,' he said.

Fox glanced briefly at the name. Then he looked up. 'Ever fancied a transfer to the Flying Squad, young man?' he asked.

'The butler didn't do it, guv,' said Gilroy.
    'Oh?'
    'No, sir. He spent the night dancing at a gay club in Chelsea, apparently.'
    'What you might call a cast-iron alibi, Jack.'

'So you want to authorize a trip to New York for you and Jack Gilroy, Tommy, is that it?' Dick Campbell, the Deputy Assistant Commissioner Specialist Operations, sat back in his chair with an amused expression on his face.
    'Yes, sir,' said Fox.
    'But what d'you hope to achieve? We can start extradition proceedings from here and the Americans will do the rest for us.'
    'Look, guv'nor,' said Fox, trying to hide his impatience, 'I want to put Harris down for every bloody crime I can conjure out of the evidence we've got. But if some smart-arse American attorney starts interfering, he'll spend years whittling it down and down and down, so that we'll have nothing left. And you know as well as I do that we can only proceed on the counts for which he's been extradited. If we're not careful, Tango Harris will walk out of the Old Bailey with a pound out of the poor box.'
    'Yes, I know all that, Tommy,' said Campbell, 'but what d'you propose to do when you get there?'
    'Have a fatherly chat with him and see if I can't persuade him to come home with me. I'll tell him we're all worried about him.'
    'Well, if anyone can do it, you can, Tommy. But don't spend too much of the Commissioner's money, will you. We have things called budgets these days.' Campbell paused. 'What the hell made him go to New York, of all places? It would have been easier for him to go down to Dover and across on the ferry.'

191

'He probably can't speak anything but what passes for English over there,' said Fox, a sour expression on his face. 'But apart from that, guv'nor, it seems he might have a friend in New York.'

Campbell shrugged. 'Just one thing, Tommy.'

'What, sir?'

'Don't cause a diplomatic incident, eh?'

'Would I do such a thing, guv?'

'And I suppose you'll be going to Disneyland while you're there.'

Fox paused with his hand on the doorknob. 'Be pretty flat after this place, sir,' he said, and waved a hand as if to encompass the whole of New Scotland Yard.

Chapter Twenty

But Fox didn't go to New York. Just as he was examining the airline tickets which the Squad office had obtained for his flight to the States, he received a telephone call from Joe Daly at the American Embassy.

'Tommy, the guy you want is a Lieutenant Joe Kobreski. He's in charge of detectives at the precinct that covers Madison Avenue. Sol Whiteman, the agent in charge of the New York office, was talking with him. He's going to see what he can find out and call back. Seems that Harris has already attracted the attention of the NYPD.'

'Doesn't surprise me.' Fox was beginning to see his few days in the States slip away. 'What's he been up to?'

'According to Whiteman's information, Harris has been trying to get involved with the local mob.'

'The Mafia?'

Daly scoffed. 'They'd like to think they are, but they aren't. Seems he's been making overtures to some of the local gangs. Trying to get a piece of the action.'

'What sort of action, Joe?'

'Prostitution, numbers, drugs. The usual.'

'He's certainly well qualified,' said Fox. 'So what are the NYPD doing about it?'

'Apart from playing it close to the chest, you mean?' Daly's deep-throated chuckle rattled down the phone.

'Well?'

'They're about to hit the whole set-up. With any luck your Mr Harris will get collared with the rest. If all goes well, he'll finish up in the pen for a long time.'

'What?' Fox was outraged.

193

'Doesn't that suit you, Tommy?' Daly chuckled again. 'I thought that's what you wanted.'

'He's mine,' said Fox, 'and I want him locked up in Parkhurst, not in some sterile American prison where he can make phone calls and give interviews to the Press.'

'Sorry, Tommy, but it's out of my hands. Unless . . .'

'Unless what?' Fox sounded desperate and hopeful at the same time.

'From what Sol Whiteman tells me Kobreski is a pretty resourceful cop. He might just be persuaded to talk Harris into coming home. He's only small fry, after all.'

'He might be small fry to you, Joe,' said Fox, 'but he's a bloody great shark to me. By the time you lot let him out, I'll have retired. And that's too long for me to wait.'

The NYPD station house responsible for the area where Tango Harris had taken refuge was close to the ugly flat slab of the United Nations headquarters which jutted out of the skyline of the East River like a tooth that's been filed down. In the same area of Manhattan was the Ford Foundation building, the Chrysler building, Grand Central station, and the Pan-Am building. If it wasn't for the Rockefeller Center, visitors could well be excused for thinking that New York was a city dedicated to transport . . . until they tried to get a yellow cab in the pouring rain.

Inside this station house, harassed detectives, who seemed to have time only for their own problems, sat sweating in shirt-sleeves, hammering away at typewriters, documenting reluctant prisoners and fingerprinting them. The officers' guns were carefully locked away to guard against some crazed prisoner seizing one and blowing away the precinct's entire detective force. There had been too many incidents of that sort in the history of the New York Police, and it made American police officers ultra-sensitive and extremely careful.

Lieutenant Joe Kobreski was short and swarthy with very black slicked-down hair and shoulders that could only have been developed by intensive weight training.

His coat hung on a hook behind the door, his tie was loosened off, and his shirt was sweat-stained. On his desk was a half-eaten sandwich on a paper bag. Next to it was a file of paper that had been faxed from Scotland Yard, and which he was now riffling through.

The previous day, he had received a telephone call from Fox, who had decided to short-circuit both the American Embassy in London and the FBI in New York. Fox knew about the rivalry between the Bureau and the NYPD and Fox was an impatient man. He and Kobreski had discussed, as only policemen can, the hurdles confronting any law-enforcement officer wishing to extradite a prisoner from one country to another, and touched briefly on the shortcomings of the FBI and the legal systems of their respective countries. At the end of the conversation they had reached a useful understanding. The phone call had been followed by faxed details of Harris's criminal record. It made interesting reading even to a New York cop.

'A detective called Fox of Scotland Yard is interested in this guy Thomas Walter Harris who's gotten in with Charles Pearson.' Kobreski pushed the file across the desk towards Detective First Grade Luce. 'Sol Whiteman from the Bureau was asking questions about him a few days back. And Scotland Yard want to talk with Harris about a few homicides and one hell of a lot of racketeering.'

'What's this?' Luce picked up the file.

'Guess that's their version of a yellow-sheet.'

Luce skimmed through the docket. 'Not bad for a Limey,' he said. 'Robbery, extortion, drugs, prostitution.'

'So where are we at?' asked Kobreski.

'We got a stake-out right now on the Pearson mob, Lieutenant. And we collared two of them for the homicide just off Madison—'

'Yeah, yeah, I know,' said Kobreski. 'They took out one of Aventura's boys. Right?' He glanced up at Luce. 'So where's this guy Harris fit in? Any connection with the homicide?'

'Nope. Harris was looking to buy a piece of the racket, but Pearson's gang wouldn't let him play. Gave him the bum's rush. Seems they got enough problems with the Aventura mob without some Limey hustling them. The guys on surveillance checked Harris out after they saw him making a mark with these characters.'

'So what was he doing? Apart from trying to buy a stable of hookers.'

Luce shrugged. 'One of Dementi's snitches says he was trying to buy a gun. Seems Harris knew Pearson from way back in London. So when Harris got in shtuck with Scotland Yard he decided to come over here to try and cash in on a favour . . . and make a fresh start.'

'Have I got news for him,' said Kobreski. 'Who's Dementi anyway?'

'He's a second-grade on Robbery, Safes, and Lofts.'

'Reckons,' said Kobreski and took a bite of his sandwich. 'And did he? Buy a gun?'

'That much we don't know, Lieutenant,' said Luce. 'But he seems the sort of guy we can do without. Got enough of our own hoods without importing them. And that's what Pearson said.'

'How patriotic. I reckon we'll go talk with this son-of-a-bitch. Where's he at? Did Dementi's snitch tell us that?'

'No, sir. The guys on stake-out put a tail on him but lost him.'

'Some stake-out. Just as well this Fox told me Harris was in a hotel on Madison.'

'Yeah,' said Luce. 'Sol Whiteman told me where he was.'

'Thanks for letting me know,' said Kobreski acidly.

'Are the Brits going for extradition? Deportation, maybe?'

'Nope. Either will take for ever and a day. I reckon we'll talk real nice to this guy. Tell him to take a health trip. For certain he'll get more time in the slammer back home in England than he will here, except we won't tell him that. I mean, what have we got? Soliciting the purchase of an illegal weapon? That's nothing.' Kobreski stood up. 'Jeez!' he added. 'As if we ain't got enough to do.'

'Does this guy know the Brits are going to collar him when he touches base?' asked Luce.

'If he doesn't, he's one dumb guy.' Kobreski took his revolver from his desk drawer and slid it into his holster.

It was a good hotel just off Madison Avenue. Lieutenant Kobreski enquired at the desk for Harris only to be told that he was out.

'Mr Harris said he was going to visit the Empire State,' said the desk clerk, smiling the ready smile that she had learned in training.

'That's nice,' said Kobreski. 'We'll wait, ma'am. But don't tell him when he comes in. It's kinda like a surprise.' Briefly, he exhibited his badge. 'And you don't want any trouble in this nice hotel of yours, do you?'

The desk clerk giggled nervously. 'I never even saw you, Officer,' she said.

Kobreski and Luce made their way to the bank of elevators and rode to the seventh floor. Once in the corridor leading to Harris's room Kobreski went in search of the floor waiter.

Eventually tracking him down to a small office, Kobreski produced his shield. 'Open up room seven-oh-five for us, feller,' he said.

The floor waiter looked apprehensively at the detective's badge. 'Say, what's this all about?' he asked, fumbling for his master key.

'Best you don't know,' said Kobreski. 'And if I was in your shoes, I'd stay outta the way. Could get caught in the cross-fire.'

'Yes, *sir*,' said the floor waiter and hurried to open the door of Room 705.

Kobreski looked round the suite appreciatively. 'This guy sure knows how to look after himself,' he said. 'Guess we'll make ourselves comfortable.' And with that, he lit a small cigar and took off his overcoat. Then he sat down in an armchair that could not be seen from the door and

197

placed his revolver on his lap. A moment or two later, he withdrew a headband with a single long feather in it and put it on his head.

The expression on Detective Luce's face did not change. 'What's with the feather, Lieutenant?' he asked.

'Helps to screw up complaints,' said Kobreski. 'If we don't convince this guy Harris to go home and he complains to Internal Affairs, they ain't going to listen too much when he tells them he was interviewed by a cop wearing Red Indian headdress. For which same reason, we don't use names.'

Ten minutes later he and Luce heard the door open and then slam.

Harris walked into the suite wearing a hat and coat and was met by the sight of Kobreski, still reclining in the armchair, pointing a gun at him. 'Hi!' said Kobreski.

'What the hell—?' Harris stood stock-still, staring first at the Red Indian feather and then at the gun in Kobreski's hand. Very quickly, he decided that the gun had priority. This was not the time for smart remarks. He raised his hands rapidly.

'I'm Lieutenant Moroni, New York Police Department. Just take your weapon out, real slow, and put it on the floor.'

'Oh yeah?' Harris had lost none of his truculence in crossing the Atlantic. 'You don't look like no cop to me. Pull the other one.'

With his free hand, Kobreski produced his shield. 'Like I said, make with the artillery.'

Harris looked pained. 'I don't have a gun, Officer,' he said. 'I'd be crazy to carry a shooter over here.' A strong hint of deference crept into his voice. 'What's this all about, anyway?' he asked.

'I sure hope you're right, feller,' said Kobreski, waving his pistol in Harris's direction, 'because carrying a concealed weapon in this city can get you in a lotta trouble. Like dead.' He stood up, walked across the room with his revolver in the ready position, and ran his free hand expertly over Harris to make sure that he was unarmed. Then he sat down again.

'I want a solicitor,' said Harris promptly.

'What in hell's that?' asked the American. 'A hooker?'

'I think he means he wants an attorney, Lieutenant,' said Luce.

'Damn right he does,' said Kobreski.

'What's coming off here?' asked Harris, still wearing his hat and coat and standing in the centre of the room. He understood English law and English detectives, but the brash New Yorker facing him, whose gun was still wavering back and forth, terrified him.

Kobreski reholstered his revolver and carefully studied the pathetic figure of Tango Harris. 'Seems like you been getting in bad company since you got here, Mr Harris,' he began.

'I'm on holiday, Officer. A tourist, like. Been seeing all the sights. I've just been up the Empire State Building. Very impressive, that is. And tomorrow, I plan to see the Statue of Liberty.'

'That a fact?' said Kobreski. 'I shouldn't go making too many plans, if I was you.'

'What seems to be the problem?' asked Harris hopefully. But he was fairly certain he knew.

'Detective officers from my precinct have had a number of undesirable persons under surveillance for some time now. These guys are members of Charlie "The Rat" Pearson's little gang, and you were seen approaching them several times. My snitch,' continued Kobreski, borrowing Detective Dementi's informant for the purpose of the narrative, 'tells me that you made several attempts to buy a shooter.'

Harris was sweating profusely now. 'I never—'

Kobreski held up his hand. 'Some of Charlie "The Rat" Pearson's guys have been collared in connection with a homicide.' He gave Harris a disconcerting grin. 'This is the State of New York, my friend. And the penalty for murder in the first degree is the electric chair.' In fact, the death penalty in New York was by lethal injection, but Kobreski felt that it just didn't compare with the threat of the chair for effect.

'I don't know nothing about no murder.' Harris's

strangled voice rose in desperation and he collapsed into a chair. 'Where did you say it was?' He took off his hat and wiped his brow with his sleeve.

'I didn't say,' said Kobreski. He glanced at Luce. 'This guy's some actor, Detective,' he said and turned back to Harris. 'Mind you, you're lucky, Mr Harris.'

'I am?' Harris looked enquiringly at the American. He thought for a moment that he must have missed something.

'Oh, sure. The State Governor ain't that keen on the death penalty. So you'll probably only do ninety years.'

'For Christ's sake!' Harris tried to control any outward signs of fear, but he was panicking like hell inside. 'I'm fifty-four,' he said in a whisper. His fingers started gripping nervously at the arms of his chair.

'That's OK,' said Kobreski. 'You'll just have to do as much as you can.'

Suddenly it came to Harris. 'It's Fox, isn't it?' he said. 'He's put you up to this, hasn't he?'

'Pardon me?' Kobreski looked convincingly mystified.

'Fox of Scotland Yard put you up to this, didn't he?' said Harris again, as though he'd just solved a particularly difficult problem.

'Never heard of him,' said Kobreski dismissively. 'But I heard of the guy your friend Charlie "The Rat" blew away. He was connected with the mob.'

'What mob?' Harris now had a hunted look about him.

'What mob?' Kobreski let out a hoot of laughter. 'D'you hear that, Detective? What mob?' He stopped laughing as suddenly as he had started, and stared at Harris in theatrical disbelief. 'In this city, mister, there's only one mob. They call it the Mafia.'

'Leave it out,' said Harris and shot a quick sideways glance at the expressionless Luce. 'I don't go about shooting people. I keep telling you, I don't know nothing about no murder.'

'This guy sure has a great repertoire of one-liners,' said Kobreski, addressing Luce. He switched his gaze back to Harris. 'That's real funny, you know that? You could

200

have made a killing in vaudeville . . . a few years back.'

'No way would I wanna be in your shoes, Mr Harris,' said Luce suddenly, still maintaining his dead-pan expression. And having said his piece, lapsed into silence once more.

'I'll explain, Mr Harris,' continued Kobreski, adopting a conversational tone. 'If we can convince the District Attorney that you were involved in this homicide . . .' Kobreski paused to stub out his cigar. 'Then you'll find yourself on Death Row quicker than that. But like I said,' he added as an afterthought, 'you'd probably appeal your way out of it.'

'Say, Lieutenant . . .' Luce leaned forward earnestly and pointed a finger in Harris's direction. 'D'you reckon if this guy decided to go back to London we might just leave him outta the indictment for this homicide? After all, the two guys we got in didn't name Mr Harris. They just gave a description and I don't reckon they'd pick him outta the line-up. Know what I mean, Lieutenant?'

'Well, I don't know about that, Detective.' Kobreski appeared to consider the matter carefully as he stared at Harris. 'We don't like people – particularly Limeys – coming across here and getting mixed up in homicides. Especially when the victim's a Mafiosi, because one thing usually leads to another. Like the next thing we're doing is investigating the homicide of Mr Harris here.'

'Yeah!' said Luce thoughtfully. 'Once these guys know who he is, they'll blow him away for sure. And we only got to take him down the precinct and then let him out and they'll know.'

'That's true, Detective,' said Kobreski. 'The officer has a point, Mr Harris. You see you've gotten between two very nasty groups of mobsters. Like I said, a week last Monday one of Aventura's mob got blown away by some friends of your friend Charlie "The Rat". So Guido Aventura'll be looking for anyone who's with Pearson. Including you. But I suppose,' he continued slowly, 'that we could save ourselves a whole lotta trouble if you went on home.' He picked up his coat and started to put it on.

201

'You see, Mr Harris, we're very concerned about your health and if these guys think that you were involved in rubbing out this godfather and they find out you're still here . . .' Kobreski left the sentence hanging in the air and shrugged. He had given a ham performance of a TV detective, but he knew that the real Kobreski would not have impressed Harris half as much.

'I'll go,' said Harris with indecent haste. 'I just don't want no trouble, Officer.' He seized what he saw as the only way out of a desperate situation. He had seen television programmes about the American police, American prisons, and the Mafia, and he wanted to have as little as possible to do with any of them.

'There's just one condition,' said Kobreski.

'What?' Harris, unable to take his eyes off Kobreski's wavering feather, looked as though he was willing to do just about anything to escape the clutches of this hard-nosed detective. 'I suppose it's going to cost me?' Harris had been brought up in an environment where everything had to be paid for.

'It will if you talk,' said Kobreski. 'You got to promise not to say anything about this to anyone. If word gets around that I let a homicide suspect go flying off to England, I could lose my badge. And my reputation with the mob would hit the deck. Get my drift, buster?' He swept off his Red Indian headband and stuffed it in his coat pocket.

'OK,' said Harris with resignation. 'I'll stay shtum.' He knew that he'd been set up, but he could see no alternative to going along with what he knew in his heart was Fox's plan. If this detective arrested him, he could be locked up for a long time. Maybe not for anything to do with a murder, but certainly while Fox arranged for his extradition. And the choice between years in an American remand prison and a few months in Brixton while his lawyers sorted it all out was no real contest.

'Great.' Kobreski lit another cigar. 'Just to show you what nice guys we are, we'll run you out to JFK right now. Make sure you catch a flight to London. How's that grab you?'

It took two hours to get Harris to Kennedy Airport and on a flight to Heathrow. Kobreski fixed it with airport security for himself and Luce to escort Harris right to the aircraft . . . to make sure he went.

Just as Harris got one foot on the steps, Kobreski took his arm. 'Be sure and have a nice day now,' he said.

Back in his office, Kobreski telephoned the head of the Flying Squad at New Scotland Yard. 'Fox,' he said when he was connected, 'you owe me one.'

Chapter Twenty-One

Denzil Evans had been disconcerted to receive a telephone call from Fox at two o'clock in the morning directing him to assemble a team and meet a flight at Heathrow Airport four and a half hours later. And as if that was not enough, Evans knew instinctively that despite Fox's instructions being quite specific, he was almost certain to find fault. Or worse still, to have changed his mind altogether about the course of action he required of Evans.

Not prepared to leave anything to chance, Evans had spent much of the rest of the night on the telephone, ordering his whole team to be at Terminal Three by six o'clock. After a miserable drive through pouring rain, he had managed to grab a quick cup of coffee before stationing himself with his men in the arrivals lounge.

Now he watched closely as the huge aircraft taxied up to the finger and the doors opened. Outside, on the tarmac, several police cars were drawn up surrounding the jumbo jet. Evans knew that if somehow Tango Harris managed to escape, Fox would be extremely angry. And Evans didn't fancy a blue suit with little silver stars on the shoulders.

Harris, still wearing the now-crumpled suit in which he had been interviewed in New York by Lieutenant Kobreski and Detective First Grade Luce, was the seventh passenger to alight. He had been on the aircraft for six hours, but it had seemed longer because he had hardly slept on the flight.

'Thomas Walter Harris,' said Evans, 'I am arresting you for conspiring with Alfred Penrose, Randolph Steel, and others, to murder William Crombie. Anything you say will be put in evidence.'

Although fully expecting to be met by the police, Harris was momentarily stunned at the reason for his arrest, but he quickly recovered. 'I'm not going to say anything, so you needn't worry about that,' he said. 'Except that you won't be able to make it stick.'

Evans treated that remark with lofty disdain and instructed DS Buckley and the other officers to escort Harris straight to the waiting police cars and not, under any circumstances, to ask him any questions. Evans was fully conversant with the law.

Fortunately for Evans's peace of mind, their journey into central London was slightly ahead of the morning rush-hour, although they encountered one or two problems in Kensington. Evans would have instructed his driver to use the siren, but he didn't want to make Harris feel that important. Even so, they reached Rochester Row police station by seven-thirty.

Harris's solicitor arrived at half-past eight, just as Fox got out of his car.

'This is preposterous,' began the solicitor.

'You took the words right out of my mouth,' said Fox, ushering the solicitor through the door. They walked in silence through the station and across the yard to the security wing.

'My client has a complete answer to the charge, you know . . . and he will refuse to answer any questions,' said the solicitor as they reached the door to the interview suite where Harris had been put only ten minutes previously.

'Which charge is that?' asked Fox mildly, settling himself and lighting a cigarette. 'There are so many that even I'm confused.' He glanced at Evans. 'What exactly did you arrest him for, Denzil?'

Evans, somewhat taken aback by Fox's question – Fox had carefully detailed the charge on the telephone – took a deep breath and wondered if he should come up with a different answer. 'Er, conspiring with others to murder Billie Crombie, sir,' he said at length.

205

'Billie Crombie?' Fox looked thoughtful. 'Refresh my memory, Denzil,' he said.

'Billie Crombie was the man who was shot dead at Catford Greyhound Stadium, sir,' said a thoroughly confused Evans.

'This is absolutely ludicrous—' began Harris's solicitor.

But Fox cut in. 'Oh yes, of course,' he said. 'Mr Blunt's job.'

'This is a bloody stitch-up,' Harris burst out. 'You set me up with those New York coppers to get me sent back.'

Fox ignored Harris and turned to the solicitor. 'Have you any idea what he's burbling on about?' he asked.

'My client tells me that he was interviewed by the New York police, Chief Superintendent, and accused of implication in a murder over there,' said the solicitor, determined not to let Fox have the interview all his own way.

'Really?' Fox contrived to look astounded at this proposition. 'Where on earth did you get that piece of fiction from?'

'My client informed me on the telephone,' said the solicitor. 'When eventually he was permitted to make the call . . . which is his statutory right.'

'What an extraordinary thing for him to have said.' Fox smiled sympathetically at Harris.

'Do you deny that such an interview took place?'

'I know nothing about the activities of the New York Police Department,' said Fox airily, 'but if anyone is going to answer questions it is your client. Not me.'

'I have already said that my client has nothing to say.'

'Pity,' said Fox. 'Now then . . . the questions.'

'I have said before, and I say again, my client is not answering any questions. But apart from anything else, Mr Harris is now under arrest and you may ask him only such questions that will remove ambiguity, assist in the recovery of stolen property, or to safeguard the life of another. I put it to you that none of those provisions applies.'

'I entirely agree,' said Fox mildly. 'He's been arrested

206

for conspiracy to murder Billie Crombie and it would be most improper to question him about that. Most improper.' He smiled helpfully. 'But he's not under arrest for the murder of Gina West, a prostitute found murdered in a West End hotel on the twelfth of October last,' he continued, drawing his list of prepared questions across the table. 'Now then, if you're ready, Denzil' – he glanced quickly at Evans, who was sitting close to the recording machine – 'you may turn on the Wurlitzer and we shall begin. Mr Harris,' he said, 'where were you on the night of the twelfth of October last?' He looked up expectantly.

'My client has already answered that question on another occasion,' said Harris's solicitor.

And so it went on. Fox asked question after question, not expecting answers . . . and not being disappointed. He had played this game before and he knew that a blanket refusal to answer any questions would not have the same impact on the jury as if each specific question was repeated in evidence . . . together with Harris's refusal to answer it. The questions were sufficiently damning on their own, and Harris's refusal to answer made them doubly so. But one question got a reply. Fox produced the envelope that Jason Morley had received at his flat in Richmond. 'I am now showing exhibit "GJ Seventeen" to Mr Harris,' he said for the benefit of the tape-recording. 'Do you recognize that letter, or the address which is written thereon, Mr Harris?'

Harris gave the envelope a cursory glance. 'No,' he said. 'Don't know anyone who lives there. And, to save you asking, I've never been to the place in my life.'

'Excellent,' said Fox. 'Do you have the form there, Denzil?' He reached out a hand.

'Yes, sir.' Evans, now on surer ground, produced a printed form and handed it to Fox.

'This form,' said Fox, 'is my authorization for the taking of an intimate sample from your client.'

'I can tell you now—'

'Just a moment.' Fox held up a hand and then swiftly wrote a few details on the form in front of him. After signing it with a flourish, he put his pen down and leaned back in his chair. 'You have a question?' He smiled benignly.

'What d'you want an intimate sample for?' asked the solicitor. 'And of what, may I ask?'

'Semen,' said Fox, the expression on his face appearing to imply that such a course of action was both obvious and inevitable.

Harris scoffed. 'I should cocoa,' he said.

The solicitor frowned at his client and turned his attention to Fox again. 'Why?'

'Because Gina West had engaged in sexual intercourse immediately before her death. Almost certainly with her killer. And I intend to submit an intimate sample from your client for DNA analysis, it being my contention that it was your client who murdered Miss West.'

'You seem to have forgotten that my client furnished an alibi for that date, Chief Superintendent.' Now it was the solicitor's turn to smile. 'Furthermore, you will be aware that an intimate sample cannot be taken without my client's consent.' The solicitor paused. 'And he so refuses.' He made a note in the book on the table in front of him and looked up. 'Sections 62 and 65 of the Police and Criminal Evidence Act refer . . . Chief Superintendent.'

'And you will be aware,' said Fox, 'that a jury is entitled to infer guilt from such a refusal. Section 62, sub-section 10, of the same act refers . . . as I'm sure you're aware.' He grinned insolently at the solicitor. 'Incidentally,' he added, turning to Harris once more, 'did you know that Miss West's post-mortem examination revealed that she was HIV positive?'

'Do what?' Harris sat up sharply. White-faced, he gripped the edges of the table and stared at Fox. 'You're bloody lying,' he said.

Harris's solicitor glanced at the ceiling and groaned . . . inwardly. Neither reaction was recorded on the tape of course, but then Harris's solicitor was a shrewd lawyer.

At the end of thirty minutes of almost totally unproductive interrogation, Fox smiled, sat back in his chair, and lit a cigarette. 'Right, Denzil,' he said, 'you may now charge Mr Harris with the murder of Miss Gina West and conspiring with others to murder Mr Crombie. Oh, and let Mr Brace know we've cleared up one of his little jobs. Once we've done that, we can start talking to Mr Harris about the unfortunate death of Mr Kevin Rix, a number of robberies from lorries, a few cases of living on immoral earnings, one or two dodgy massage parlours, several cases of causing grievous bodily harm . . .' He smiled at the solicitor. 'Never rains but it pours,' he said. 'Much the same in your trade, I suppose?'

Morrie Isaacs had been assured that no criminal proceedings would be taken against him and that he had really been in custody for his own protection. He was further assured that Tango Harris and the Crombie brothers were now locked up along with most of their respective henchmen. This last piece of information had a remarkably restorative effect on Morrie Isaacs's memory and, in what proved to be an unsuccessful attempt to ingratiate himself with the police, he now claimed to be almost certain that he could recognize the malcontents who had thrown petrol bombs into his West End restaurant thereby reducing it to a smoking shell and killing his barman into the bargain.

There was, however, one slight problem. In any crime where proof relies upon identification, it is customary to hold an identification parade. But police cannot submit suspects to this ordeal without their consent.

Gary and Kenny Crombie were ill disposed to assist the police under any circumstances, and when their solicitor advised against such a course of action, they were only too ready to agree with him. After all, that was the sort of the advice they were paying him for. Or the British taxpayer was.

The alternative, in the face of such a refusal, is to hold what is called a group identification. And police, if they think it is warranted, may go ahead and do it . . . even if the suspects don't much care for the idea.

Consequently, Detective Superintendent Gavin Brace, a Uniform Branch inspector, two sergeants, and enough officers to ensure that the Crombies didn't run away were gathered at Waterloo Underground station in the rush hour.

Standing in a corner, and surrounded by a ring of policemen, the uniformed inspector faced Gary and Kenny Crombie . . . and their solicitor. 'Right,' began the inspector, 'I'll tell you what it's all about. First, Mr Gary Crombie will go up on one escalator and the witness will come down on the other one . . .'. The inspector coughed self-importantly. 'Then we shall repeat the exercise with Mr Kenneth Crombie going up ditto.'

'I can't stand heights,' said Gary Crombie.

The inspector looked at him over the top of his clipboard. 'There is no need for jocularity,' he said, and coughed again. 'This is a serious business.'

At a signal from the inspector, a police officer at the top guided Morrie Isaacs on to the downward escalator at the same time as Gary Crombie was told to start the upward journey. In among the crowds of other passengers were a number of detectives whose task was to prevent the escape of either of the Crombies.

But things did not go quite as planned. As the downward Morrie Isaacs passed the upward Gary Crombie, Crombie waved vigorously at him and shouted: 'Morrie. Morrie Isaacs. How are you? Long time no see.'

Isaacs, unnerved by this greeting from the suspect, half waved back. 'Oh, hallo,' he said lamely.

'Bloody brilliant,' said Brace from his vantage point near the booking hall. As the officer in the case, he was allowed no part in the proceedings.

The same thing happened again when it was Kenny Crombie's turn to go up the escalator. 'Morrie, darling,' he yelled. 'How ya doing? Still churning out that muck you call food, you old poofter?' And he waved again. Gary and Kenny Crombie were taken from top of the escalator, placed in a police van, and driven straight back to Brixton prison where they were being held on remand.

'Well?' asked the uniformed inspector. 'Did you recognize anyone?'

'Of course, Officer,' said Isaacs. 'I recognized them both. And they recognized me. Didn't you see them wave?' He paused and glanced at a man stepping on to the escalator. 'And that's the third one,' he said excitedly. 'That's Billie Crombie. Him there.'

'Bloody brilliant,' said Brace again and, disgusted with the whole proceedings, turned on his heel.

'It was a blow-out, guv,' said Brace savagely. 'I reckon Morrie Isaacs had been got at in stir.'

'How so?' asked Fox.

'We put the Crombies up on a group identification at Waterloo tube station . . . on the escalators.'

'And did the bold Morrie Isaacs pick them out?'

'Couldn't fail,' said Brace. 'Both Gary and Kenny Crombie waved like boy scouts taking their semaphore badge and shouted at the tops of their voices. Isaacs couldn't have failed to see them. And if that wasn't enough, he identified some passing bank clerk as the late Billie Crombie.'

'So their mouthpiece is now going to claim that Isaacs picked them out because they drew attention to themselves, I suppose.'

'Exactly, sir.' Brace looked downcast about the whole business.

'Not to worry,' said Fox cheerfully. 'We'll put Sharon Scrope in the box. She's willing to testify that she saw Gary and Kenny – and the late Billie – set off to torch Isaacs's restaurant, and that they came back and told her all about it. They insisted on watching the television news to see if there was a mention of it, so she says.'

Still Brace looked doubtful. 'D'you reckon she'll stand up and say all that, guv?'

'Too true,' said Fox. 'She'd do anything to put those two down. By the way, there was something else you ought to know, Gavin.'

'What's that, guv?'

'Sharon Scrope said that Billie told her they'd worn stocking masks when they torched Morrie's restaurant.'

'Thanks very much, guv'nor,' said Brace.

'Randolph Steel, you are charged in that you did murder one William Crombie on Saturday, the twentieth of October, at Catford Greyhound Stadium, against the peace. You are further charged in that you did murder one Kevin Rix on or about the tenth of November, in Greater London, against the peace. Do you wish to say anything in answer to the charges? You are not obliged to say anything, but anything you do say will be put in evidence.'

'Get stuffed,' said Randy Steel.

The custody sergeant duly wrote it down.

'D'you reckon you'll get them down, Tommy?' Deputy Assistant Commissioner Dick Campbell poured two stiff measures of whisky and placed one in front of Fox.

'We'll give it a run, sir,' said Fox, taking a sip of Scotch. 'Now that we've got all the baddies in custody, most of the not-so-baddies will be prepared to give evidence . . . I hope.' He grinned and put his glass down.

'As a matter of interest, Tommy, how did you manage to persuade Tango Harris to come home?' asked Campbell.

'Had a few quiet words with the New York police and they explained the error of his ways, sir. Apparently, he was quite amenable. Wouldn't surprise me if he became a born-again Christian.'

Chapter Twenty-Two

The trial of the surviving members of Crombie Incorporated was a lame affair, and Fox saw it as little more than a programme-filler to precede the main event, the extravaganza of Tango Harris.

The proceedings were enlivened throughout by Arlene Fogg who occupied the dock as she had occupied everything else in life. Bang in the centre. Her two sons flanked her together with those of their cohorts who had not switched allegiance and earned themselves a place in the later, more prestigious, Harris trial.

But the Crombies were beaten before they started. Counsel tried their desperate best to shake the prosecution case, but the jury weren't having it.

On several occasions, the judge was tempted to have Arlene Fogg removed from the dock for her vociferous outbursts but decided to bide his time until the verdicts were delivered. Then he gave her ten years.

Gary and Kenny Crombie were sent to prison for life for the murder of Harry Dodge, Morrie Isaacs's barman, and collected quite a few concurrent sentences for other lesser offences.

The small fry went down for anything between eighteen months and ten years.

Sharon Scrope, who was commended by the judge for her courage in coming forward to give evidence, later sent a packet of condoms to each of the Crombie brothers . . . care of Parkhurst Prison.

And Fox bought a case of Scotch for the Flying Squad.

'The Gina West murder, Tommy,' said DAC Campbell.

'Down to Tango Harris, sir. He killed her because she wouldn't accept him as a ponce, but mainly to send a message to Billie Crombie that he was taking over. She was one of Billie's girls, you see.'

'Yes, I know, but have you got enough to get him down for it?'

'Piece of cake, guv'nor,' said Fox. 'Alfie Penrose has admitted that he took out the lease on the flat at Richmond in the name of John Phillips. And he told the solicitor that his previous address was Harris's place at Buckhurst Hill. Once the John Phillips credit card arrived at Richmond – which was the only reason he'd taken the place – he spun the solicitor this fanny about having to give up the lease for business reasons. But Penrose claims that he was acting on Harris's orders.'

'What was the point of all that?' asked Campbell.

'It was a sort of double bluff, sir. Harris knew we'd track it straight back to him but he thought that it would be so bloody obvious that we'd think it had to be a set-up by Billie Crombie.'

'But you'll need more than Penrose's testimony.'

'Tango Harris gave us the rest, sir. After he'd killed Gina West, he over-egged the pudding and sent a letter to Crombie at Richmond, knowing bloody well that the Old Bill would get to hear of it. Unfortunately for Harris, he's not too well up in forensic science. The blank sheet of paper in the envelope bore a couple of nice fingerprints. Harris's fingerprints. On top of that, he refused an intimate sample, which entitles the court to infer guilt, because it's pretty certain that it was him who screwed her before he topped her. Or someone did,' he added with a laugh. 'The application form for the credit card had a print on it too, and although Fingerprint Branch are sure it's Penrose's, there are only seven points of similarity. Not that it matters. Penrose is giving evidence for the Crown.'

*

214

'Put up Thomas Walter Harris.'

The full panoply of the law was arrayed in Number Two Court at the Old Bailey. The jury, apprehensive and in awe of the responsibilities that had been thrust upon it, sat silently taking it all in.

Huge masses of paper, the result of hours of painstaking statement-writing by countless detectives, stood in piles on a table in the centre of the courtroom. Alongside the paper mountains was the fearful collection of weaponry that members of Fox's team had seized from the warehouses at Greenwich and Wanstead and from sundry other places with which Tango Harris was connected, either directly or through the co-conspirators who now crowded into the dock with him. There were revolvers, a rifle or two, four or five sawn-off shot-guns. a sledge-hammer that the prosecution hoped to prove had smashed first a man's hands, then his feet, and finally and fatally his skull. There was an electric drill, said to have made holes in more than one kneecap, or to have been used for unlicensed dentistry, and lastly the small electric generator that had brought incredible suffering to several of Harris's enemies – usually through their genitalia – among whom, the Crown alleged, was Kevin Rix.

Harris himself was dapper, and ostensibly unconcerned by it all. His light-grey suit, white shirt, gold cuff-links, purple tie, and matching pocket handkerchief all testified to his perceived station as a leader of the criminal fraternity. His immaculately cut hair – what little remained of it – manicured fingernails and horn-rimmed glasses gave the impression of a successful businessman, which is how he saw himself, rather than the worst possible type of villain . . . which is how Fox saw him. To the casual onlooker, Harris could as easily have been standing trial for some fraudulent breach of company law.

Beneath Harris were seated the pick of the English bar, their briefs marked at amounts some wage-earners would have been happy to take home in a year. In Harris's eyes, their task was a simple one. To get him off at all costs. Privately, these barristers had expressed grave

215

reservations about their chances of succeeding; the counts on the indictment were, in their view, overwhelming. But, as has often been said before, there is nothing quite as fickle as an English jury.

Day after day it dragged on, much of the time in the earlier stages taken up by sophisticated wrangles between counsel and the judge over the admissibility of evidence. These esoteric legal joustings usually took place in the absence of the jury, many of whom started to wonder whether they were really needed.

Counsel for the prosecution, a shrewd and competent QC, made much of Harris's refusal to give a sample of his semen. 'Why, members of the jury,' he enquired with contrived naïvety, 'should a man decline to assist the prosecution to prove the very innocence which he so vehemently protests?' He dropped his arms and allowed his shoulders to droop at his own apparent inability to grasp the archness of the accused. 'Surely, ladies and gentlemen,' he continued, 'there is but one construction that can be put upon that refusal.' He paused dramatically. 'And that is the knowledge that such a sample would prove categorically his guilt.' Then, just to make sure, he drew attention to the letter addressed to Billie Crombie which had been sent to the Richmond address and which bore Harris's fingerprints.

Inevitably there was some light relief too. And just as inevitably, it was the cross-examination of Fox that provided it.

'Detective Chief Superintendent.' Harris's counsel rose from his seat with a magnificent flourish of his gown and carefully adjusted his half-lensed glasses as he peered down at his brief. Then he looked up, sweeping his glasses off again. 'My client asserts that at your instigation, he was interviewed in New York City by a . . .' Counsel raised his glasses momentarily and stared through them once more at his brief. But Fox had given evidence too often in his career to be intimidated by the theatricality of barristers. 'By a Lieutenant Moroni who, my client says, was wearing a Red Indian headdress at the time.'

He paused irritably as a ripple of laughter ran along the public gallery . . . and certain parts of counsel's benches. 'And that this officer attempted somehow to implicate my client in a murder which had been committed in that city. Furthermore, Chief Superintendent, my client claims that he was threatened with the electric chair. I put it to you, Chief Superintendent, that instead of seeking his return under the extradition treaties which exist between this country and the United States of America, you deliberately arranged for my client to be threatened by the police in New York so that he would be coerced into returning to the jurisdiction of this court.' He threw his glasses on to his brief and pushed his hands into his trouser pockets.

'Really?' said Fox.

Counsel's mouth opened slightly before he returned to the fray. 'Well, do you have an answer?'

'If you have a question, sir,' said Fox with a benevolent smile.

'Let me put it another way,' said counsel, suddenly aware that the police witness was no fool. 'Did a Lieutenant Moroni threaten my client in New York City to the extent that he was terrified into returning to England?'

'I don't know.'

'What d'you mean, you don't know?'

'Firstly, I wasn't in New York. In fact, I've never been to New York. Secondly, I don't know whether your client was, in fact, coerced into returning to England,' said Fox. 'I was not privy to his state of mind at the time. But return he did.'

'I do wish that counsel for Harris would refrain from asking convoluted questions.' The rasping voice of the judge broke into the proceedings, and he glared at the high-lofted ceiling.

'My lord?' Harris's counsel glanced at the judge, barely able to conceal the annoyance he felt at being interrupted.

'These are fatuous questions,' said the judge, raising his glasses to peer disconcertingly at the barrister. 'This officer' – he nodded towards Fox – 'has stated that he

217

wasn't in New York and he cannot possibly know what went on there. You must know that any answer to such a question would be hearsay.' The judge gave a dry cough. 'If you are trying to put forward the proposition that your client returned to this country under some sort of duress, then so be it. Perhaps he should have been extradited, but he was not. I would remind you, however, that this court is not concerned with the manner in which your client was brought before it. He's here and that's all there is to it.' The judge sighed. 'Red Indians. Really!'

'But, my lord—'

'Have any enquiries been made of the New York police?' asked the judge, determined to thwart any grounds for a later appeal.

'Certain enquiries have been made, my lord, yes,' said defence counsel reluctantly. He was beginning to regret his attempt to score points about the New York interview. He had raised it in the hope that Fox would be made to look unreliable and devious, a policeman who would cut corners. If that could be shown to be the case, the jury might well be doubtful about other parts of his evidence. That was the theory of the thing, anyway. But now that the judge had decided to pursue the story, it promised to blow up in counsel's face.

'And has this Lieutenant Moroni been traced . . . or interviewed?'

'My enquiries indicate that there is no officer called Moroni in the New York police, my lord.' Harris's counsel looked quite crestfallen.

'And no Red Indians either, one presumes?' The judge smiled and the occupants of the public gallery took this as licence to laugh again.

'No, my lord,' mumbled the barrister.

'I see. And is counsel aware that the death penalty in the State of New York is carried out by way of lethal injection and not electrocution?'

'So I believe, my lord.'

'And what was the *locus in quo* of this murder your client was allegedly accused of having conspired to commit?'

218

Counsel looked decidedly unhappy. 'There are many murders in New York, my lord, and I'm afraid that it has not been possible to identify the one which the New York police were allegedly discussing.'

'I'm sorry,' said the judge, leaning forward. 'I didn't quite catch that.'

Harris's discomfited counsel repeated his statement and the judge smiled sympathetically at the jury. 'I can only apologize, ladies and gentlemen, for this waste of time,' he said and returned his gaze to the well of the court. 'So,' he continued, 'it amounts to this. Your client says that he was interviewed by a police officer in Red Indian headdress – a police officer now found not to exist – about a murder that seems not to have occurred, and threatened with a penalty which is not enshrined in the State of New York's laws . . . such as they are.'

'Er, yes, my lord. I suppose so.'

'Perhaps then, you would oblige us all by asking questions of a less factitious nature, Mr, er . . .'

'As your lordship pleases,' said counsel and turned to glower at the solicitor who had prepared the brief.

'I do,' said the judge.

The trial ended one month after it had begun. The jury, unimpressed by the glittering array of legal talent, found the accused guilty of the most serious charges. But just to demonstrate their independence, they threw out a few of the minor counts. And Alfie Penrose, who had turned Queen's Evidence, actually walked free from the dock. That he was mysteriously run over and killed in East India Dock Road three days later by a car which did not stop, did not invoke anyone's sympathy.

When the verdicts had been returned, the judge delivered sentences that he thought would dissuade anyone else from emulating the activities of Harris and company. With little ceremony, Steel and Guerrini were given life sentences for the murders of Carter, Crombie, and Rix, but the judge reserved his most swingeing address for Harris himself.

'Thomas Walter Harris,' he began. 'For many years you have behaved as though you are above the law and

219

you have conducted numerous nefarious enterprises that have netted you vast sums of money. During your felonious rape—'

'I never raped no one,' shouted an agitated Harris.

'Shut yer gate,' said the prison officer next to him.

The judge frowned. 'During your felonious rape of the society in which you live,' he continued, 'you have ridden roughshod over your fellow human beings. But like those of you who have gone before, you have to learn that there comes a day of reckoning. You will go to prison for life, and to ensure that you will not benefit from your ill-gotten gains, and to act as a salutary warning to other like-minded persons, I shall recommend that you be not released before the expiry of thirty years.' The judge paused. 'Oh, and I shall make an order of criminal bankruptcy,' he added. 'Put him down.'

'Well, guv'nor, what have you got to say to that?' asked Gilroy.

'A large Scotch, please, Jack. See you in the Magpie and Stump in ten minutes.'